Published in 2025 by Provoco Publishing who own the publishing rights.

ISBN: 978-1-0686412-8-2

Cover Artwork - © Provoco Publishing
Cover Design – © Jane Murray at Provoco Publishing
Logo Design - © MJC at Martyn Carson Creative
Edited by Jane Murray

Passing Through

Jacqueline Dixon

Prologue

He hovered, peering through the iron railings outside the school, watching one particular girl playing and laughing with a group of her peers in the playground. He could not take his eyes away from her and stood there trying to look inconspicuous. When she turned towards him, still laughing, her expression changed and as if in a trance, she began to walk slowly towards him. He moved quickly away from the railings when a teacher appeared at the main entrance and her eyes turned towards him with an alarmed look on her face. The teacher rushed over to the young girl and quickly took hold of her arm, guiding her towards the main entrance of the school.

He turned momentarily for one last look at the young girl as she was being led away by the teacher. He realised how sinister he obviously appeared, just standing there watching the young children in the playground. He would have to be very careful in future as he was sure the teacher had noticed him on numerous occasions, peering through the railings in such a conspicuous way. He had no doubt that he looked like a very unsavoury individual skulking around outside a girl's school and suspected that he would no doubt be approached next time and questioned as to why he was constantly loitering outside a playground, watching children play.

All the same, he had no choice, as he felt compelled to watch over that particular young girl. As he continued walking, he had conflicting emotions of happiness, and deep sadness but he knew he would have to bide his time and be patient.

Part One

1965 - Transitory Life

Chapter One

Celeste Harrington awoke as usual with a ferocious, thumping headache. She hauled herself out of bed and stumbled into the bathroom where she threw up into the toilet, choking and spluttering all the while. She ran some cold water into the wash hand basin to splash over her face and when she looked at her reflection in the mirror overhead, she gasped at the sight of her swollen eyes and blotched complexion. She was only nineteen years old, but she looked, and felt, like a dissipated, much older woman,

'What a disgusting, awful state I am in,' she growled to her reflection.

She had lost quite a bundle of money at the casino during the early hours of the morning, although she considered that there was plenty more where that came from. All the while, she had drunk so many glasses of champagne that she had had to be carried into a limousine and driven home.

As usual he had been right there, ready to pick up the pieces of her broken self and rush her back home where he would undress her, tuck her into her own bed and then he would be gone. The face now staring at her would seem to interchange from one image to another and she could barely differentiate or even recognise them in the fog of her befuddled mind.

During the past year, she had spiralled down into a pit of misery, and she had no recollection of how, when or why she had begun that journey of self-destruction. After all, she had everything that she could possibly wish for, and she could go anywhere she wanted – the world had been her oyster.

Celeste was an extremely vibrant, attractive young woman standing just over five feet ten inches tall, with pale blonde hair and a creamy, flawless complexion, brilliant blue eyes and an hourglass figure. She had been born into wealth and had enjoyed a good, solid upbringing. Both she and her older brother, Vincent, had grown up in an extremely privileged environment, wanting for nothing.

Vincent had always been the ambitious one, and as soon as he had graduated from the Royal College of Art, he had gone straight into business as an interior designer, only catering for exceptionally affluent clients with opulent mansions. Celeste, on the other hand, never had any specific desire to be particularly successful in life or achieve great things – she never had the inclination or the need to pursue any such ambitions. Her only plan upon leaving school was to have complete freedom to do as she wished without being fettered to full time employment. Her parents were good, kind people, and had allowed her to travel as and when she pleased with a very generous monthly allowance. When she was eighteen, they bought her a house in the fashionable area of Cromwell Gardens in South Kensington, London. Her brother took care of the interior design of the property and together with their mother, Grace, they made the house a lavish and elegant home for her. She adored living alone, making her own decisions, and her life in those earlier times had been full of excitement and social whirls. Much to her parent's relief at that stage, she had shown them that she could be a very responsible young woman, able to take care of herself.

Nevertheless, without making it too obvious, her brother always kept an eye on her. He always tried to instil in her that her one flaw was that she was far too gullible and impressionable. He worried that she had no sense of the bad in people and just went flitting about her life regardless, like a beautiful but fragile butterfly. He was very protective of his beautiful sister and always dreaded that she would be swayed by some young man out to exploit her.

At one particular social function held by her brother, she met Olsten Ryder, a successful businessman and owner of a very prosperous and reputable company that manufactured collectable ceramic dolls. She instantly struck up a friendship with him despite his more mature years. Olsten was impressed that such a beautiful young woman of vast wealth was so innocent and unspoilt and like her brother, he also felt protective of her. Celeste thought Olsten was a real gentleman and enjoyed his company – he was so different to a lot of younger men that she frequently met, who she felt were only interested in her wealth.

Olsten had been so mesmerised by her beauty and stylishness, that with the approval of her parents, he sought to have a life-sized ceramic doll made in her likeness. Celeste had been thrilled with the idea – she had felt flattered and had insisted that she be allowed to make her own personal choice of the attire for the finished creation.

When the doll had been successfully finely crafted and adorned in fashionable garments specifically selected to Celeste's very own preference of clothing, complete with a set of authentic jewellery, it was proudly put on display in Olsten's office reception area, to be admired by clients and guests alike.

Soon after Celeste had moved into her house in Kensington, she met Lewis Rutherford, a close friend of her brother's and they were immediately smitten with each other. Lewis was also born into wealth and had no interest whatsoever in Celeste's money, much to her relief. They spent all their free time together and although she did not work herself, she often hosted various functions held in Lewis's art gallery in New Bond Street.

Both parents on each side were delighted to see them so happy together and soon after that first meeting Lewis had moved in with Celeste and six months later, he proposed to her - she had leapt at him knocking him clean off his feet. They planned for the wedding banquet to be held at the Ritz Hotel in Mayfair, and it was going to be a huge lavish event with friends, family and business acquaintances all invited.

'Is that a yes, then?' he had said, laughing with tears in his eyes. From the very first meeting, he had more or less made up his mind that he was going to marry her.

'What do you think!' she had replied, playfully straddling him as he lay flat out on his back on the carpet.

One evening as Celeste had sat quietly in her luxurious lounge, listening to music while she went through their wedding invitation list, her phone rang. In her excitement to answer, she had rushed over to the phone, breathing quite rapidly when she had picked up the handset.

'This is the residence of HRH Celeste Harrington,' she had gushed flippantly, expecting the caller to be Lewis.

'I'm sorry to disturb you, Miss Harrington – this is Olsten Ryder's driver speaking. Mr. Ryder wonders if you would like to accept an invitation to join him for dinner this evening in his private quarters? If you accept, I could pick you up in an hour or so.'

'Oh – is that Kyle?' she had asked drumming her long red varnished, talon-like fingernails on the tabletop.

'No,' the driver had replied. 'Kyle has the evening off, and I am his brother covering for him - a temporary driver. Mr. Ryder would be honoured if you could join him. If you would like to accept the invitation, I could pick you up by – say, eight o'clock?'

'Well, let me see,' Celeste had replied checking her wristwatch. 'It's already a quarter to seven. I suppose I could easily be ready for eight. Yes – why not, tell Mr. Ryder that I would be honoured to join him for dinner – that would be lovely, and I am looking forward to it.'

'That's settled then – I will be there outside your house promptly at eight o'clock to pick you up,' the driver replied briskly and hung up before Celeste had even had a chance to say goodbye.

She hadn't been absolutely sure at the time, but she could have sworn that she'd heard him actually click his heels together as if in a salute before he had hung up. *What a polite young man,* she had thought to herself, smiling. She had then leapt up from the seat, sprinted up the stairs, taking two steps at a time, to her bathroom to prepare herself for the evening, which she viewed with anticipation.

She had never before been invited into Olsten's private quarters in his office building. She was very intrigued and wondered how many other people were attending, or if it was just a special invitation for her alone. Lewis had been away in Paris for the past week, and she had not seen any problem in accepting Olsten's invitation at that time. He was, after all, one of Lewis's business acquaintances through her brother and she had known Olsten for quite some time now – so what was the harm in it, even though she was soon to be a married woman, she had persuaded herself.

She was never to be the same after what happened that evening and her life completely changed. In her befuddled mind, she could never even remember the exact details of that ill-fated evening when everything began to go wrong for her. She began to drink heavily and self-destruct, much to the amazement of her parents, her brother and Lewis, and she abruptly broke off their engagement. Following his departure, her mother had constantly called by to see her throughout the following weeks, but Celeste had eventually put her off, insisting that she was quite capable of looking after herself and that she just wanted to be left alone.

At the same time, her father advised her to undergo counselling and arranged for her to see a renowned psychoanalyst to assess her mental stability.

For a short time, she attended at the clinic determined to help herself, but for some inexplicable reason that she could not even begin to comprehend, she seemed determined to destroy her own life. That incessant voice in her head kept telling her to do things that she didn't want to do, and she had no control over her own destructive actions.

She ran her fingers through her lank greasy unwashed hair – she knew that she looked a complete mess, and she was disgusted with herself. Stumbling into her kitchen to make some hot strong coffee, her tongue felt like a huge, furry swollen slug in her mouth and while she waited for her coffee to brew, she drank a large glass of water straight down causing her to choke and splutter again.

She was suddenly startled by a shrill noise that seemed to drill right through to her throbbing brain, causing her to drop her cup of coffee, which shattered when it hit the kitchen floor.

She hesitated for a few seconds feeling completely disorientated, as she stared at the spilt coffee and shards of crockery, fear rising in her throat, until she realised that it was her phone ringing. As if in a trance, she slowly walked towards the phone and picked up the handset. Standing in complete silence, she listened to the speaker on the other end of the line.

'Yes, I understand – I will get dressed right now and should be at your office very soon, my darling,' she whispered down the line.

Chapter Two

Olsten Ryder smiled as he replaced the handset after making an important business call. He stretched out in his chair with his feet up on his magnificent ornate dark oak-wood desk in his office, pondering over the previous day's unfortunate incident involving the young girl, Amitola. He had earlier been attending a meeting and then later, he had found himself outside the Marylebone library in New Cavendish Street, just missing the full impact of some falling scaffolding that had come crashing down towards the young girl standing on the pavement below. They had both just escaped potential serious injuries although Olsten sustained a gash on his head from a falling plank and the young girl had some minor cuts on her knees.

Today, although not of such a serious nature, had turned out to be a particularly hectic day. Numerous meetings with fashion editors, material manufacturers and marketing campaigners had been held to promote their exciting and incredible successful new line of collectable dolls. Millicent Bradley, his personal assistant, was always by Olsten's side making notes and ensuring that all arrangements were made to meet the various deadlines which they were committed to.

Olsten was relieved to finally put his feet up and relax in his office for a short time, at least a few minutes without any interruptions from his telephone constantly ringing by his side. It was one of those hazy early afternoons and he felt quite drowsy, his lids felt heavy, and he could hardly keep his eyes open. He freely succumbed to his feeling of lethargy, closed his eyes and languorously drifted off into a light but restless slumber.

He dreamed that he was walking through swirling dark shadows that completely overwhelmed his senses and then he saw her waiting for him, standing in a brightly lit compartment - the light was dazzling, almost blinding him. She was wearing a long, flowing white, shimmering satin gown - her long dark hair glistened under the bright light. He went to her and held her close - her laughter wafted around him like an exquisite perfume permeating into every porous membrane of his senses.

Suddenly she froze - her eyes widened with fear, the bright light began flashing on and off and before his very eyes, her body began to shrink and slowly spiral into a pitch-black never-ending tunnel. She began to get smaller and smaller until she completely disappeared out of sight.

Olsten's whole body shuddered - he stirred, struggling to awaken from the repetitive dream, feeling mentally exhausted and groggy. The sweat poured down his face and his heart pounded so loudly that he felt the sound vibrating through his brain. He rubbed his eyes and looked around at his surroundings, momentarily forgetting where he was.

A shiver ran through his body like a current of electricity. The recurring dream never failed to bring back that tragic day so vividly - never far from his mind and he wanted desperately to temporarily blot the whole awful disaster from his mind, even for just a few hours in a day. But he knew that he never would until the time came when he could put everything right and his normal life could resume in his own beloved realm.

He closed his eyes again for a few seconds while he struggled to regain all his senses. He sighed loudly to himself - *who was he kidding, he could not forget for one second, let alone for a few hours.* How could it have happened - he had asked himself that question a million times over. He had no way of knowing that such a disastrous mishap could have been grossly overlooked in their sophisticated environment and the obvious cunning tampering of such seemingly highly developed machinery was to have such a devastating effect on his life.

It seemed like a monumental number of years had passed since that ill-fated day, but in reality, it was only thirteen years ago – the longest thirteen years that he had ever lived through. He buried his face in his hands - he felt weary as he swivelled around on his chair away from his desk and stood up. He needed to stretch his limbs and move around to get the blood circulating through his tired veins. He walked into his adjoining private suite, through to his bathroom and splashed cold water on his face. Reaching for a monogrammed towel, he dried his face and walked back into his lounge where he strolled over to his drinks cabinet and poured himself a glass of whisky.

He then wandered back through to his bedroom and stood for a while gazing out of the window, overlooking the magnificent view of Berkeley Square and the adjoining garden lined with wonderfully tall trees swaying in the wind. The stream of people constantly milling back and forth never seemed to amaze him. He loved the hustle and bustle of London and knew when the time eventually came that he would have to leave, he would be sad and reluctant to depart from the beautiful old, musty, sometimes corrupt, but mostly exciting city of

London. But, for now London was where he needed to be.

His office, cluttered with a curious collection of Victorian knick-knacks, resembled an ethereal film set with various items littered on his desk and side units. Unlike his office, his adjoining private quarters were ultra-modern and were well equipped with the most up to date furnishings and facilities. Whilst he rarely stayed in these quarters overnight, it was just very convenient for him to have the luxury of being able to rest on his laurels when absolutely necessary, whenever he chose to take a short repose to refresh his mind and body after a particularly long day working in his office.

Olsten's company, based in a grand old house in Berkeley Square, Mayfair, was situated in the heart of London's dazzling West End - one of the city's most affluent and desirable areas. It was his pride and joy. Within the plain Georgian exterior of the house, the interior still retained much of its eighteenth-century grandeur with sweeping stairs, high, ornate plaster ceilings, over-mantle mirrors and marble floors and fireplaces. Although it had been renovated to bring it back to its former pristine state, the overall elegant style of the interior had not been changed or altered. The house was believed to be haunted but neither Olsten, nor any other members of staff, had ever had any experience of ghosts floating around the building. *Except in my own head,* Olsten thought as he picked up a photograph of himself with his arms around a beautiful dark-haired woman. She had looked stunning that day, wearing that gift that he had given her – a set of emerald jewellery that had complimented her dark eyes and hair so well. She had looked like a princess – his princess. It should have been a day to remember but tragedy had struck, and they had suddenly been hurtled into the depths of despair, and he alone would have to wait patiently for time to restore what had been lost.

He sighed deeply as he placed the photographs back on the side unit next to his bed. His mind wandered and he thought back to when he had begun his journey to the present day and all that he had achieved along the way – ever seeking to find peace of mind through the passage of time.

Now located in London, he somehow felt more at peace, and especially loved his large stately, opulent home, Hanover Lodge in Holland Park. He had always been used to living in a spacious environment and although the house was not as grand as he was ordinarily accustomed to, it suited his needs for the time being. The property was a plush family home in the heart of this wonderful affluent area, but it was especially perfect for entertaining large numbers of guests, which at times was imperative for his business. Arranged over five floors, complete with two grand drawing rooms, a large library which he also used as a study, six bedrooms with en-suite bathrooms and two separate fully fitted and furnished apartments in the lower level, this magnificent and meticulously refurbished house provided a real sense of glorious space.

The house had an expansive dining kitchen with French doors leading onto a superb south facing private garden where he held social and business cocktail gatherings during the summer months. In the basement area he could spend time in his modern gymnasium complete with a range of cardio and toning equipment and separate shower room. Even though he never understood the craze of pushing a body to its very limit to achieve ultimate fitness, he felt that he needed to keep himself strong in mind and body, and without his previous superior scientific rejuvenating equipment, it was the best alternative.

He suddenly felt an unexpected but somewhat fleeting rush of elation and a feeling that not all was so bad, and everything would work out in the end. He would savour this sentiment for a short while for as long as it lasted - he knew that it would not last very long. He gulped down the last drop of whisky in his glass and walked back into his office area. *At least I am halfway through the long, never-ending passageway,* he thought as he felt the warmth of the whisky trickle down his throat.

He was just about to leave his office when the phone rang. He leaned over the desk and picked up the handset. His personal assistant, Millicent Bradley, spoke to him in a succession of short informative sentences. She knew that he did not particularly like communicating by phone and always said what she needed to say as simply and as quickly as she could. Olsten often told her that he always knew what she was going to say before she had uttered one single word, which horrified her. She sincerely hoped that he was joking although she sometimes had an eerie feeling that he was not.

Millicent had been working with him as his personal assistant in London for the past five years and mutual respect had been instant on the first meeting. She was a hardworking and very loyal young woman who, likewise, seemed to be able to anticipate some of his thoughts and movements to some extent. Where

Olsten was concerned, this was a remarkable feat – he was an extremely mysterious and secretive character. He often joked with her about her apparent accurate perception of his mood and requirements in general in the office. Millicent knew that this was probably the case with most secretaries. It was an important necessity to be one-step ahead at times, although she realized right from the start that he was not an easy man to understand. Occasionally she couldn't help feeling intimidated by his sophisticated demeanor and acute perception of people and life in general – it was apparent that he was a cosmopolitan and experienced man of the world – well travelled. But at times she felt a distinct feeling that there was a darkness hovering around his persona and at these particular times she couldn't help feeling a slight unease in his presence which she was not entirely able to explain to herself.

Although Millicent had been quite nervous and timid initially during the first few months when in the presence of Olsten, his own easy manner soon put her at ease. She quickly began to gain more and more confidence, dealing proficiently with the day-to-day business operations and was able to handle situations in his absence. Olsten had complete faith in her ability as his personal assistant.

Millicent's manner was always calm and composed even when all around there was chaos. She brought a feeling of tranquility to Olsten's office that he certainly needed in times of panic and rush deadline periods when dealing with various meetings involving fabric samples and material choices, dress design, and marketing campaigns. He suspected that, sometimes, during the deadline periods, she may have felt some panic herself, but she still displayed a composure he admired. He liked that quality in a personal assistant, although he did feel as though he would have still valued her even if she had been a ridiculous, flustered, accident prone young woman. She was part of the team, and he could never imagine the office without her and felt blessed to have found her.

Millicent now informed Olsten that she had called Mrs. Defoe, to check how Amitola was after her nearly serious accident the previous day and had been told that she was absolutely fine apart from bruised knees.

Amitola was a young girl who Olsten had seemingly taken under his wing after he had saved her from imminent danger. As a toddler she had run blindly out into a road in front of an oncoming lorry - Olsten had rushed out and had grabbed her in the nick of time. He had thereafter befriended her parents, Mr. and Mrs. Defoe, and had kept in touch with them over the years.

This recent accident had also been a dangerous situation, and it was incredibly fortunate that he had yet again been around to save the young girl from serious injury. Amitola's parents regarded Olsten as their daughter's very own protector – he always seemed to be around when she needed help. Although they never expressed their reservations or questioned his somewhat inexplicable and intriguing existence in their daughter's life, they could never imagine or believe the ultimate motivation behind his ever-watchful eye over her.

Millicent also told Olsten, as he had requested her to do earlier on in the week, that she had selected a perfect birthday gift for Amitola. This had been one of her duties religiously every year since she had begun her employment with Olsten as well as shopping for Christmas gifts for the young girl. This year for Amitola's thirteenth birthday, Millicent had chosen one of the collectable dolls, which she hoped Amitola would love.

Olsten frowned, slightly puzzled at her choice of gift, which he felt might not be suitable or well received for a young, growing girl who would probably expect something far more exciting and sophisticated like a small, portable transistor radio. Aside from that, to a young soon to be teenager, such an expensive collector's doll would seem to be an extremely and outrageously extravagant gift, not to mention a little bizarre for her age and one that would not be fully appreciated and certainly not for its value. But Millicent insisted that if Amitola loved beautiful things, she was sure to be thrilled and completely mesmerized with a doll not only adorned in a beautiful gown and genuine miniature jewels, but one that came complete with a miniature armoire containing several gowns and a miniature faux fur coat. What girl would not, no matter what age, Millicent assured Olsten.

It was indeed an extravagant gift, but one that Amitola's parents would probably frown upon all the same, Olsten thought. Despite his reservations, Olsten thanked her and asked her to arrange to have the gift boxed up, wrapped and forwarded as soon as possible together with flowers and candy.

'I am sure she will be thrilled with her gift, and I can't wait to see her face when she opens it,' Millicent told him. 'At that age, I would have been absolutely ecstatic to have such a doll with its very own wardrobe complete with a selection of ballroom gowns and not to mention genuine miniature jewellery.'

There is going to be a party for her this weekend with some of her friends and family and you, as you know, are also invited. Thinking about that doll, though, as I have said she may well prefer something a bit more grown-up. However, I can tell that you yourself are a huge fan of the dolls, which I hasten to add, is an important factor while you are working here. I certainly know what to get you for Christmas,' Olsten laughingly told her before ending the call and setting down the handset.

Millicent smiled as she replaced the handset although she had a slight frown on her face. Despite his constant easy-going attitude, she couldn't help noticing that he had looked thoroughly and completely worn out today. Apart from a deep gash on his brow because of the accident, the dark circles under his eyes had started to look particularly bad during the past few months. She understood he was accustomed to late nights in his study at home, busy with his various projects. She would make sure that he was not disturbed during the afternoon, or more importantly, the evening. Any urgent matters would have to wait until the following morning.

Olsten walked across to his closet, pulled his jacket from one of the hangers and slung it over his shoulder - it was a very warm afternoon, and he would not need to wear it. He gathered some papers that he would possibly go over in the evening, tucked them in his briefcase and closed his office door securely behind him.

On passing Millicent's desk, he stopped and told her that he would be in the office very early the next morning in time for his scheduled nine thirty meeting, but in the meantime, she could contact him at his house during the evening, if needed.

'Well, I'm sure that will not be necessary, Olsten – everything has been dealt with that required your attention today and as the afternoon is free of appointments, I will not be bothering you at home,' she told him, smiling.

'That's fine, Millicent, I was hoping you would say that, but just in case, do let me know if something urgent comes up. You know you can call me at home any time if there is something vitally important that needs to be dealt with immediately.'

This had always been their habit although he hoped that they would not have any pressing matters to deal with today. He was looking forward to a good relaxing evening - he needed to replenish his soul. He was planning to have a soothing soak in a hot Jacuzzi with a glass of Bourbon. It was a much-needed exercise and one which he was certainly going to enjoy.

He often worked in the evening at home where he could concentrate more on important details without a telephone constantly ringing and interrupting his train of thought. This evening, in particular, he needed to be alone with his thoughts more than anything else.

Millicent also couldn't help noticing that he had been displaying some signs of disorientation and lack of concentration during the morning. She hoped that he was not suffering from a concussion from the blow to his head. She had been amazed when she heard that although he had miraculously missed the full impact of some falling scaffolding in order to shield Amitola from possible fatal injury, he had nevertheless sustained a head injury from one particular piece of timber whacking him over the head. She had taken the liberty of making a doctor's appointment for him and although he had seemed initially annoyed, he promised to pass by his physician on his way home. She hoped that he would keep to his promise.

It was most unusual for Olsten to leave his office early afternoon, but he felt that he could do with a bit of rest, especially as it was such a gloriously sunny, warm day. In fact, if he was honest with himself, he needed a short holiday and after he had tied up some important matters with his solicitor James Lambert, he hoped to arrange a short break for himself and maybe head off to Italy where he could take time to revisit an old friend or two and those wonderful buildings and artwork over there.

Italy had always held a very special place in Olsten's heart; he found its considerable architectural achievements, such as the construction of arches, domes and similar structure during ancient Rome, absolutely fascinating. This had been a particular passion of his during his short period of time there where he was studying art history and architecture before venturing over to the USA. His fascination with monuments, including statues, churches, art galleries, historic houses and archaeological remains were still a great source of fascination to him and was something that he would never tire of.

He smiled now as he noticed Millicent busy at her desk making notes of various tasks scheduled for the following day. Her desk was always full of sketches and fabric samples strewn all over. He knew that she had developed an interest in the design side of the business, especially when it came to historic period costume design, which she had been researching quite extensively lately, and he fully expected her to present some designs of her own when she felt ready. She had put forward an idea recently that she thought a collection of period collectable dolls would be an exciting and interesting scheme and had already sketched an Elizabethan doll complete with a selection of various bustling costumes of that particular era which she believed could be successful.

Olsten was impressed and knew she would strive to fulfill her dream of becoming more involved in costume designs. He decided that he was going to offer her all the encouragement, support and help that she needed and certainly deserved.

Olsten was such an imposing man and Millicent admired and respected him so much. He was an extremely striking and attractive man in his appearance; he was well used to towering above most people, being six foot six inches in height. His hair was very thick, dark blonde and wavy, which he wore combed straight back from his forehead, giving him a very sophisticated and wholesome look. He had a very sensual face with a good strong, square masculine jaw line; his eyes were a deep, dark penetrating brown outlined with thick black lashes. His thick black batwing eyebrows gave him an especially dramatic look. He was a very fine-looking individual, completely unaware of his very attractive physical allure, which caught the attention of many a female passing by.

As Millicent watched him walking over to the small life just outside her office door, she couldn't help thinking that it was such a pity he seemed to surround himself with a barrier to thwart various people from getting too close to him. It was as if he was almost afraid to become too familiar with the people who knew him the most, or thought they knew him. He was certainly a man shrouded in mystery.

'Be sure to pass by the doctor's clinic,' Millicent called out to remind him. She realized that she was nagging him, but it really was the only way to get him to do something that he adamantly refused to do. She knew him so well in that respect and knew also that he only agreed to such a request purely to appease her.

'Don't worry, Millicent. I've specifically left the office early with every intention of passing by to see the doctor. I won't hear the last of it if I miss *that* appointment.' He laughed as the iron doors on the old-fashioned lift snapped shut, making a loud clanging sound. He had not intentionally left the office early to see the doctor, but he knew now that he would have to keep his promise.

Although he was loathe to go, Olsten also knew that Millicent would continually nag at him. He had no time for doctors of any kind and their so-called medications, but just to please Millicent, he would go through the motions to put her mind at rest.

At the same time, Millicent suspected he was under some pressure where a certain young socialite by the name of Celeste Harrington was concerned, whom he had met at one of the many social parties and gatherings that he had to attend from time to time. Millicent had witnessed quite a few unpleasant scenes when this particular young woman had swept into his office unannounced, ranting and raving and making ridiculous accusations about him. Millicent had observed how kind and considerate Olsten was at all times with Celeste, but she felt all the same that the woman's behaviour was a great worry to Olsten, and she felt a dangerous unhealthy tension building up between them.

How it had all begun remained a mystery to Millicent as Olsten had never once mentioned Celeste as anything but a friend and sister of one of his business connections. Celeste had previously been invited to various cocktail parties at his home and had been a perfectly behaved guest in those days before she had gone through some sort of drastic personality change. Millicent wondered if Celeste's brother knew of her escapades, and if so, why had he not admonished his sister in some way, given the circumstances. She had on one occasion mentioned this to Olsten but at that time, he had told her simply not to worry about anything and had insisted that he was certainly not going to involve Celeste's brother in the matter unless it became absolutely necessary.

As much as Millicent tried not to interfere, she found it increasingly difficult to ignore the poor woman's state of wellbeing. After offering to assist Celeste into the elevator one day when the young woman had stumbled, and as a result nearly having her head chewed off for her trouble, Millicent had retreated well back after that. Although she knew that it was none of her business, she could not help feeling sorry for Celeste, who she could clearly see came from a very affluent background. It was tragic to see her when she came barging into the office, wearing the most elegant outfits and dripping in diamonds, but floundering around completely inebriated. Millicent worried that one day she would be mugged on her way home or worse, although fortunately she always departed in a limousine waiting for her outside.

Chapter Three

The owner of a small, but successful fashionable collectable doll corporation, *Sir Ryder & Company*, Olsten Ryder had enjoyed considerable success as his company had rapidly grown over the last five years. It was one of the most triumphant and celebrated doll manufacturers of its kind and he was immensely proud of the quality of his creations. The dolls were of the highest quality, made with the finest bisque porcelain.

He was particularly selective in his choice of creative staff members and, being aware that the making of a doll is one of the most exacting art forms requiring a whole host of talents in the process, they had all been meticulously chosen based on their exceptional skill and knowledge of their craft. He had made sure that he had a team of the very best and talented group of people he could possibly find - they were all extremely invaluable in his business.

After spending a short time in Italy studying art history and architecture, Olsten had then gone on to study in the Parsons School of Design in New York. Following his graduation, he had been invited to join a prestigious group of designers and was part of an internationally recognized force in the fashion field - he soon became one of the country's top celebrated designers. His fashion ideas were particularly inventive and almost had the look of being futuristic; many critics dubbed his flair as being avant-garde.

Throughout his career, Olsten's vision of how a modern American woman should dress continually caught the eye of the fashion world's trend-spotters;

his designs were featured regularly in such publications as *Women's Wear Daily*, *Town & Country*, *New York Magazine*, *The New York Times* and *Vogue*.

Despite his passion for the clothing design industry, Olsten had been interested in collectable dolls for some time and decided to try his hand at the doll sculpting process. He subsequently received a glowing review from an esteemed panel of judges at the National Institute of American Doll Artists Conference in NYC, for the model-like fashion doll he had entered for critique.

During the years that followed, Olsten turned more and more of his attention to developing and perfecting his doll designs, while still pursuing the career of a rising fashion designer. He finally made the decision to leave the fashion industry to concentrate more on his doll manufacturing venture and after purchasing one of America's oldest doll companies together with its rich legacy, he made it into his own small, but extremely successful corporation.

All of Olsten's dolls and costumes reflected his particular fashion industry background and in particular, his intricate passion and desire for absolute beauty and perfection. These creations were subsequently prominently featured in national and international media including *People* magazine, *CNN*, *Entertainment Tonight*, *Women's Wear Daily* and British *Vogue* magazine. Several of his creations were added to the permanent collection of the Louvre Museum of Decorative Arts in Paris, France.

Olsten also part served as Standards Chairman and President of the National Institute of American Doll Artists (NIADA) and regularly aligned his company and creative spirit with a variety of charitable initiatives. His magnificent and perfected dolls were regularly featured in worldwide doll and toy specialty retailers and featured as a fine doll boutique in the Manhattan stores.

Olsten's collectable dolls were adorned in fine, sophisticated clothing, as befitting a work of art, involving the use of magnificent fabrics. A great deal of care and attention was put into the choice of fabrics and lace ordered from manufacturers, which were of the finest and most beautiful materials, including Calais lace, silk taffetas and silk chiffons, an exquisite wardrobe of hand-beaded silks, luxurious cashmere and camel hair - a myriad of exclusive haute couture fabrics.

All moulds for the dolls were specially crafted and handmade by the company and not produced on an assembly line like most contemporary doll companies. To ensure that the products were made with care and consummate quality, a great deal of thought and time was put into the whole process, right down to the very last detail.

Olsten was immensely proud of their unique style and preferred a modest production line of any model. He was primarily a fanatical perfectionist and wanted his collectable dolls to be not only unique, but also absolutely and irresistibly perfected, right down to their miniature painted toenails. He adored beautiful women and elegant women's attire and wanted the dolls to look like living mannequins.

Their latest line of models was to include a line of legendary movie stars. This had been a great idea of Danielle Fontaine, his French-born doll clothes designer, and he wholeheartedly agreed that they would be a huge success. They were presently working on an Audrey Hepburn look-alike doll, depicting her role as the elegant and sophisticated woman in the movie *Breakfast at Tiffany's*. The doll was to be adorned in a black simple cut empire-line waist dress, arm length gloves, a string of pearls and a high-quality miniaturized fur shoulder wrap.

All the dolls were produced and marketed, complete with a selection of miniature beautiful full-length gowns, fur coats and authentic hand-crafted miniature jewellery, to include diamond earrings, necklaces, bracelets and, of course, ornate hats and scarfs. Each model came complete with the doll's very own trunk and miniature armoire.

The fashions represented some of the finest women's clothes miniaturized to fit their eighteen-inch models, using classic dress making techniques with vintage fabrics and designs to create the ultimate pieces for the cultivated buyer and dedicated collector.

In addition to the numerous miniature porcelain models, he had a very select and highly sought after specialised life-sized assemblage of collectable dolls including wax, bisque, porcelain and composition dolls, earning a highly reputable name with antique and collectable doll enthusiasts worldwide. He had many customers requesting a life-sized doll made in the likeness of their loved ones. He himself had one special ceramic life-sized doll close to his heart standing on display in his office which customers admired. This doll, of course, created a lot of interest but when questioned about the history of the doll, Olsten would always just smile saying nothing.

As Olsten now stepped out of the building, Kyle Fenton, his driver, was waiting for him at the front of the entrance. Kyle promptly opened the door of the limousine and Olsten settled in the back seat relaxed and ready for the drive.

When they pulled out from the kerb, Olsten sighed loudly, feeling slightly irritated when he heard the engine of another vehicle immediately start up behind them which slowly began to follow them closely. He smiled to himself in a cynical way at how the driver of the vehicle could not be more conspicuous if he tried and Olsten was becoming increasingly tired of being constantly under surveillance. He decided not to worry about it for the time being as he was determined to have a more relaxing afternoon and evening.

Olsten studied his driver in the rear-view mirror as they drove along through the busy streets of London. He really did not know much about his background at all, but he had come with excellent references. He was extremely smart in his appearance and although appearing to be very polite in his manner, there was something curiously callous about him - it was just a certain odd look in his eyes that Olsten had observed at times. His previous much trusted driver Demetrius Stafros, one of the two sons of his office cleaner, Mrs Agno Stafros, had left quite suddenly without giving notice. His mother had been stunned, having no idea of his whereabouts at the time. It was a tragedy when she had later been notified that his body had been discovered washed up on a beach on the Greek island of Lesbos by a Greek coastguard. The local authorities believed that he had taken his own life as there had been no suspicious circumstances surrounding his death. Mrs Stafros refused to believe that he would take his own life considering that suicide was a sin in their faith.

In the meantime, Millicent had been instructed by Olsten to contact a reliable recruiting agency for personal chauffeurs. A short time after interviewing one or two candidates, Kyle had been selected with excellent character references. Olsten was very adept at reading a person's character but in this case, he was not able to do that with Kyle – he found it quite extraordinary. Olsten had initially gone to some concerted efforts to become familiar with the young man to get to know his character, but Kyle retreated every time. Kyle made it very clear that he was not interested in a congenial relationship with his employer. Olsten determined that the young man was best left alone - after all, he was a reliable driver although as a young man, in his opinion, he was far too serious for his own good. He concluded that Kyle was a very private type of person and Olsten could easily relate to that, as he very much valued his own privacy. Kyle's appointment had been offered with the privilege of being afforded a small studio apartment in the basement within Olsten's house and included the luxury of having all meals, on and off duty, prepared and served in the staff kitchen by Olsten's housekeeper and cook, Nancy Murray. Olsten could afford to be very generous with his members of staff at work and at his home – he believed that all staff should feel happy and comfortable in their jobs and in return, all he asked was their loyalty to him and commitment to their work.

'How are you today, Sir?' Kyle now asked – his eyes narrowing slightly. He was very aware that Olsten was observing him closely, almost studying him meticulously in the rear-view mirror.

Kyle's manner was always polite if nothing else, although this seemed to unsettle Olsten in a puzzling way. Demetrius had always been slightly cheeky in his manner, but with a touch of charisma which had appealed to Olsten. Their conversations together had been easy and comfortable, whereas with Kyle, it was almost painful to conduct a simple conversation with him.

'Good, very good,' Olsten said. 'How are you enjoying your job – have you settled in well?' 'Yes – thank you, Sir,' Kyle replied. 'Oh, before I forget – I need to stop by to see Dr. Oleg at the clinic in Harley Street prior to going home,' Olsten then said. 'Sure Sir,' Kyle replied as he turned into Grosvenor Street, towards New Bond Street. As they drove through the streets, Olsten gazed out of the window, constantly amazed at the huge quantity of people seemingly rushing around the area whatever time of day it was – he wondered where they all came from. So many different people from all walks of life going about their day-to-day business, marching along like an army of ants. Olsten, still deep in thought, now flinched as the car suddenly came to a halt outside the clinic in Harley Street. When he reluctantly climbed out of the car, walked up the steps and pushed open the heavy front door, he had a fleeting urge to turn on his heels and flee back out down the steps. He sighed heavily as he continued walking towards the young lady behind the reception desk.

'Good afternoon, Sir,' she said, smiling radiantly.

'Good afternoon,' he replied smiling in return. 'My name is Mr. Ryder, and I am here for my one thirty appointment.'

'Please take a seat, Mr. Ryder – the doctor will be right with you,' she replied, after checking her appointment book.

The very smell of the inside of a medical institution made him feel extremely restless and as he sat down, the young lady behind the reception desk glanced at him and again smiled.

When he was ushered into a clean smelling, stark white medical room for an assessment, the physician proceeded to examine the pupils of his eyes and then carried out a general test of Olsten's coordination and sense of feeling, his memory, orientation, and concentration capacity.

'Are you experiencing any double vision?' the physician asked Olsten, as he leaned closer towards him. 'What about a ringing sensation in the ears?'

'No, I'm fine, apart from a slight headache and lack of sleep these days, I feel okay, honestly,' Olsten insisted, as he stood up ready to leave.

'We just need to take precautions here – if you feel any loss of ability to concentrate or have any feelings of anxiety or depression, or worse still, any blackouts, I would like you to make another appointment to see me,' he told Olsten with a definite look of concern on his face.

'I will for sure, but I can tell you now, I have certainly not been experiencing any blackouts – not to my knowledge, anyway,' Olsten joked, as he put his hand out to shake the physician's hand. 'And thanks for all your concerns,' he continued, 'but there is really nothing to worry about - I feel just fine'.

'That's a matter of opinion,' the physician muttered almost to himself as he watched his patient quickly stride towards the door.

As Olsten walked out of the door and closed it softly behind him, the physician sat at his desk making notes in his file. He was concerned about the patient's cold touch, faint pulse and the dilation of the pupils. He always felt extremely irritated when a patient was nonchalant and uncaring about their overall wellbeing, and he certainly felt annoyed by Olsten's drollness in the circumstances.

'Well, I've done my bit,' Olsten muttered to himself, as he walked out of the building. 'At least it will keep Millicent happy.' He knew that the physician had been concerned about his overall condition, but he felt fine in the circumstances. In fact, he decided that he would return the following week just to assure the physician that he had sustained no serious damage from the accident. He would try to concentrate the next time, though, to ensure that the physician did not suspect anything unusual in his condition. He had been thoroughly bored and agitated during the whole examination, so much so, that he had consciously switched himself off during the ordeal causing his heartbeat and pulse to slow down at a most alarming pace. He had willed himself to retreat into a somewhat stupefied, almost unconscious state of mind and body – that was the extent of his loathing of medical environments. But, even so, he determined that he would really try not to show his irritation so obviously the next time. Olsten had called his housekeeper Nancy earlier, to let her know that he was intending to leave the office early afternoon and had asked her to prepare a dinner of succulent salmon, potatoes and asparagus with a creamy spicy sauce that evening before he retired to his hot steamy Jacuzzi. He was now very anxious to get home and relax.

Nancy had been employed as his housekeeper a short time after he had arrived in London and he was very happy with her although she was an incessant chatterbox, as he often told her. Nancy was invariably familiar with Olsten's routine - sometimes he would be away for weeks at a time out of the country and other times, he would work very late in the evening at his office. She always maintained and kept his huge house scrupulously clean and conscientiously planned and prepared nutritional meals for him.

Although at times she felt almost invisible to the naked eye working with Olsten, she was aware that she was very much valued as far as he was concerned. He was generous to a fault and often presented her with flowers, chocolates and small gifts.

When she first worked with Olsten, she had the most curious sentiment that he seemed to be almost of an imperial background; his manner and character were so eloquent and noble – she could not even explain it to herself. It was just a strange sense that she felt in his presence and at times she had to stop herself from almost curtsying.

She had been a little apprehensive and doubtful when she had first applied for the position. When she had received a call to meet with his secretary, she had expected to be positively drilled at the interview, but she was pleasantly surprised when she was finally introduced to her prospective boss. He seemed to need no more than a firm handshake and the position had been offered to her. She need not have worried as

Millicent had pointed out to her at the time - his firm warm handshake and reassuring smile had put her completely at ease immediately.

Millicent had mentioned to her that he had an uncanny way of being able to read a person's character by just looking into their eyes. She had explained to Nancy at the time that when she had been a new recruit herself, she had been extremely nervous at the prospect of meeting her new boss but assured Nancy that he was a wonderful man to work with and how quickly she herself had settled into a very comfortable daily routine with him. Similarly, Nancy had also quickly adapted to a very comfortable working relationship with Olsten. For his part, Olsten could not have wished for a more conscientious and loyal housekeeper.

She had been amazed when told at the onset of her offer of employment that her job also came with her very own apartment within the house. This additional part of her employment offer had come at a critical time in her life, and she couldn't quite believe how incredibly fortunate she was when she accepted the role. Her husband had died the year before and she had been left not only lonely and desolate but horrified to discover that her husband had left her with no financial security.

Chapter Four

Later, when Olsten climbed into bed just before midnight, feeling completely exhausted, the phone rang and rather reluctantly he picked up the handset, and instantly wished that he had not when he heard the voice of his solicitor James Lambert. He rubbed his chin in annoyance as the fatigue that had crept up on him during the late afternoon now completely overwhelmed him and he wanted nothing more than to drift off into a deep, undisturbed sleep.

Although he had promised himself the sheer luxury of soaking his aching body in a steaming hot Jacuzzi, he never quite got around to it. After eating the delicious meal that Nancy had prepared for him, he had retired to his study to go over some papers which he had brought back with him from the office, not noticing how quickly the hours went by, before finally admitting to himself that it was time to retire to his bed.

'I'm sorry to call you at such a late hour, Olsten,' James said before immediately launching into the one subject that Olsten did not particularly want to hear about at any hour of the day or night.

'I just thought I should let you know that Celeste Harrington called me this evening. I must say that girl is acting very strangely these days. I just cannot imagine what has gotten into her. It is almost as if she has gone through a severe change of personality, and it is most disturbing to witness. She was such a confident young woman, full of the joys of spring, when we first met her and it is scary the way she is behaving now - I don't know about you, Olsten, but I am extremely worried about her.'

He paused for a second while he took a puff of his cigar – Olsten could almost smell the smoke down the line. He knew that James was partial to a cigar and a glass of Cognac before retiring for the night. Listening patiently and wondering at the same time how James could sit up halfway through the early hours of the morning puffing on his cigars and drinking his endless glasses of Cognac and still arrive at his office at the crack of dawn, Olsten knew that, like himself, James was a workaholic and spent most of his waking day working right through and beyond.

'If I'm honest,' he continued, 'I don't really like to harp on about Celeste and her feelings of rejection, but I thought I would just warn you that she may pay you a little visit sometime during this week. And, I have to say, God help you – the mood she is in now, I dread to think what the outcome of that meeting will be. Plus, her mother has been on to me and insists that I ask you to desist from interfering with her daughter's life and spoiling her relationship with Lewis.

Desist, desist – what an incredibly melodramatic word to use, Olsten thought as he listened to James. He could hardly keep his eyes open, and he felt his head lolling forward, almost feeling that he was about to lose consciousness any minute.

Apart from being his solicitor, James was a very trustworthy and close friend to Olsten, and he very much valued his friendship although James could be extremely annoying at times. This was such a time, especially so late at night and Olsten did not feel the least bit eager to continue talking to him.

'Yes, she is certainly behaving so peculiarly and unpredictably, James, and I can assure you that contrary to what Mrs. Harrington is saying, I have never tried to interfere in her daughter's life,' Olsten said, sighing in complete exasperation as he shook his head trying to stay awake.

'How did this all come about, Olsten – surely you must have realised at some point how serious she was feeling about you. Her mother is adamant that you are the cause of her mental and physical breakdown and has asked me to implore you not to contact her and to stay out of her life. She said that she has no doubt whatsoever you have led Celeste astray with absolutely no regard to the fact that she is so much younger and that you knew she was a vulnerable and sweet natured girl, ripe for the picking.'

Implore – now that's another dramatic word, Olsten thought as his eyelids began to droop again.

'Hah, that is absolute nonsense, James, and you know it. I think Mrs. Harrington is getting carried away – she should stop trying to put the blame on me and concentrate more on getting help for her daughter,' Olsten replied.

'But what makes her so certain that you led Celeste on, or astray, as she puts it? She was so upset and said that you have deliberately deceived her daughter purely for your own egotistical enjoyment and self-indulgence.'

James heard Olsten take a sharp intake of breath at that point.

'If anything, Celeste is interfering in my life, although I feel so sorry for her - that poor young girl, I just wish I could help her more, but she just goes hysterical every time she comes near me. If she is so besotted with me, why on earth does she behave as she does in my presence – now what can you say about that?'

'*Because* according to her, you are not being totally honest with her,' James replied. He knew that the conversation was going around in circles, but he just could not understand why a young girl would make such seemingly false accusations for no reason.

'Did you know that she has hired somebody to follow me? I just don't understand what she thinks she is doing by hiring that private investigator, although I rather suspect that he is just a bodyguard from one of those clubs she frequents these days. The man is practically on my back from the minute I leave my house to the time I leave my office and back again. He skulks around in every dark corner, deluding himself that he is invisible to the naked eye. What has gotten into the girl – I had no idea she felt like this about me. She was engaged to be married last year, so what happened between then and now, I do not know - I am completely and utterly astonished. I've given her absolutely no reason whatsoever to think that there is or has ever been anything other than friendship between us – believe me, James.'

James then heard Olsten grunt down the line, before he appeared to have dropped the handset by the side of his bed – the sound of it clattered loudly in James' ear, making him flinch and grunt in return.

'Sorry about that - the phone slipped out of my hand,' Olsten mumbled down the line. There were a few seconds of silence, apart from heavy laboured breathing and realizing that Olsten was maybe struggling to keep awake, James decided to end the call, but before he was about to say goodnight, Olsten began speaking again.

'What that man, whoever he is, finds to do with himself in between times of following me everywhere I go, hiding around corners waiting for me to come into his view, I really cannot imagine. But I know one thing, if he keeps it up, I will have to pull him aside and talk to him. So far, I have found it quite amusing, as the man is very young and obviously inexperienced.'

'No, don't even think about accosting him, Olsten – if he is acting on Celeste's behalf, it will only give her another excuse to retaliate,' James said, his voice full of concern. 'Why she keeps confiding in me,' he continued, 'I just don't know - I'm your solicitor, after all, not hers. It is almost as if she is intent on fabricating all kinds of stories to cause as much trouble as she can just to provoke you. But listen, Olsten, don't forget she is a woman scorned, and she has made a conscientious effort to pry into your private affairs and has come up with some information, which has convinced her that you are some kind of devious character.'

On hearing this last comment, Olsten suddenly started laughing. James could not help feeling irritated himself at this point and sighed loudly down the line.

'Don't be so ridiculous. And what information, may I ask, has convinced her that I am some kind of devious character? That is outrageous– defamation of character. Now listen, I've had enough of this nonsense,' Olsten said, his voice sounding croaky – he suddenly felt dog tired. 'Why do you keep saying that she is a woman scorned and why would she want to provoke me? How can she be a woman scorned when I have never ever given her the slightest sign of any romantic? I have never even kissed the girl for God's sake – well apart from when she literally lunged at me on one occasion. She was a fun-loving girl one minute, thrilled and excited about getting married to that young man she spent most of her time with last year and then suddenly she becomes this obsessive, demented and hysterical woman and all the attention is suddenly on me. I just do not understand it, James – there is something very wrong here, I am telling you. I am seriously starting to wonder if she is maybe taking prescription drugs that are having some kind of adverse effect on her. I certainly do not need all this aggravation in my life – I have enough excitement to contend with as it is.'

'Is that so? And what kind of excitement is that, then?' James asked, laughing now trying to make light of the situation.

'This is no time to joke. I am not in the mood. It just seems all so ridiculous to me,' Olsten replied gruffly.

'I know this is really none of my business, but I can't help wondering *what* exactly is going on between the two of you because she absolutely and emphatically insists that you are involved in a romantic relationship with her, which she says you are now denying. I really think you ought to invite her over one evening for a good talking to and set out to gain her affections again. Don't get me wrong, I know that this is not what you want to hear, but could you not just give her a little encouragement to keep her in high spirits, if you know what I mean.'

'No, I don't know what you mean. To give her a little encouragement would be the worst thing for me to do in the circumstances. There never has been and there never will be any romantic relationship between myself and Celeste – *why won't you believe this*,' Olsten retorted.

'*Why* would she make it up?' James replied irritably.

'James – if you are not careful, I'm going to come round there and punch you right in the mouth. Now leave me alone and let me get some sleep.'

'I'm telling you, Olsten, when a woman like this sets her sights on a man and he is not cooperative, she can become deadly. The woman, or should I say young girl, remember now, she is barely twenty years old, is used to getting all her own way and it is you she is relentlessly pursuing with a passion.'

Olsten suddenly felt completely tired of the whole subject.

'JAMES,' he shouted down the line. 'YOU ARE NOT LISTENING TO ME - I have no idea what is going on here. I am going to say this just one more time and then I don't want to hear another word about it. All I know is that she began behaving completely out of character sometime late last year. I have always treated her as I would have treated my own daughter - she is just an impressionable young woman, and I would never have taken advantage of her in any way. I am certainly not going to encourage her now in any way.'

'Okay, alright, just calm down, Olsten. For goodness' sake, it's like talking to a bear with a sore head. If you are not up to this now, we'll leave it until tomorrow. I can see I am just wasting my time trying to talk to you at this late hour, or should I say, early hour. I'll call you again tomorrow and we can discuss it over dinner somewhere – your choice. I'm off now.'

Before hanging up, although not meaning to pry any further into Olsten's personal affairs in the circumstances, he quickly added, 'Oh, yes, and Millicent said that you had been able to rescue Amitola from yet another near accident when she stepped out of a library and some scaffolding became loose overhead and just missed her head by inches. Are you sure, you don't have hidden antenna's that alert you to would be accidents where that girl is concerned? No, second thoughts, don't answer that. We'll not bother to go into all that just now, I'll see you tomorrow – goodnight, sleep well.'

Without answering, Olsten just slammed the handset down loudly, leaving James feeling very uneasy. He'd regretted having to call Olsten about something that he knew his friend and client would clearly not want to discuss especially at such a late hour He had known Olsten for some years and knew only too well what a very secretive man he could be. Anything concerning his personal life was not something that he was prepared to divulge with anyone. Even if there was something going on with Celeste or any other woman, James knew that Olsten was not about to share this information with anybody, not even somebody who was seemingly close to him, like himself.

Although Olsten had annoyed him – well, they had annoyed each other, if he was honest with himself, James felt a sense of dread and foreboding creeping up on him and he felt a huge amount of concern for his close friend. He knew that there was something very odd going on, but he could not fathom why or what was happening. Whilst he may have appeared judgemental, he had spoken with fondness in his heart and had not intended to criticise Olsten's conduct in any way. But he knew that Olsten mistakenly regarded Celeste as a mixed-up harmless young girl.

After an explosive confrontation between them the previous year, Olsten had nevertheless tried to always steer well clear of Celeste if possible. James knew that Olsten did not want to hurt her feelings in any way but felt that it was for the best to keep her well out of his way. All the same, despite Olsten's fervent denials of any such romantic attachment, James couldn't help wondering just how much he was actually involved with Celeste.

James personally felt that Celeste was a serious threat to the wellbeing of Olsten's future - he had seen her kind of woman before, and in his experience, they were extremely lethal and dangerous. It was the very nature of her accusations and the extent of her paranoia that worried him - they were the kind of accusations that could not only ruin a man's reputation, but also his whole life.

After speaking with Olsten, James sat in deep thought remembering how troubled Olsten had been when he had called around to see him late one afternoon the previous year and Celeste had flounced into his office soon after.

At that time, Celeste had physically attacked Olsten, pummelling him with her fists. She had gone into a jealous rage when she had come across a photograph of Olsten and a dark-haired woman, whilst snooping around in his private rooms adjacent to his office.

Olsten ordinarily did not allow anybody in his private quarters but to keep her from having one of her tantrums, he had let her run free. On seeing the photograph, she had literally gone berserk, demanding to know all the facts about his personal history. James had been shocked and had taken hold of Celeste, pulling her away from Olsten.

'Who is this woman to you and why do you keep her hidden from me – I have a right to know,' she had screamed at Olsten, struggling to pull away from James who had been holding onto her tightly.

'I don't think that is really any of your business, Celeste,' he had told her calmly.

'As your future wife I think I am entitled to know everything about you and if you are not prepared to share that little piece of your life that you seem determined to hide from me, I shall have to find out for myself. I know your dirty little secrets, Olsten, and I am going to make it my business to expose you for what you really are – you are nothing but a deceitful and despicable monster,' she had spat at him.

'Now, come on, Celeste, you don't know what you are talking about. I have never tried to deceive you in any way. I think we should call your brother to pick you up and take you home,' Olsten had replied, walking towards her.

She had then dropped the picture frame and despite James still holding onto her, she had strained to lung again at Olsten – spitting and hissing like a wild cat.

Olsten had gone to great efforts to pacify her in the circumstances but, by the time Vincent had arrived, she had gone into a trance-like state, barely able to speak, which had immediately shocked James. Olsten had given her some brandy, laid her down on a couch in his private lounge and had tenderly covered her with a blanket. After a short time, she had fallen into a deep sleep.

Olsten, James and Vincent had sat talking for some time during that afternoon through to the evening, and although Vincent had been reluctant to leave her in Olsten's private quarters later that evening, he felt in the circumstances that as she appeared to be sleeping quite peacefully after her outburst, it was best to just let her remain there. Olsten had assured both James and Vincent that he would stay with her until she was ready to go home, and they had both left feeling confident that she was in safe hands. He had then picked her up and carried her into his bedroom, where he had laid her down to sleep more comfortably, while he settled himself down on his couch to sleep.

He had awoken very early the next morning to find that she had already left and although he had called several times during that day to check on her, she had refused to speak to him. He had thought about sending flowers but decided that it was better to leave her for the time being. He had hoped that she would, in turn, call him some time later to explain her irrational bouts of bizarre behaviour and apologise.

After that particular attack, Olsten had been deeply concerned about Celeste's unhinged state of mind. She was not the cool sophisticated female that he had thought she was - she had become a very unstable and possessive young woman, dangerously obsessed with him. She was unpredictable and he had then considered her a loose cannon ready to explode. James knew Olsten had realised at that time; he would have to be very cautious in dealing with her in future.

All the same, James had been stunned and completely baffled by Celeste's ramblings about a proposal of marriage that Olsten had apparently made to her.

On setting down the handset, after patiently but grudgingly listening to James and his obvious concerns, Olsten switched off the side lamp and settled down for a good night's sleep - he very soon drifted off.

As always, she was there waiting for him in that brightly lit glass compartment - her satiny smooth black mane of hair sweeping down her back like a cloak. She put her arms around his neck and held him close, as he lifted her up, swirling her around and around until she laughingly begged him to stop. He set her down rather clumsily in his dizzy state after feeling hands on his back pushing him forward and she fell backwards in the glass compartment against a switch which set the operational process into a faster pace. He watched helplessly as she began to rapidly shrink until she was a small dot – and then she was gone.

He cried out in his sleep and thrashed about struggling to awaken from the haunting recurrent dream. He woke up dripping in sweat - he could feel his heart beating furiously and he almost fell out of his bed as he stumbled towards his bathroom. Standing in front of the bathroom mirror, squinting at his reflection, he saw his eyes were bloodshot from endless sleepless nights and dark shadows under his eyes gave him a sinister appearance. He bent over the sink to splash his face in cold water. After drying his face with a hand towel, he stood for a while contemplating the dark circles under his eyes.

'I look like a bloody vampire,' he whispered to himself as he turned out the light and walked back to his bedroom. He threw himself back onto his bed and very soon drifted off into a much-needed deep sleep, dreaming of travelling miles and miles over many oceans and many realms - his journey seeming never to end.

Chapter Five

Olsten arrived at his office early the next morning, as promised, and promptly sat at his desk to go through all his messages. Millicent appeared, looking as fresh as a daisy, as usual. She set down a tray containing a pot of steaming hot coffee, some Danish pastries, and a jug of grapefruit juice, which he firmly believed gave him enough energy to boost start him for the rest of the day.

'Good morning, Olsten. I hope you had a relaxing evening,' she said, cheerfully, as she held out a cup of strong coffee for him, after he had gulped down a glass of fresh grapefruit juice.

'Well, not exactly – I ended up going through some paperwork and then going to be quite late, which I had promised myself not to do. So, I really need this,' he said, gratefully as he drank the scalding coffee. Having said that, Olsten felt surprisingly fresh despite his restless night and, after having taken a long hot shower once he had hauled himself out of his bed early that morning, he felt ready for another busy day at the office. He was scheduled to meet with Danielle Fontaine, his clothes designer for the dolls, at nine-thirty – it was already twenty past now, he noticed, and she had still not arrived. It was just as well, as he was really enjoying his Danish pastries – just the way he liked them, freshly baked, coated with sticky apricot jam and sprinkled with almonds. He munched away as Millicent quickly went over some important papers received in the early morning mail.

He was looking forward to seeing Danielle again with her new designs and although they had lots to do, he wanted to make her visit a pleasant one as always. Apart from dealing with the necessary business matters, they usually dined together once or twice during her stay in London, at one of her favourite restaurants. He very much enjoyed her company – she spent most of the time gushing about her designs that she was hoping he would like as much as she did, although he had to admit at times that he thought them a little too risqué for a doll.

'Well, you certainly look a lot more refreshed today after your half day yesterday,' Millicent answered, if somewhat a little sarcastic. He glanced at her and noticed that she was smiling mischievously. At the onset of their working relationship, she would not have had the nerve to make such a light-hearted comment to him but now that she was extremely relaxed in his presence, she had come out of her shy self somewhat and had gained more and confidence as their work relationship developed.

He looked up at her smiling – he was so pleased that she seemed to enjoy her job, and it was evident right from the beginning that they worked well together and even though she did seem to want to pamper or nag him at times, he did not mind in the least.

'It certainly was a most pleasant change for me to take off so early on in the day although, and I have to say I was loathe to do it, but I made a concerted effort to attend at the physician's clinic as promised, so I don't want any more of your nagging, young lady,' Olsten said, laughing.

'And how did that go? I hope there were no repercussions from the accident,' Millicent replied somewhat more seriously, leaning a little closer over the desk towards him to watch his facial expression.

'No – none, although I had to endure an overall examination, which is something I despise, as you know. But it's all done now, and I don't want you worrying about my health for a considerable while.'

Millicent was an only child and had been the apple of her parent's eyes. Her father had died very young when Millicent had turned fourteen and she had been heartbroken. Soon after, her mother had met and married her second husband Roberto Giordano, who owned a very popular Italian Restaurant in St. James' Street. When Millicent left school, her mother had encouraged her to go into the business with them, but it was not the life that she had wanted for herself. She had set her heart on fashion design and although she began working with Olsten as his secretary, although she now classed herself as his personal assistant, she knew that she ultimately wanted to become involved in costume design for the collectable dolls.

She was a lovely young woman with masses of curly auburn hair, which she kept neatly pushed back from her face with a large black hair band, giving her a severe appearance older than her years, although when she became extremely busy and began rushing about, stray tendrils of her curls escaped, lending her a much softer look. She had the most attractive green eyes that seemed to sparkle like huge emeralds from amidst all the freckles she had spread all over every area of her face.

While dining out with Olsten one evening, Millicent had confessed that these freckles were the curse of her life and that if she had not been inflicted with them, her life would have been entirely different, as she would have become a famous ballet dancer with pale porcelain skin and straight silky hair flowing down her back as she pirouetted around on a stage.

During the course of the evening, she had been slightly preoccupied and a little maudlin as a current love affair had ended rather abruptly, although Olsten managed to cajole her to laugh about it, eventually. It had been a very relaxing and charming occasion, and they had not discussed any business matters the whole evening. The next day, she had told him that he had made her feel so much better and she had forgotten the rotten swine in question already. Olsten could not quite see what on earth she had seen in the man to begin with, from what she had told him. He tried to counsel her about how women were such strange creatures and seemed to want a man who treated them badly.

As far as Olsten was concerned, Millicent was like a breath of fresh air and whenever he came into the office a little tired or ill tempered, she always cheered him up. He could be very demanding and a trifle impatient at times when he felt anxious that they were not going to meet a deadline, but she appeared to be able to always deal with the pressures of the job regardless.

Millicent poured Olsten another cup of coffee and then sat down opposite him, to open the incoming mail while he went through his messages. It was the most peaceful part of the day for them both and a ritual they both enjoyed immensely. Millicent always arrived at the office well before him and by the time he showed up at the office, everything was well organized and ready for him – she was the perfect assistant.

He drank the second cup of steaming hot, strong coffee practically straight down again and then poured himself another, all the time grinning. She knew he was teasing her.

'Did you manage to get the flowers and candy delivered yesterday?' he asked, without looking up. He took a huge bite from his second Danish pastry and gulped down his third cup of coffee.

'Yes,' Millicent answered frowning now, looking a bit concerned. 'I just don't know how you can gulp down cup after cup of steaming hot coffee – it's a wonder you don't burn your mouth and throat.'

Olsten chuckled. 'Oh, don't worry about me – that's the only way I can drink coffee – strong and steaming hot. You should know that by now!'

Millicent nodded. 'Yes,' she then continued, 'after ordering the flowers, I called her parents to let them know to expect a delivery. I am sure she will be delighted with her gift. Mrs Defoe was telling me that for a teenager, Amitola is remarkably mature and chatters non-stop about everyday matters.

He glanced up from his appointment ledger with all its various notes attached.

'That's good. I'll call Mrs Defoe later this afternoon to check on how things are. Thanks for doing that, Millicent – I know it's not part of your duties, but I do really appreciate it,' he said softly, almost absentmindedly, seemingly distracted by something else on his mind at that point.

'Did I by any chance receive a call from Miss Harrington yesterday afternoon?' he asked, trying to sound unconcerned.

'No, not that I can think of but maybe Roy took a call from her,' Millicent replied, looking up at him again and watching his expression closely. 'Would you like me to call Celeste for you?' she ventured.

'No, no, that won't be necessary,' he quickly replied.

Millicent observed the concerned expression on his face at the mention of Celeste's name. She knew that the young lady in question was a cause of considerable worry to several people, and she especially felt sorry for Celeste's ex-fiancé who must be forever worried about her antics since she had surprisingly and abruptly cancelled their wedding seemingly without any prior warning. In the circumstances, Celeste's ex-fiancé had been very understanding – *too understanding in the circumstances,* Millicent thought and wondered if he was far more distraught than he let on. It was just such a strange situation and one that she could not really understand – she could not imagine that Olsten could possibly be involved with such an erratic young woman so much younger than himself. He was always very kind and sympathetic to Celeste at all times although she persistently berated him for his cruel unfeeling treatment of her.

Millicent sat there in deep thought, carefully watching Olsen's face attentively. He was very guarded about showing emotion, but it was clear that Celeste was troubling him. Much as she wanted to, Millicent could not even attempt to discuss any such matter with him as she knew that his guard would go up and he would retreat immediately.

'And, by the way,' Olsten said quickly changing the subject. 'I know that I was not entirely in agreement with your idea of gifting a collectable doll to a teenage girl as a birthday present -I do think that the doll you selected was an excellent choice. Mind you, although that model does not include a particularly vast expensive collection of authentic miniature jewellery - I would hate to think that the doll would inevitably be stolen.'

'Oh, I doubt very much that anybody who is not a serious collector of such dolls would even expect for one moment that the jewellery on any of the dolls is real. I know that all of the models are very expensive collectable items, but I would not imagine that anybody would take any interest in stealing a child's doll unless it was another child or a genuine collector of such dolls,' Millicent replied.

'Yes, you are probably right but all the same, as a growing girl going into her teenage years, I hope she really appreciates it.'

As Millicent stood up and stepped back to walk away from Olsten's desk to refill his cup of coffee once again, he looked up and smiled at her and then said cheerfully, 'You know Millicent, you have a particular passion for those period dolls that we are hoping to perfect to the highest quality. I want you to become a little more involved in the dress design side and coordinate with Danielle. It'll be another line of dolls for us to seriously think about.'

Millicent beamed at this remark - he was right, she did have a particular interest in the period fashion designs and loved the grandiose of those costumes. She absolutely adored romantic period dramas and historic period costumes especially fascinated her;

beautiful, flouncing, bustling dresses and hats with ostrich plumes looked spectacular to her.

Apart from *"The Barretts of Wimpole Street,"* Millicent had many favourite period movies including *"Marie Antoinette," "Private Lives,"* and *"Idiot's Delight,"* which had fabulous clothing and accessories. The little beaded Juliet cap that Norma Shearer wore in *"Romeo and Juliet"* became the rage among stylish women of the day. She also adored the movies starring Katherine Hepburn, including *"The Philadelphia Story,"* and *"Woman of the Year."* In these particular movies, Hepburn's sporty-yet-glamorous image was well displayed – the fashions had been so well cut and were incredibly elegant and chic.

It was safe to say that Millicent was a movie junkie and a profound and incurable romantic. She should have lived in days gone by as an eighteenth-century romantic heroine that she spent so much time reading about.

Just then the phone rang, and Millicent immediately picked up the handset. It was Roy Bolton, the ground floor reception attendant cum security man, ringing to inform her that Ms. Fontaine had just arrived in reception. Millicent quickly gathered all the relevant papers, put them in a file ready for the meeting in the boarding room before going down to the reception area to greet Danielle. Several minutes later, she escorted the other woman into the office and watched with barely concealed amusement as Danielle dramatically swept past her to greet Olsten in her usual gushing manner. He stood up and bent over to receive her customary kisses on each cheek.

'How was your flight over, Dani?' he asked in between her kisses to each side of his face. 'I hope you are not too tired for this early morning meeting. I have booked our usual place for lunch and then afterward, perhaps you can go straight back to your suite of rooms for a rest, if you need to. We can call by the workshop area tomorrow to go over the jewellery designs with Lily.'

Although Olsten repeatedly offered to accommodate Danielle in his own house during her visits to London, she always insisted on staying at her favourite hotel.

'Oh, the flight was so so – you know how much I hate flying,' Danielle replied, still holding onto Olsten's hand. 'I'm not in the slightest bit tired, though – it's only a couple of hour's flight time, after all. I am used to all this hectic travel, Olsten, my dearest man. But I would very much appreciate going straight back to my hotel after lunch for a short nap, as I have promised to take Millicent out for dinner later this evening - isn't that right, my darling,' she said, winking at Millicent. 'We have got a lot of news to catch up on – and what about that shy little Lily creature, maybe we can drag her out as well,' she added, winking again at Millicent.

'Oh, I am looking forward to it, Dani,' Millicent said. She loved to spend time with Danielle when she was in London, generally strolling around London's leading fabric retailers, found in and around Tottenham Court Road and Soho, selling a huge range of quality textiles although she bought most of her fabrics in Paris.

'I've already asked Lily, and she says her mother particularly needs her this evening,' Millicent paused, now lowering her voice slightly and adding. 'It was such a shame when Olsten's previous driver died.

They had been dating for some time and when he left suddenly without even saying goodbye, she was beside herself. When we later heard the awful news of his death, she was, of course, broken hearted. It was reported that due to depression, he had taken his own life. We have all been so worried about her - she is such a shy, vulnerable type of girl.'

'Oh, what a shame – such a tragedy,' Danielle said, looking shocked. 'That poor girl needs to get out more. Please let her know that she is quite welcome to join us if she changes her mind. The best thing she can do is to drown herself in her work – that has always been the best solution for me.'

'Yes, you are right Danielle. I think she is doing exactly that – she does love her work, but she is obviously still pining for him.

'Time heals a broken heart, and I should know,' Danielle replied, suddenly looking pensive.

Lily Reynolds was the jewellery designer, who invariably had to coordinate with Danielle to create matching jewellery to enhance the miniature clothing designs. Lily had a great talent in her chosen craft and although Olsten did not deal directly with her, he very much valued her as a member of their team. Lily was, without doubt, an indispensable and essential cog in the wheel of the business and without her expertise, he was very aware that he would have to search far and wide to find another such skilled specialist. As far as Olsten was concerned these skilled artists were a rarity, and Lily was definitely one of a kind.

When away from her workplace, Lily took care of an ageing mother and was often unable to join them at the various functions that they attended. Millicent often tried to persuade her into going out to the theatre or the odd evening out for dinner, but she always inevitably cried off with excuses of having to take care of her ailing mother.

They both suddenly turned towards Olsten as he loudly cleared his throat to attract their attention. They could see that he was amused by their general gossipy chitchat.

'Are you ready, you two agony aunts – I know you have a lot to talk about, but we need to make a start and get on with the business side of things,' Olsten said, as he stood shaking his head at them. He certainly did not approve of office gossip, but he couldn't help all the same laughing at them both – they were so amusing and were incorrigible whenever they got together.

However, the particular piece of information about his previous driver, well, that was very interesting, and it was something that he had not been aware of. As a general rule, he did not entirely approve of members of staff dating one another, as it always ended up creating an uncomfortable atmosphere in the workplace.

'I am raring to go Sir,' Danielle said laughing, as she stood to attention, mock saluting him.

Danielle was a petite woman in her early thirties; she had to stand on tiptoe to kiss Olsen, even though he bent down to oblige her. She was a very bubbly and passionate type of woman with impeccable taste in clothes, perfume and jewellery, especially pearls and often wore a pearl choker and matching earrings to accentuate her usual smart and fashionable attire.

Her makeup and hair always looked perfectly fresh and elegant. She kept her fingernails very long and sharp, and Olsten often found himself on many occasions staring at them, fascinated by the length and wondering how on earth she could do the simplest of day-to-day tasks without those nails obstructing her every movement. For as long as Olsten had known her, she had always kept her hair in a short bob style, which looked very feminine and chic.

Olsten relieved her of her heavy portfolio of designs and steered her towards his conference room, where she immediately sat down and set out various fashion illustrations and a selection of sample materials on the large conference table in preparation for their meeting.

Millicent followed with more steaming hot fresh coffee and some fruit juice before promptly sitting down at the table with her notepad. Danielle launched into her designs and ideas for materials to be used for the new dolls. Her designs were spectacular, and each miniature outfit was clearly thought out to the absolute last minute detail.

They carefully went over all the designs and discussed the various materials to be selected in detail, as it was very important that the gowns looked exceptional. The ornate hats would need a lot of work as they were so exquisite, and special care would need to be taken in selecting materials to be used for such miniature, fiddly items.

'I have the most wonderful ideas for some of the gowns – one particular style I have in mind is a full length, off-the-shoulder ball gown, made of pilled silk chiffon. The strapless bodice will consist of sheered chiffon, caught up with silver cord and beaded embroidery, ball length voluminous skirt made of

Lurex and silk chiffon. To keep the chill off her shoulders, the gown comes complete with a Lurex and silk chiffon jacket, trimmed with faux fur to compliment the gown. Accessories are to include a full net petticoat, button opera length gloves, satin shoes, a beaded evening bag and genuine pearl or crystal jewellery. The dress will be fully lined, complete with a structured bodice, boning, zipper closures and rolled hemlines,' Danielle enthused, eyes shining.

All in all, the designs were stunning. The completed ball gowns and accessories would be breath taking; the fur coats and matching hat designs were wonderful. Danielle proceeded to go into various ideas about the doll's hairstyles.

Around mid-morning, they decided that they were too engrossed with the session and far too busy to go out for lunch. Millicent stepped out to make a telephone call to order some snacks for lunch and returned with a selection of sandwiches, salads, some spicy meat pastries, and two bottles of chilled white wine.

'I think it would be a wonderful idea if the doll actually came with various miniature wigs. Some of the wigs could be long and flowing, and others in a sophisticated pinned up evening style to accommodate some of the more elaborate hats. You know the collectors will be absolutely thrilled with a doll that comes complete with her very own set of wigs and miniature wig stands, don't you think so,' Danielle gushed, as she turned to Millicent, munching on a salmon and cucumber sandwich.

'I think that's a great idea,' Millicent replied. What do you think, Olsten?'

'Yes, for sure, I think it is a fantastic idea - in fact,' he turned to Millicent, 'make a note to get on to one of the leading miniature wigs and accessory suppliers – try Madam Gigi's Trading Corp. We will need some contemporary styles as well as some classic styles. Although I must remind you both that these dolls are not designed in mind for children to play with – these are collectable dolls to be kept in a glass show cabinet and are worth thousands of pounds.'

'Oh, yes, of course, we do know that it is not a small girl's item to be dressed up and played with, but we do think that several accessories will make each doll that extra special for the passionate collector,' Millicent quickly said.

'No, no, don't misunderstand me, I am not ruling out the idea. As I said, I think a selection of wigs and hats, apart from a variety of gowns in a beautifully crafted miniature armoire, would be a very appealing addition,' Olsten replied, making his enthusiasm plain for both women to see.

Danielle clapped her hands together and then leaned towards Olsten across the table. 'Olsten, I really have a good feeling about this line of dolls, they are going to be bestsellers. The collectors will be delighted with the versatility of these dolls – I just know they will be charmed with a change of wigs for the dolls. I do think we need to have the very best quality, just like a regular sized wig. The netting scalp cap will need to be stretchable, and the weaving of the actual hair should be exactly as a life-sized regular wig. Lily has designed some of the most divine miniature jewellery, tiny diamond stud earrings, necklaces and bracelets! I am so excited about these models!'

Millicent reached across for the photographs of the jewellery.

'I can't believe how exquisite they actually look – I wouldn't mind having one of those bracelets myself – a regular sized one, of course.'

'And, for the hats,' Danielle almost purred in an exaggerated version of her French accent. 'It is going to be millinery in miniature magnificence – it will be a selection of doll's hats to die for. My aim is to create miniature hats that have the same quality and design of full-sized hats. My designs include a chic fedora, fashioned in white fine-grained leatherette with a sporty hatband of black and white polka dots and a black straw trim edged around the brim – a black and white ensemble for a chic fashion statement.'

She paused to catch her breath before continuing. 'Another style will feature the classic snood, crocheted in raspberry chenille and dotted with tiny sequins, complete with a lovely, black tulle veil. The hat will be lined in black taffeta. One of my designs also features the classic turban style hat, which will be made in luminous lavender velvet - this hat will be lined in white satin. No amount of expense will be spared – I will use felt, satin, taffeta, velvet and other rich and glitzy fabrics. The doll-scale trims will include feathers, fur, leather, jewels, ribbon, tulle, flowers and special shaped trims. Veiling will even include the glamorous Russian veiling. Each hat will be completely finished inside and out with quality linings, headbands and trims.'

Millicent sat there staring in complete fascination and admiration of her. 'That all sounds so fabulous,

Danielle. I wish I could create such magnificent designs,' she gushed.

'Well, I certainly think this deserves one of our best bottles of Champagne, Millicent,' Olsten said, as he stood up. 'I will be right back. You two make a start, I just need to make a call to James – I promised to have dinner with him this evening for a serious discussion.'

'A serious discussion, you say,' Danielle said, as she looked up with an inquisitive expression in her eyes. 'Now what are the two of you cooking up this time? I want to know every little detail.'

'Nothing for you to worry about, although the entire discussion will probably end up about you – you know how obsessed James is with you,' Olsten said, laughing.

'I know nothing of the sort. I am far too busy when I get into London to notice any such thing. Although I have to say that I think he is a very charming man, if a little too rough around the edges for my liking,' Danielle replied.

'Oh, and don't forget to give Mrs. Defoe a call, Olsten,' Millicent interrupted, as she opened the refrigerator beside the drink's cabinet.

'Yes, well, I'll leave you two ladies to enjoy a glass of champagne while I make a couple of calls. I'll be right back to join you both.'

'Oh, and who may I ask is Mrs. Defoe? Is this a new love interest of yours, Olsten that you have kept very hush-hush from us until now? We all know what a very mysterious man you are. I bet there are a bucketful of secret ladies hidden away somewhere.' Danielle winked at Millicent as Olsten rolled his eyes and strode out of the room, sighing loudly.

Although Danielle had not appeared to have noticed, Millicent had seen a slight look of annoyance on his face before he turned to leave them. Her remarks had obviously touched a sore point.

'No, it's nothing of the sort, Danielle. It's just that an incident happened the day before yesterday and could have been quite serious if Olsten had not been in the area at the time. It was just so incredibly lucky that he was. Mrs. Defoe is Amitola's mother – you may recall that he has mentioned her several times before. Amitola could have been hurt quite seriously; he is just checking to see how she is.'

'Oh, I see. He is a proper softie on the quiet, isn't he, and a regular Mr. Superman. My mother always told me – be careful of the quiet ones, they are the most lethal,' Danielle said, laughing, and then winking again at Millicent.

Later that afternoon, Olsten told Millicent that she could go home an hour earlier than usual, and he also instructed Kyle to drive Danielle straight back to the hotel after their meeting; she had been tired, especially after the two bottles of champagne they had drunk together. After concluding a short meeting with his chief ceramic artist, who was an expert in old and contemporary doll sculpting techniques, Olsten soon after left the office himself.

Chapter Six

Mrs. Defoe walked back from the vestibule, through to the dining room and stepped through the French doors onto the veranda after speaking with Olsten. Mr. Defoe and Amitola were both tucking into their hearty brunch of pancakes with sausages and eggs, flooded with glorious golden maple syrup. Mr. Defoe, as usual, had his head tucked into a newspaper scanning the news while sipping his strong, black coffee.

'Who was that on the phone, Constance?' he asked without looking up from his newspaper.

'I've just been talking to Olsten – he wanted to know how you are feeling today, Amitola. I told him that apart from your bruised knees, you are just fine – up and about as usual. He is looking forward to your birthday party tomorrow and he says that he may also bring his solicitor, James Lambert and Danielle - you know, his French dress designer and, of course, Millicent. You may remember that Mr. Lambert came by with Olsten when he visited last time to go over some paperwork. I think Olsten is trying to play the matchmaker with James and Danielle – could be we may see some wedding bells in the not-too-distant future.'

'Oh, I don't know about that, dear. Mr. Lambert is a confirmed bachelor these days after that acrimonious divorce of some time ago now, especially after his wife accused him of being a serial womaniser,' Mr. Defoe said, glancing up from his newspaper peering over the top of his glasses.

'Who said they had an acrimonious divorce – they were both very civil and understanding to one another and. in fact, still remain good friends to this day, even though his ex-wife has since remarried,' Mrs. Defoe replied. 'Besides, a handsome man like that will not be single for much longer and, of course, with that charm of his, I will not be at all surprised if Danielle is not smitten by him already.'

'Yes, as I said, a serial womaniser,' Mr. Defoe replied. 'Although when I think about it, that description could very well fit Olsten,' he added.

'What on earth makes you think that? You are such a cynic – Olsten is most certainly not a womaniser and both he and James are confirmed workaholics more than anything else. I suspect that they are both biding their time before they find that one special woman to spend the rest of their life with,' she replied.

'You are such a romantic, Mother,' Amitola said, still tucking into her pancakes. 'I am looking forward to seeing them all tomorrow, especially Millicent – we have such fun together when she comes around. And yes, I do remember Mr. Lambert,' Amitola said. 'He's the one who told me that I have an unusual name and how on earth you both came up with such a strange name for a tiny, cute baby.'

They both turned and glanced at each other, slightly amused.

'You must admit, my dear, that it is a very unusual name, and I suspect no other young girl has any such name - or similar name, even. I think it's a name to be proud of and I have always thought that it is a name fit for a princess,' Mr. Defoe now said, smiling at her.

'Oh, of course you would say that, Dad. Every father thinks his daughter is a princess,' Amitola said, with a mouthful of sausage.

'Please don't speak with your mouth full, dear,' Mrs. Defoe said, laughing.

When they had been selected as her Special Guardians on a long-term basis, Mrs. Defoe had contemplated changing the name, but it was stipulated at that time that this was her given name and it was not on any account to be changed, although just between them, they often shortened her name to Mira. Although Amitola, as far as they knew, currently had no idea of her true origin and the circumstances of her real connection with them, they had wanted to ensure that she grew up in a loving home believing them to be her true parents. It was decreed that the true nature of their relationship was not to be revealed until her twenty-first birthday.

Constance Defoe had been thirty-one and her husband thirty-five when they had decided to become foster parents after years of trying for a child of their own. Constance had for some time desperately wanted a baby and when they were given the chance of taking a baby girl into their hearts and home, Constance had decided to give up her job permanently to take full-time care of Amitola. They had both been living and working in America as young, successful architects at the time, before ultimately deciding to return to the United Kingdom.

James had been recommended to them to administer all arrangements for the processing of official paperwork involved and was given legal authority to take control of the management of Amitola's financial allowance throughout her life until she reached the age of twenty-one.

Although Mr. and Mrs. Defoe were not fully aware of the precise details of Amitola's true origin, they had been given to understand that there were varying conflicting reports and mysterious circumstances surrounding the birth of the child. One such belief was that she had been found outside a convent in Italy and had thereafter been transported to the United States by an unknown benefactor. Being of a romantic nature, this information had fascinated Mrs. Defoe and although she attempted to inquire into records available, there had been no other concrete information available about the real identity of the birth mother or the unknown benefactor. They secretly hoped that the undisclosed benefactor would just disappear by the time that Amitola turned twenty-one. They could not bear the thought of losing her to a stranger that she had so far never met. Holding that baby for the first time, after years of waiting for a child, had been the happiest moment for them and they had decided that they would not fret about specific details of her birth.

At the time that the official arrangements were being processed for Special Guardianship, Mrs. Defoe had quite by chance come across a news release reporting a scandal that had taken place in Italy. A young, unmarried Italian girl, Claudia Aragona, of noble birthright, had been whisked away to a clinic for the duration of her pregnancy and on the strict instruction of her parents, she had been ordered to relinquish the infant to an adoption agency immediately after the delivery. The young girl in question had been publicly shamed shortly after and had ultimately gone on the run and thereafter reportedly become a nun.

Mrs. Defoe convinced herself that this young girl was the real birth mother of Amitola and no amount of other possible explanations from her husband could persuade her to doubt this belief of hers. She promised herself that one day she would take a trip to Italy and track down this unfortunate young girl to give her some sort of solace and ensure her that her daughter was being loved and well cared for. At the back of her mind, she hoped that this was the case and that the young girl in question would ultimately be more than willing to legally hand over the child to them permanently and allow them to officially adopt her.

Amitola had always been a very happy child and through the years, they never had any cause for regret about taking her into their family. Constance had heard so many stories of children taken in by foster parents only to find that the child in their care caused them endless problems. But she had no need to worry about Amitola as she was just a delightful baby and through the years never failed to give them unconditional love - they were very proud of her.

Throughout Amitola's childhood, they enjoyed all the joys and occasional heartbreaks of parenthood. In the beginning Mrs. Defoe often watched the tiny infant in their care sleep, at times terrified that she would suddenly disappear during the night. The very first time when Amitola wrapped her little arms around her neck for cuddles and told her that she loved her, had brought tears to Mrs. Defoe's eyes. That little hand that had slipped into hers while they walked to school never failed to give her an immense feeling of pure joy.

Chapter Seven

Olsten had suggested to James that they meet in a Mexican Restaurant called El Paso, tucked away in the Soho area. He knew James was very fond of Mexican food and although they would basically talk business, they would have a relaxing evening in a cosy atmosphere of authentic Mexican folk art and sizzling spicy food. Before ordering dinner, they sat at the bar for a drink. They both ordered a three-shot cocktail Tequila.

Pausing for a moment before taking a sip of his drink, Olsten glanced around the bar area, his eyes scrutinizing everything and everyone in the bar. He turned back around on his barstool and suddenly winked at James.

'Don't look now but we are both under surveillance,' he said, grinning.

James immediately tried to swivel around on his barstool, but Olsten put his foot on the base to restrain his movement.

'Don't tell me - it's your guardian angel friend, compliments of Celeste,' James said, shaking his head in dismay and amusement. 'He is certainly onto a good thing here. This has got to be a dream of a job, just trailing around after you day after day,' James laughed, as he stood up. 'Let's go eat, I'm starved.'

'What I would be very interested to know, Olsten, is just how much she is paying this character for this charade. If it is good money, I want that job myself,' James was still joking as he sat down at their allotted table and took the menu from the waiter. 'Some people must have money to throw away on a whim.'

After scanning over the menu James finally decided on a cactus salad for starters followed by a grilled filet mignon with wild mushroom and tequila sauce.

'That should put some fire in the old veins. Talking about fire in the veins, where is Dani this evening? She called me earlier to let me know that she is in London - I asked her to join us tonight, but she said she would see me tomorrow evening. Now that woman certainly puts some fire in my veins. Although she acts as if I am just a little distraction for her while she is in London, I am going to try my very best to convince her otherwise,' James confided to Olsten, who rolled his eyes and laughed.

'You do worry me, James; sometimes I think you are a fourteen-year-old boy trapped in a man's body,' he said as he quickly scanned over the menu, ordering a zucchini and carrot salad in chipotle vinaigrette for starters and a grilled skirt steak with salsa, guacamole and flour tortillas for his main course.

'I can't keep up with you and your many women friends,' Olsten said, sarcastically.

'There is always room for Danielle,' James replied.

'Of course, I knew we would get around to the subject of Danielle. We had quite a busy morning going through all the designs and ideas. I had booked a luncheon to follow the meeting but, in the end, we decided to skip going out for lunch and ordered some food to eat in the office. Dani is so excited about her new designs for the dolls, and we decided to celebrate with a bottle of champagne, or two. Dani and Millicent had already made plans for this evening, otherwise, I did think of suggesting that they join us, although we would have found it a bit awkward to discuss the business of Celeste and her fatal attraction.'

'Okay,' James said as he moved his chair closer to the table, 'Going back to *that* subject, is there something that you are not telling me here – some secret from way back in your past, because if this is the case, just tell Celeste that it is really none of her business.'

Olsten appeared not to be listening; he seemed to be in a world of his own with his head turned towards the other side of the restaurant scrutinizing every face. James leaned forward and jokingly waved his hand across his face to capture his attention and that's when he spotted the marking on the side of Olsten's neck which he had never noticed before. As he leaned a little closer and peered more closely at the marking, he could see that it was a tattoo of a small blue crown. This puzzled James as he would never have believed Olsten was the type to go for tattoos, especially on his neck even though it was a fairly small image.

Well, he is full of surprises, James thought as he examined the small image. It was not the usual tattoo that men usually go for. He had a small lion's head image on one of his forearms which he had acquired more or less as a dare when he was a teenager, and not to mention being extremely drunk at the time.

'What is that strange marking on your neck – I've not noticed it before?' he asked.

Olsten suddenly flinched and reached for his glass. 'You know,' he said, after taking a gulp of his drink completely ignoring James's question. 'I certainly do not owe anybody any explanations about my private life, whether past or present and I'll thank you not to make any references alluding to whether or not I have a secret hidden away or have a murky past.'

'Now, listen to me, Olsten,' James said, suddenly becoming sombre. 'Did I say that you had a murky past? I don't think for one minute that you are some sort of pervert – I know you too well. I am just trying to give you an idea of how Celeste interprets and twists everything. She is searching for any little thing that she can hurt you with. She feels that as she has become especially close to you, she expects you to confide in her your innermost secrets.

'Just stop right now,' Olsten said, becoming more agitated by the minute. 'I'm only going to say this *one more time* - I have *never* had any kind of a romantic relationship with Celeste and I have certainly not become especially close to her. I do not owe her any explanations about my personal life, past or present. She came to many of my exhibitions and seemed to be a very secure and fun-loving young girl with lots of friends always milling around her, with not a care in the world. I would never have guessed that she would slowly turn into this deranged young woman that she seems to have become. I just cannot understand what has caused such a drastic and totally unexpected change in her. If it is drug related, I would not hesitate to help the girl – I hate to see her so desperately unhappy. I can't tell you enough that I would do anything to help her, but it seems that I am only in her company for a few seconds, and she becomes hysterical and accuses me of all sorts of atrocities. Where it all comes from, I cannot imagine.'

Their starter dishes arrived, and they both became silent and sat back while the waiter set down their plates of food. After he had then poured out a little wine into one of the glasses as a first taster, standing back while James took a sip and then nodded his approval for both glasses to be filled.

'Let's just tuck in,' James said as the waiter left. 'I'm ravenous. He lifted his glass in salute to Olsten. They were both very hungry and as soon as they had finished their starter, the plates were immediately cleared away and their sizzling main courses were in turn served up.

'I think that the best way of handling this in the first place, is for me to call Celeste and try to talk to her calmly and rationally. 'James said as he beckoned the waiter back to their table. 'Give us a bottle of your best red wine here, please.'

'James, I *do not* want you calling Celeste! Stay out of this. It is getting completely crazy, and I don't want it to escalate into some big scandal. You must admit that it could turn very ugly for me. As you well know, she is not just trying to disclose information leading one to believe that I have a small skeleton in my cupboard, she intends to muckrake more out of it than that, and you know what I mean.

'No, I don't know what you mean – what on earth are you talking about?' James replied.

'Apart from the fact that she continually accuses me of refusing to acknowledge that I have a wife secreted somewhere, she has actually accused me of doing away with her and hiding the remains somewhere in my office. I mean, for God's sake, what on earth goes through that woman's mind, I just can't imagine.'

He paused while the waiter stood over them pouring more wine into their glasses.

'Maybe at some time during the dark hours of the night, I have a blackout and turn from a Dr. Hyde character into a monstrous Mr. Jekyll and run amok around the dark alleys of London attacking and murdering women. Mind you, joking aside, I don't mind telling you that the way I am feeling at the moment of this business with Celeste, I could quite honestly wring her neck and have done with it,' Olsten declared.

'How can you say such a thing - you don't mean that for one minute,' James said shocked by Olsten's sudden casual glib comment. It was so out-of-character. 'Are you drunk, or what? Don't even joke about such a thing. I don't presume to know you inside and out, but I can certainly say that for as long as I have known you, you have always acted like a gentleman where women are concerned and would certainly not even slap a woman, let alone choke her to death.'

'Well, thank you for your vote of confidence. I can assure you that I always act like a gentleman where Celeste is concerned, and she can't possibly dispute that for a fact.'

'Ah, but that's the problem, she *does* dispute that for a fact,' James replied. Olsten never failed to make him feel angry and frustrated at times with his surprisingly naive outlook where women were concerned. He seemed to want to protect them, especially Celeste, despite her accusations of his alleged abusive treatment of her.

'Well, you certainly do seem to give the impression that you care very much about her wellbeing – apart from wanting to squeeze the life out of her,' James retorted.

Olsten raked his fingers through his hair seeming to be more agitated by the minute, then drank his glass of wine practically down in one gulp. He suddenly laughed and turned to James with a twinkle in his eyes and said, 'Let's just enjoy the evening. Why don't I call Millicent and Danielle and invite them over to join in some serious salsa dancing tonight.' He glanced at his watch - it wasn't even ten o'clock! The night was still young, and he felt like he suddenly needed to let his hair and guard down, something that he rarely did.

'I thought you did not approve of employees fraternising or dating outside of business hours,' James said, laughing.

'Did I say that? Yes - well, I do not approve of employees dating and this will certainly not be classed as a date, not in my case, anyway. All I'm saying is that we should just enjoy the evening, and a little bit of dancing can't do any harm.'

'Now you're talking, and I will certainly consider this a date in my case,' James said. 'Now that's my idea of an exciting evening. I haven't seen Dani now for a couple of weeks. She is a fine-looking woman – I wouldn't mind a salsa session with her any day,' he said, chuckling into his beard. 'It's just an indulgent fanciful psychological need of mine and part of my lascivious fantasies.'

'I do worry about you sometimes,' Olsten said, raising one of his eyebrows in a mock suspicious way.

As Olsten stood up from the table and began to walk away, he stopped for a second and then turned back to James.

'I'll call Celeste myself tomorrow and ask her if we can meet,' he said, with a determined expression on his face. 'I'll try to deal with this in my own way. Don't get me wrong, I am not going to give into her, I'll try to appeal to her feminine nature. As much as she is so disgusted with me and is trying to paint me as some kind of perverted creep, she does want to give me another chance, as she so graciously put it when she last called in one of her tanked-up states. God knows when she started to drink so much - I mean, she hardly drank when I first knew her, and she certainly never seemed to have any particular romantic interest in me during the earlier days on first meeting'.

James roared with laughter. 'What kind of an expression is that to use when talking about a lady – "in one of her tanked-up states". Anyway, don't you worry, I know exactly the situation here, Olsten, but you be very, very careful all the same.'

James scrutinized Olsten's expression before he walked away from the table. He had a strange, foreboding feeling at that point that Olsten's troubles were far more than he was letting on.

'Unfortunately, you don't know exactly what the situation is here, and you would never believe it even if I told you,' Olsten muttered to himself as he walked off to use one of the phones in the lobby area.

The presence of the man keeping a close watch over him had once again not escaped Olsten's attention. He hovered by the side of the doorway behind a large, tree-like plant in the shadows of the low-lit lobby, watching Olsten as he stepped into the phone booth.

After dialling the number of Danielle's hotel suite, Olsten waited for some minutes as he listened to the constant ringing tone and when there was no answer he hung up and quickly stepped back out of the phone booth. He hesitated for a moment of two as he stood watching the figure still lurking in the semi darkness of the foyer.

He was not surprised that he had not been able to find Danielle in her hotel suite – she would be dining out in a quiet, elegant restaurant and would no doubt not wish to join them in such a noisy environment as the Mexican restaurant that Olsten and James seemed to enjoy.

The man loitering behind the plant immediately turned his back as Olsten strode past him as he made his way back to the table where James was waiting, expecting to hear good news.

'Sorry James, it seems you will have to put up with me for the rest of the evening,' he said as he sat back down at the table. 'I couldn't get hold of the ladies, but we will see them at the birthday party tomorrow.'

'Oh, that's a shame - well, in that case let's order some more drinks,' James replied as he turned to catch the attention of one of the waiters.

Much later when they left the restaurant, they hailed a taxi to take them to the gaming casino in the Ritz hotel, where although Olsten did not take pleasure in, or believe in, gambling, James enjoyed a wide variety of games and was particularly fond of Roulette. I gave Olsten no end of amusement at the way James suddenly took on the persona of a hard-core gambling man.

Thinks he's James Bond, Olsten thought as he stood there, all the time watching the many faces around the table and beyond. It never failed to amaze him how these people played these games for hours on end, all through the night and early morning, not caring how much money they lost. But then, he knew that the majority of the punters were seriously rich.

There were all kinds of people gambling in the casino; rich Arabs and Russians, German businessmen, the successful con-artists and of course, the rich and famous. He couldn't help noticing in particular, all the young girls standing close by the rich punters – some of them looked barely sixteen years old – ripe for the picking and they all seemed to stick like glue to the rich men. All the girls were dressed in the most expensive gowns and were dripping in diamonds.

Although James was well aware that Olsten did not indulge in any kind of gambling, it did not escape his attention that he always seemed far more interested in watching all the people coming and going, especially the young ladies.

Olsten patiently hovered around James watching him play his game of Blackjack, all the while looking out for that one face that he was expecting to see.

This was also a frequent haunt of Celeste's and as much as she had always kept it a secret from both her parents, her brother and Lewis, Olsten knew only too well that she always found the gambling environment very exciting and could never resist it.

'Well, that's me done for – I've lost my limit of one hundred pounds,' James said, turning to Olsten, but found that he was talking to himself although he was not at all surprised to see that Olsten was no longer by his side. He quickly scanned the room above all the heads of the people in the casino until he spotted him talking to a young, scantily dressed cocktail waitress with a tray of drinks.

He quickly walked towards Olsten and the waitress. After informing Olsten that he was all ready to call it a night, he suggested that they have one last drink.

They both walked through to the bar where they ordered a glass of Champagne. James was surprised when Olsten then informed him that he wanted to stay a little longer and mix with the crowd. Although James was feeling very tired, he offered to stay a little longer to keep him company, but Olsten insisted that he just wanted to mingle on his own.

'You get yourself home, you look dead on your feet. I'm not planning to stay too long. I've just got a little business to take care of,' Olsten said as he turned and quickly walked away.

As James collected his coat and was about to leave the bar, he noticed that Olsten was now standing a short distance away with his arm around Celeste, practically supporting her as she clung to him looking very unsteady on her legs.

He also noticed the young man that they had observed earlier in the restaurant now standing close by, again watching Olsten's every move. Olsten suddenly began walking towards the man, while still holding tightly onto Celeste – practically dragging her along by his side, but the young man immediately turned and quickly scuttled away, bumping into James as he passed by him.

'Hey, watch where you're going,' James said. The man mumbled an apology half-heartedly under his breath before rushing out of the door.

Now – what was that all about, James thought, as he reluctantly walked out of the bar, through the lobby and outside, where he threw himself into one of the courtesy limousines waiting outside. He felt exhausted and as much as he had offered to stay behind a little longer, he really did not have the energy, even if he was more than a little tempted to literally spy on Olsten himself. Despite all Olsten's denials about there not being anything between himself and Celeste, he was now very much intrigued by what he had just seen.

That sly devil — he who is in denial, he thought, as he sat back in the limousine smoking his cigar.

Chapter Eight

The events following that ill-fated evening the previous year had not only been the start of Celeste's own problems but had slowly begun to effect the life of Olsten and all who worked closely with him.

Celeste's strange behavior grew worse during the subsequent year and a tragic end seemed foreseeable in the not too distant future.

The whole episode had been a foggy, giddy whirl of muffled shapes and obscure memories in Celeste's mind when she had awoken the morning after *that* evening. She had been vaguely aware she had acted not only foolishly impulsively, but that she had had no control whatsoever in her actions – she had felt almost possessed and compelled to act out of character.

There had been only one thing on her mind after that haunting evening and it was to be with Olsten again as soon as possible, throw her arms around him and confess her undying passion and love for him.

The following day, as if in a hypnotised state of mind, she had picked up her phone to call Lewis, who she had decided to tell that she no longer wanted to marry him. *As simple as that,* she had told herself.

She had been planning to join Lewis in Paris for a weekend but after that evening, she had absolutely no interest in being with him even though she adored Paris. She had been anxious to get the call over with as quickly as possible so that she could rush to be with Olsten.

'Hello darling – where have you been hiding? I'm so glad you've called,' Lewis had said excitedly on hearing her voice. 'I was calling you every hour last night - I was worried about you. I hope you have packed your glad rags for a romantic weekend in Paris.'

She grimaced and sighed heavily down the line. W*hat a bore,* she thought to herself. She wanted to get the whole issue over and done with as quickly as possible. It would have been so much better to *have just simply sent a telegram informing him – it would have been so much easier and less of a bore for her,* she thought. She needed to paint her toenails after all and had not wanted to waste time having to make such a tedious call.

'I'm sorry I missed your call last night, Lewis. I had the most wonderful, delicious evening - I was out having dinner with a friend and stayed the whole night with him. I didn't get back until this morning. We need to talk… I have been thinking about everything and I, well, I …,' she stopped in mid-sentence, when he interrupted her.

'What's all this about, Celeste. I don't understand. You sound so strange. And who is this friend that you had dinner with? What exactly are you saying? That you spent the whole night with him?'

'For God's sake – what do you think I mean? I wasn't exactly playing marbles with him the whole night,' she said, sarcastically.

She wanted to simply hang up on him at that point. She was anxious to end the call as quickly as she could.

She knew that Lewis was shocked by her whole demeanour– even her voice sounded harsh and one that she could hardly recognise as her own at the time, but she did not care.

'Is this some kind of joke, my darling, because if it is, it is not very funny,' he said, sounding slightly baffled at that point.

'Well, as I am trying to tell you, we need to talk,' she replied, indifferently. She did not feel the slightest bit of concern about his feelings. He was suddenly not important to her now and she wanted him out of her life as quickly and painlessly as possible. She felt so bored by the whole conversation. *Why didn't he just accept it like a cultivated gentleman and be civilised about the matter.*

'We can talk all you like when you get here,' he had replied, fear creeping into his voice. 'You are still coming this weekend, aren't you?' he asked.

'Well, that's just it, Lewis – no, I am not coming this weekend *or any other weekend* for that matter,' she answered coldly.

'What are you trying to say to me, Celeste? Has something happened? Tell me, I want to know,' he had almost shouted down the line.

'There is no other way to say this - I don't want to marry you, Lewis. I want to cancel all the wedding plans. I am not in love with you anymore, can't you get that into your thick head?' she blurted out, coldly

She heard him almost choke on the other end of the line in utter disbelief at the tone of her voice.

'I can't believe this, Celeste! You are not in love with me anymore and you don't want to marry me – *just like that*? It's not like you to be so cruel and unfeeling. Give me a chance to talk things over with you,' he pleaded with her.

She heard the raw desperation in his voice, but she had not felt any remorse at all.

'Is there someone else?' He asked her.

'Yes – the penny has finally dropped,' she replied, callously. 'He is all that I have ever wanted and more and I want to be with him. He is exciting and makes me feel like a princess and we are going to get married as soon as he can get away from his business work schedule and I can't wait,' she gushed without hardly taking a breath.

There had been a few seconds of silence. She had known that he was struggling to keep calm.

'How long has this been going on – I just can't understand any of this. How is it that you could hardly wait until next month for the wedding and now you have decided that you are no longer in love with me? It's just too ridiculous,' he said, sounding as if he was about to burst into tears.

'Oh, for goodness' sake, don't be such a bore, Lewis. I've simply changed my mind and that's that. There is nothing more to say,' she said before hanging up on him.

Lewis immediately dialled her number, and she had let it ring continuously until it rang off. Then she picked up the handset and placed it off the hook. She knew at that time that Lewis would continue to call her throughout the day, but she had no intention of talking to him again.

She pulled off the large sparkling expensive diamond engagement ring from her finger and tossed it carelessly into an ashtray. She would arrange to have it returned to his parent's house.

She had suspected at that time that Lewis would rush back from Paris to confront her, but she intended to make sure that she would be unavailable at all times. She planned to have all his clothing and personal possessions boxed up and sent over to his parents because she wanted to avoid seeing him at all costs. *He'll get over it. Well, he'll have to – he's got no choice in the matter,* she thought flippantly as she walked up the stairs towards her bathroom. After removing her dressing gown and dropping it on the floor, she stepped into the shower nonchalantly humming to herself.

After she had showered and dressed, she called Kyle to pick her up and drive her to Olsten's office. In spite of having her own car, a Triumph Spitfire sports car, which her father had bought for her eighteenth birthday present, the very thought of being chauffeured around in Olsten's car was something that she thought she was now entitled to. *And why shouldn't she? After all, what was his was now hers,* she had thought smiling to herself.

Kyle had not been at all surprised when she had called him to pick her up – it was as if he had expected her call.

'How did your little trip go yesterday evening?' she asked Kyle when she had positioned herself comfortably in the back seat of the limousine.

'Fine, Miss,' he replied, smiling at her in the rear-view mirror. 'And how did *your little evening* go?' he had asked making a clicking sound with his tongue.

'Oh, you know about that,' she said, suddenly feeling a little uncomfortable at the tone of his voice and the suggestive way he had made reference to her *little* evening, *which she had felt had some sexual overtone.* She had not been absolutely sure if he had been making innocent playful small talk or if his intent had been to insult her, although she had been spitting furious about the clicking sound that he had made with his tongue,

'I certainly do, Miss – as brothers we discuss everything that goes on. But don't you worry about it, doll-face – it will be our *little* secret,' he had replied, a little too cocky for her liking.

She had gasped as he winked at her in the rear-view mirror with a menacing expression on his face. She felt for sure at that point that he was being extremely disrespectful in a decidedly malicious manner. She did not in that moment immediately pick up on the comment made that "as brothers we discuss everything that goes on" – but she suddenly remembered when the driver had called that first time to arrange a meeting with Olsten, he had distinctly said "Kyle has the evening off, and I am his brother covering for him - a temporary driver". She shook her head as if trying to clear her scrambled brain – she felt extremely confused and determined that Kyle had maybe been covering his tracks so that she would not be able to identify one brother from the other if there was, in fact, a brother. She felt sure that Kyle was playing mind games with her.

She felt her face redden – the thought of being discussed by him and his brother, whoever that was, infuriated her, and *how dare* he call her 'doll-face.' After lighting up a cigarette and noticing annoyingly that her hands shook, this had further enraged her. She sat there fuming - puffing on her cigarette and blowing out the smoke towards the back of his head. A feeling of murderous anger washed over her at that moment, an uncontrollable urge to loop the strong, leather shoulder straps of her handbag around his neck, pulling tightly until he choked to death.

She closed her eyes tightly trying to block out all the horrific thoughts that were racing through her mind. *What is happening to me,* she thought sitting there feeling helpless and vulnerable.

A sudden rush of conscience and an overwhelming sense of wretchedness and shame had washed over her in that moment, and she desperately regretted having spoken to Lewis in such a cruel and heartless way. She realised how unbelievably unfair she had been to him, and she suddenly missed him so much. Something stirred in her soul that she recognised as her true self and not the uncaring person she had suddenly become overnight. She promised herself that she would call Lewis when she returned home to apologise for her cruel and insensitive behaviour and beg his forgiveness.

But she still felt that urgent and all-consuming need to see Olsten and nothing could have changed her craving to be with him again at that time.

'Is Mr. Ryder expecting you?' Kyle's question coincided with her thoughts about Olsten.

She visibly flinched when his spiteful tone of voice interrupted her thoughts. She knew he was tormenting her.

'I don't see that it is any business of yours whether or not Mr. Ryder is expecting me,' she snapped back at him. *The nerve of the man,* she thought. She wanted to shout out for him to stop the limousine immediately so that she could get out and be as far away from him as possible.

She had been determined to mention his offensive attitude to Olsten when she arrived at his office. It really was too much that Kyle should talk to her so disrespectfully - she much preferred Kyle's brother, and she would suggest to Olsten that, in her opinion, he would be much more suitable as his permanent personal driver. He had been so much more polite and respectful than Kyle.

But then vague thoughts of flirting outrageously with Kyle's brother came to mind and she felt more ashamed. Her face again reddened just thinking how reckless she had behaved during that evening – she couldn't even remember his name.

'So where is your brother – what's his name?' she asked him, nervously.

'As far as I know he is on another job, Miss – maybe not as *exciting* as his last one, if you know what I mean,' he replied, again with that same infuriatingly cocky attitude and click of his tongue.

She flinched as a small voice began to talk to her in her mind and she raised her hands to clutch at her head. Kyle continued watching her in the rear-view mirror, sniggering all the while. She felt as if he was mocking her with those cruel eyes staring constantly at her. When the bile had threatened to erupt from her throat, she wanted to scream and escape from the car, but she was unable to move a muscle. It was as if she was strapped in that car. *Take me back to my house immediately - I want to go home;* she had screamed inside her head.

'It won't be long now, doll-face. We are nearly there,' Kyle told her. His tone of voice was dripping with sarcasm and his manner so contemptuous at that stage that she was practically reduced to tears.

She spent the rest of the journey in silence. Several thoughts of how to take her revenge out on him raced through her mind. She felt her face twitching uncontrollably, becoming redder by the second.

That will show him not to mess with me – such a contemptible little rat, she thought to herself.

She almost choked when she heard Kyle suddenly laughing out loud and she was overcome with a sense that he was actually reading her mind - she sat there trembling with fear.

When they had pulled up outside the building in Berkeley Square, Kyle immediately climbed out of the car and opened the door for Celeste and as she alighted from the car, he had bowed to her mockingly and sarcastically clicked his heels together.

'Good luck, Miss – you'll need it,' he said, as she flounced past him with her head held high and headed towards the front door of the building. She turned when she had heard him sniggering again and immediately walked back to him and slapped his face hard. He threw his head back and laughed out loud as she glared at him and raised her hand again to slap him, but he had grabbed her wrist holding onto it tightly.

'You are hurting me,' she hissed angrily at him.

'I wouldn't do that again if I were you, Miss,' he said, through clenched teeth.

'How dare you – I'll be talking to Mr. Ryder about your behaviour, and I am sure he will dismiss you instantly,' she spat out as she pulled back her arm, visibly shaking. She stood rubbing at her wrist – the whole area had gone bright red as a result of his rough treatment before storming in through the front door and standing in front of Roy at the reception desk, still shaking uncontrollably.

'I need to see Mr. Ryder right now,' she demanded, her eyes wide open with fury.

'Are you well, Miss Harrington?' Roy asked as he stood up and walked around the reception desk, immediately taking hold of her arm and assisting her towards the plush seating.

'I just feel a little faint,' she replied as she had slumped onto the seat, barely able to stand on her feet for a second longer.

'Now, you sit there while I call Mr. Ryder,' he told her.

After speaking to Millicent and informing her that Celeste was in reception asking to see Olsten, Roy told Celeste she could go straight up – Mr. Ryder could see her straight away in his office.

As soon as Celeste had been ushered into Olsten's office, she burst into tears and rushed into his arms. He had stood there, puzzled, with his arms around her, waiting for her floods of tears to subside as he peered over her head, looking at Millicent in total bewilderment.

'Would you bring a pot of coffee in,' he asked Millicent who stood at the door watching and looking just as puzzled as Olsten.

'I'd rather have something stronger,' Celeste said as he steered her onto a nearby sofa. Olsten sat patiently by her side on the sofa while she sobbed uncontrollaby. His one thought had been that something terrible had happened to her fiancé Lewis. He poured a glass of whisky for her which she promptly gulped straight down and then asked for another.

'I insist that you dismiss your driver immediately – he has been consistently rude to me and making offensive innuendoes and lewd remarks about our dinner date yesterday evening,' she finally blurted out, much to his astonishment.

Olsten stared at her, totally baffled by what she was saying. He had been away for a two-day business trip in Paris and had arrived back early that morning feeling quite worn out.

Millicent, who had remained at the doorway, looked on wondering what on earth was going on.

'I am so upset, Olsten, I just feel so guilty now after talking to Lewis this morning. He was extremely upset when I told him I had spent the whole night with you and could not marry him now that I am in love with another man,' Celeste continued, still sobbing uncontrollably.

At this point, Millicent's mouth dropped open as she looked from Olsten to Celeste shocked by what she was hearing – she had had no idea that there had been a romance going on between them. The thought of Olsten being with Celeste when he was supposed to have been in Paris on business for the last two days stunned her – it couldn't possibly be true! But if it was, why had he felt the need to keep it secret and actually lie about his trip to Paris? But then, it was none of her business, she told herself and they were, after all, two consenting adults.

She cleared her throat nervously, not knowing what to do – she realized that she should have left them both alone, but as she turned to walk out to make some coffee, Olsten gestured her to remain in his office.

'I don't understand what on earth you are talking about, Celeste,' Olsten said, all the while looking at Millicent's face and shaking his head in astonishment.

'You told me to break off our engagement last night while we were together, Olsten, and I have done exactly as you have told me. I want you to know that I have sacrificed everything just to be with you now. Lewis is horrified that I have broken off my engagement,' she told Olsten, as the tears had rolled down her face.

'Go ahead and prepare some coffee, would you please, Millicent,' he said, shock making his voice sound peremptory.

When Millicent returned, holding a tray bearing a pot of strong hot coffee, she set it down on a small table in front of the sofa,ready to pour when Celeste suddenly leaned over and pushed the tray away causing the cups and saucers to topple over onto the floor.

'Millicent, can you put me through to Lewis in Paris – he is staying at the Ritz Hotel – you can find the number in my diary,' Olsten said.

'NO, NO, PLEASE DON'T CALL HIM,' Celeste suddenly screamed at him and before she could do any further damage to his office, he had stood up to take hold of her again, nodding to Millicent to go and make the call, while he restrained the sobbing woman.

'I'm sorry, Olsten, but now that things are different between us, I couldn't go through with the wedding. I just want to be with you now. Please tell me that nothing has changed your mind after last night – I couldn't bear it if you left me now. We had such a wonderful time together and I realized that you are the man I want. I have always wanted you, Olsten - just you and nobody else.'

Olsten released her from his grip and stood looking at her, completely baffled by her whole demeanor. His immediate thought was that she had taken some kind of medication that had caused her to become disorientated and delusional.

At that point, the telephone rang and Olsten strode over to his desk to answer it. Lewis's irate voice was on the other end of the line.

'Yes – good morning,' Olsten said quietly not wanting to alarm Celeste. 'You need to get back here today. There is a situation here that you need to deal with. Yes, I do know the circumstances ... no, I can't explain now, but we can talk when you get back and believe me, this is not what you think and have been led to believe. Okay, I will talk to you later,' he said, looking over at Celeste before hanging up.

Celeste was strangely quiet by that time, seeming to have calmed down considerably. Olsten noticed a strange, distant look in her eyes; she had appeared to be in another place.

Sitting down next to Celeste again, he put his arm around her to comfort her, when she suddenly lunged at him, kissing him passionately on the lips and then biting him, causing his lip to bleed. He immediately pulled away.

He was stunned, and realised that there was something seriously wrong with her; – he felt quite certain that she was under the influence of medication that had resulted in having an adverse effect on her.

Celeste sprung up from the sofa like a demented being and began to run around his office and then through to his private quarters, screaming at the top of her voice.

Millicent rushed back through into his office, alarmed at the commotion. She ducked when a portrait came hurtling through the door from his private sitting room, which crashed into the far end wall of his office near to the doorway. She had to turn her face away from the flying glass that shattered from the framed portrait. It had not escaped her attention at that time that Olsten's upper lip had been bleeding and there had been traces of lipstick smudges around his cheeks and on his lips.

She looked on, horrified, when Celeste charged at Olsten, still screaming at the top of her voice.

Chapter Nine

Millicent sat next to Lily on a wooden bench in Berkeley Square Garden across from where they worked, eating their sandwiches during their lunch break. It was a beautiful sunny day, and they both felt relaxed watching all the people strolling by.

They had a busy schedule for a Monday morning and were both feeling quite relieved that the morning had passed by fairly smoothly. Olsten appeared to be slightly distracted by something or other during their usual morning conference and Millicent couldn't help glancing at him from time to time feeling a little concerned - he had not even touched his Danish pastries.

After the evening out on Friday with Danielle and the birthday party on Saturday for Amitola, Millicent felt a little ragged around the edges, although she had spent half the day in bed the following Sunday. It was a well-deserved rest for her as she was not used to going out two nights in a row.

'How did the party go?' Lily asked.

'It was absolutely fantastic; I had such a good time, but I am so exhausted today. You should have joined us, Lily. I know how much you worry about your mother and need to be there for her, but you really should get out from time to time for your own good. I don't mean to be rude, Lily, but you do look so peaky sometimes and you seem to be getting thinner and thinner – if you are not careful, you will just disappear,' she said, trying to make light of it, not wishing to offend her too much.

Lily averted her eyes and Millicent noticed that her hands shook slightly. She immediately leaned over and placed her hand over Lily's to reassure her when she saw her eyes beginning to tear up.

'Oh, I'm so sorry, Lily. I didn't mean to upset you. I know it's none of my business, but I do worry about you. You must get out of the house sometimes for your own sake.' Lily smiled then, as she drew her hand back.

'No, it's fine, Milly – it's nothing to do with my mother, we do have a set routine, and I can deal with caring for her as well as being able to cope with my work. Mother is so easy to look after and not at all demanding, as you probably imagine. We have always had a good relationship and enjoy spending time together. You will have to come over one of these evenings to meet her and have dinner with us. She has a wonderful sense of humour and is an excellent cook. I know you probably envision that I spend my evenings with a grumpy and depressing old, sick woman, but it is really nothing like that.'

'I didn't mean to pry,' Millicent said, feeling slightly embarrassed. 'I just thought that she was unable to do anything for herself and relied entirely on your help.'

'Although she is now in a wheelchair, she quite happily copes during the day while I am at work and is able to make cups of tea and light snacks for herself. I often leave sandwiches for her lunch - like today, but otherwise she is quite capable of heating up some soup for herself. In fact, she quite often prepares a meal for when I get home in the evening. She always loved cooking when I was growing up and Dad and I always thought she was a great cook. So don't imagine that I have to go home, and spoon feed a bedridden woman unable to do anything for herself. She even wheels herself around and does the housework as much as she can.'

She looked up then and Millicent could sense by the expression on her face that she was hesitating to say what was really on her mind.

'I have been seeing somebody,' she finally blurted out. 'I didn't say anything about it before because he is actually a colleague that we both know, and he asked me not to mention it to anybody at work. He was quite insistent about it.'

Oh, not another co-worker affair – she seems to have a perpetual need for workplace romances, Millicent couldn't help thinking. She did not want to see Lily hurt again.

'Oh, I don't see anything wrong with dating somebody from the workplace, but in the circumstances ...' Millicent paused, not knowing exactly what to say as she leaned closer, wondering who the current boyfriend could be. She knew how long it had taken Lily to recover from the heartache of losing Demetrius.

Although she had been inconsolable when she had heard that he had taken his own life in Greece, she had later been stunned to hear that he had planned to marry a Greek girl, although he had proposed to her before he disappeared.

'Yes, I know that I have probably surprised you, after losing Demetrius, but I am over that now,' Lily said, as if reading Millicent's mind. 'I'm sure you think that I just go home every evening and don't have any life other than my work and looking after my mother.'

'So, how long have you been seeing this new man?' Millicent asked, being careful not to question her too much, but dying to know who she was actually talking about.

'For around two months, although I have a feeling that it is all over now. I actually thought it was becoming quite serious, but he has suddenly become very distant, and I don't really know where I am with him half the time - I can't think what I have done wrong. We have never ever said a cross word to each other, and he has always seemed to enjoy my company, as I have his.'

'In what way has he become distant with you? Have you asked him why he has suddenly changed with you?' Millicent asked, taking hold of Lily's hand. She couldn't believe that once again Lily had gotten herself involved in yet another relationship that was going tragically wrong for her - doomed to failure by the sounds of it.

The tears had begun to well up in Lily's eyes again and Millicent took out a tissue from her handbag and handed it to her. Lily sat there dabbing her eyes.

'I don't mean to be rude, Milly,' she said, sitting up straight on the wooden bench. 'But I would prefer to talk about something else now before I get really upset and seriously blubber. I feel so embarrassed now talking about this and I feel a little guilty as he did specifically ask me not to mention it, especially to you.'

'Oh, okay, but I want you to promise me that you will come straight to me when you feel you need to talk about this again. Don't think that I don't have any idea of what you are going through. Not so long ago, I was going through exactly the same thing, and I can tell you now that I am completely over it. I just cannot think what I saw in the man in the first place

– he was an arrogant, fat Italian bastard,' Millicent suddenly blurted out.

Lily's hand flew to her mouth shocked by what Millicent had just said – it was so unlike her to make such a remark, but she found it hilarious all the same. They both suddenly burst out into loud and slightly hysterical laugher, ignoring a few strange glances from some people passing by.

All the same, Millicent was intrigued by what Lily had just told her, that the man concerned had specifically asked Lily not to divulge their secret with *her* in particular. She found that very strange and wondered why on earth he, whoever his was, had specifically asked Lily not to discuss it especially with her.

And what I don't understand in the circumstances, is why she feels embarrassed and guilty talking about it when he is obviously not worth her loyalty, Millicent thought, as she sat there.

'Anyway, you haven't told me about the party,' Lily said after their fit of laughter had subsided.

'Well, for a start, Amitola loved her gift - she was absolutely delighted with the collectable doll selected for her in spite of Olsten's reservations about the choice of gift. Her parents could not believe that Olsten had given her such an expensive and finely crafted creation. Amitola said that she will treasure it forever and she actually said that the miniature jewellery was so amazing and found it fascinating that you could produce such tiny pieces. So, you should be very proud of your work, Lily. You are very talented.'

'Oh, thank you Milly. That's so sweet of you,' Lily replied, smiling.

'I mean it, Lily – you are so incredibly talented. Mr. Ryder is always praising you and has said on many occasions that your work is outstanding and that you are a gifted and valuable member of his team. He says you are indispensable, and he could not possibly do without you. I wish I was half as talented as you.'

'Were there many people at the party?' Lily asked, looking more than a little self-conscious and embarrassed by Millicent's flood of admiration for her work. She knew that Mr. Ryder was well pleased with her work, although he never personally praised her to her face, so, it was good to know that her work was recognized as outstanding. Her face began to glow with contentment, momentarily forgetting her troubled love life.

'There were quite a number of family and friends from Mr. and Mrs. Defoe's side; some school friends of Amitola's, and from our side there was, of course, Olsten, me, Danielle and James,' Millicent replied. 'Oh, and Kyle. He had driven us all there and when Mrs. Defoe came to the door, she insisted that he join the party,' she quickly added.

Millicent had the distinct impression that Lily was really probing to find out if that certain person who she had just been talking about had been at the party. She couldn't be sure, but she thought she detected a slight twitch in Lily's eyes – a slight fluttering of her eyelashes, when she mentioned Kyle's name, or was it the mention of James? She had noticed on many occasions that whenever Lily was in the company of James, her face would noticeably flush. James often teased and playfully tormented her, trying to coax her out of her obvious painful shyness when in his presence. Of course, there was absolutely no question of it being Olsten.

Although it couldn't possibly be James, she pondered as she sat there gazing fixedly at Lily's face, then quickly turning away blinking in awkwardness as Lily stared back looking slightly bewildered by Millicent's unwavering stare.

'For a minute there, Millicent, I had the distinct impression that you were inspecting every little line on my face,' Lily said laughing, but with a certain tension behind her smile.

'Oh, I'm sorry, Lily. I went off into a daydream for a minute there,' Millicent said, quickly averting her probing eyes.

'A daydream about something nice, I hope. But anyway, you didn't finish telling me about the party.'

'Oh, yes, well, Mrs. Defoe certainly knows how to put on a delicious spread, I can tell you. I ate so much that I thought I was going to burst. I don't think I will need to eat anything else for a good few days,' she said, laughing.

'The one interesting thing about the party is that James and Danielle appeared to be getting quite close. James seems to be besotted with Danielle and although she does give the impression that she is not at all interested, she certainly seemed to be enjoying herself. They spent the whole evening dancing together. Mind you, Kyle seemed to constantly buzz around Danielle, although she seemed to swat him away like an annoying fly and I for one certainly didn't blame her for that – the man was making a right pest of himself until James warned him off.'

She immediately noticed a distinct frown appear on Lily's face at that point. It was not her intention to cause friction with Lily by enlightening her with such information to hurt her feelings in any way, but she just wanted to draw out some sort of response from her to find out who she was involved with and offer some advice in the circumstances, if necessary. Not that Lily would listen for one minute what Millicent had to say to her – she seemed intent on doing exactly what she wanted regardless.

All the same, Millicent felt a bit mean, after all, Lily was old enough to know her own mind and it was up to her who she spent her time with. The main problem with Lily was that she was so easily impressed and had obviously not had very much experience where men were concerned in the first place.

But then, Millicent had to admit to herself that she could be exactly the same. Her mother had constantly warned her about making wrong decisions in life where men were concerned and couldn't stress enough that women learnt hard lessons by poorly thought out and impulsive actions and decisions. Of course, so far, she had not absorbed as much of her mother's valuable advice as she should have – but she was getting there, she hoped anyway.

Millicent glanced sideways at Lily still waiting for some sort of response, but Lily appeared not to have been listening and had certainly not taken the bait.

She quickly looked down at her wristwatch. 'Our times up – back to work,' Lily said as she stood up abruptly.

Millicent sighed loudly as she reluctantly also stood up and together, they strolled back through the expansive garden and across the road back to work. As much as she loved her job, on such a glorious sunny day, it was a crime to be kept shut away in an office.

'It's such a beautiful day I could sit out here all day,' Millicent said. 'What do you think, Lily, shall we play hooky today and go window shopping in Knightsbridge or shall we wander around St James' Park? Oh, wouldn't that be just wonderful.'

She turned to Lily, waiting for her to answer, but she seemed to be a million miles away, staring straight ahead.

'Are you okay, Lily?' she asked.

'What? Yes, I'm fine,' Lily replied, a little distractedly.

As they were both about to step into the front door, Lily suddenly held back saying that she had left something on the wooden bench back in the garden. Millicent watched, puzzled, as Lily quickly ran back across the road towards the garden entrance. She could not think what Lily could possibly have left; she could see that she was still carrying her handbag, and she had definitely not been carrying an umbrella. She couldn't possibly be going back for her partially uneaten package of sandwiches which she had inadvertently left on the wooden bench instead of tossing in the stone garbage bin.

But then Millicent noticed a man standing on the other side of the road, who when he saw Lily crossing over towards him, quickly began walking away in the opposite direction. Lily began running after him, calling him to wait and when she caught up with him and took hold of his arm, Millicent couldn't help noticing that he was trying to shrug her hand away – the action was noticeably aggressive. Although he had his back to Millicent's view of him, it was obvious that he was angry, and she could hear him yelling at Lily.

'You've been a naughty girl, tittle-tattling behind my back when I specifically told you not to talk about us to anybody and especially not her.'

Feeling hesitant to stand at the doorway any longer before being spotted by either one of them, Millicent quietly closed the door and quickly ran up the staircase to return to her office on the fourth floor of the building.

'Is everything alright, Miss,' Roy called after her as she had scurried past him with an anxious look on her face. He looked towards the door waiting for Lily to follow but when there was no sign of her, he resumed reading his newspaper.

When Millicent reached her desk, which was situated by a window overlooking the park area, she saw the man still outside with his arm now around Lily. He kissed her on her cheek and then walked quickly away from her. Her heart went out to Lily when she could see that the young woman was devastated by what had just been exchanged between them. When the man had walked far enough away, Lily literally collapsed onto her knees and Millicent could see that she was in tears, her whole body shaking with emotion.

She immediately ran back down the stairs and out of the front door into the street but by the time she had reached the outside area, Lily had gone.

When she again scurried past Roy with that same anxious look on her face, he stood up then to follow her out of the door, wondering what on earth was going on.

Millicent stood outside frantically scanning the area hoping to see Lily, but there was no sign of her. She decided to walk further along the road and then she stopped dead in her tracks as she then caught a glimpse of the man that she had seen with Lily – she gasped now as he turned to face her. He smiled and winked at her, and she was taken aback at that moment by a bright light flashing before her eyes, nearly blinding her. She stumbled slightly by the impact, squinting, and held up her hand to shield her eyes. Without saying a word, he abruptly turned from her and walked away with not the slightest indication of any unease at being recognised. There was no mistaking those eyes staring into hers, rendering her frozen on the spot, unable to move for a few seconds as she stood there watching him walk away.

Turning, she walked back in a complete daze, her heart beating so fast that she felt as if she was going to faint. When she reached the front door, Roy stood there waiting for her with a puzzled expression on his face.

'Are you alright, Miss,' he asked again. 'Was that man bothering you?'

'I'm fine, Roy,' she muttered as she walked past him towards the stairs.

'Well, you don't look fine, Miss, if you don't mind me saying so,' he said, looking really concerned by her whole demeanour.

When she again returned to her office, she slumped down on the chair and laid her head on her desk. She suddenly had a pounding headache, and everything began to spin in front of her eyes and then there was blackness.

'MILLICENT, MILLICENT,' she heard a voice calling. She lifted her head still in a dazed state to see Olsten leaning over her looking very worried.

'What on earth has happened to you,' he said, placing his hands on her shoulders.

'I – I must have dozed off,' she answered, looking around the office somewhat puzzled. She could not believe that she had fallen asleep and when she glanced over at the clock on the wall, she realized with dismay that she had actually been asleep for almost an hour. Although she was relieved that Olsten had obviously been out of the office for some time and would not have known how long she had been sleeping in the office, she felt completely mortified as she sat there trying to avoid looking up at him.

He narrowed his eyes as he peered closely into her face, noticing that her eyes looked inflamed and red. 'Whatever has happened? You look upset Millicent, and I want to know what's upset you,' he said, leaning over to her more closely and willing her to look up at him.

Her face turned red, and she quickly averted her face from his.

'I'm fine – I told you, I just dozed off. I'm just a little bit tired after the weekend. I suppose I am just not used to two late nights in a row,' she replied, a little too harshly. She shrugged his hands away from her shoulders as she suddenly stood up so abruptly that her chair was thrown back from her.

Olsten stepped back bewildered at her behaviour. It was just not like her to act in such a strange way. He stepped forward again to pick up the chair and as he did so, she immediately moved quickly away from him like a startled, frightened rabbit.

'Don't touch me – please stay away from me,' she said, visibly shaking.

He frowned as he stood looking at her completely puzzled. She was visibly shaking from head to foot.

Seeing her obviously so distressed, he felt reluctant to question her too much even though he could clearly see that something had certainly seriously disturbed her. He wondered if she had drunk a glass or two of wine during her lunch break and had nodded off in the office; she looked bleary-eyed and definitely out of sorts. He could see she was embarrassed that he had found her sleeping in the office but could not understand her all too obvious aggressive and odd manner towards him.

'I don't know what on earth is going on with you, Millicent, but I suggest you go and get yourself some strong coffee and take some time to rest yourself and then please go straight home. I am just off to another meeting and when I get back, I don't want to see you still here. When I see you tomorrow morning, I fully expect to see you back to your normal self.'

Millicent nodded as she stood there watching him stride off without a backward glance at her. He seemed quite angry with her. She shuddered then as she felt a feeling of panic slowly wash over her. She shook her head, wondering what had gotten into her to act in such a strange way; she was only too aware that she had a pounding headache, and her eyes felt as if they had been scorched by lightening.

What on earth had Olsten thought of her – she would most definitely need to apologise for her behaviour, she thought as she locked up her desk and picked up her bag ready to leave. She felt totally humiliated that she had fallen asleep at her desk. It was most unusual for her and so unprofessional. It was something that she had never done before in all the time she had worked in an office.

She decided to go straight home and get into her warm bed where she could sleep and sleep and hopefully think about this whole episode tomorrow. When she went down to the lobby, Roy looked up at her as she passed him by with a sheepish grin on her face.

'Feeling better, Miss?' he asked, smiling back.

'Yes, I think so, Roy, but I have a terrible headache – I feel as if somebody has tried to suck my brain out,' she replied almost absentmindedly. 'I think it's best if I go home and try to sleep it off.'

Yes, I'm sure you need to sleep it off - by the looks of those red eyes, I think you have probably had one too many glasses of wine during your lunch break, Roy thought as he watched her stagger out of the door and then almost stumble down the step. He immediately jumped to his feet, rushed over to her, took one of her arms and steered her back in through the door.

'Now, you just sit yourself down while I make you a cup of strong coffee and then you can be on your way,' he told her, gently guiding her onto a seat.

'I do feel a little odd, a cup of coffee does sound good Roy, thank you,' she replied.

After drinking the hot, strong cup of coffee, she felt a little better and assured him that she could stand on her feet without feeling wobbly and she was ready to be on her way.

'Yes, well then, get yourself onto a bus and go straight home to your bed – hope you are feeling better tomorrow,' he replied.

'I might just take a slow stroll back home; it will probably clear my head. I just can't understand where this awful headache came from. I was feeling fine this morning although a little bit tired from the weekend.'

'I wouldn't recommend a stroll back home in this heat, especially not with that headache. It will no doubt make you feel even worse. No, the quicker you get home, the better. I really think it would be better if I called Kyle to pick you up. I'm sure he would not mind at all, and he could get you home in ten to fifteen minutes,' he said, picking up the hand-set ready to call a number he had listed, where Olsten was attending at a meeting. Kyle, of course, would be waiting outside ready to transport Olsten back to his office after the meeting. Roy knew that Olsten would not object at all if Kyle took off beforehand to drive Millicent home.

'No, absolutely not, Roy, I would rather take a bus,' she said, noticeably flustered by the very mention of Kyle's name. 'Please do not bother, Roy – I will definitely take a bus, I promise,' she said, a little calmer now, although she suddenly slumped back on the sofa looking as white as a ghost.

Roy immediately hung up the phone. 'Just you wait there for a little longer before you go running off – I'll make some more coffee,' he told her before going through to the small kitchen for staff members, where he began to prepare some more fresh coffee. When he returned to the reception area with another two cups of coffee, Millicent had left already. He stood there puzzled, thinking what on earth had caused her to behave in such a way. It was just not like her at all.

Chapter Ten

When Roy had securely locked up before departing for the evening, after working a little later that day, he sauntered along through Mayfair thinking about Millicent. He couldn't get her face out of his mind and wondered what had gotten into the girl earlier. That dazed expression in her eyes had worried him all afternoon and he hoped that she had gotten herself straight home and gone directly to her bed. Apart from suffering with a splitting headache, she was clearly experiencing some sort of anxiety by the looks of her.

He couldn't understand her attitude when he had insisted that he call Kyle to drive her back home rather than taking a bus. He knew that Kyle had driven Mr. Ryder to a meeting sometime earlier that morning and then again after lunch, but he had not been too far away and could easily have run Millicent home and returned back for Mr. Ryder when he had concluded his meeting a little later. He was puzzled that Millicent would not hear anything of the sort and made it abudantly clear that she did not want him to call Kyle to drive her back to her flat. In fact, Roy couldn't help noticing at the time that she became quite agitated by the very mention of Kyle.

It had not escaped Roy's attention that Kyle did not exactly endear himself to females as he always appeared to go out of his way to intimidate them in a subtle way. His whole demeanour, either consciously or unconsciously, especially while interacting with females in the office, seemed to reveal an arrogant and a particularly unfortunate challenging manner, which obviously had not gone unnoticed by Millicent and as far as Roy could see, she had taken a particular distinct disliking to him.

All the same, when Roy had insisted that Millicent stay a little longer, he had been puzzled and surprised when she had left so abruptly without a word while he was preparing more coffee. If he had had his own way he would have gladly escorted her home himself but, of course, he could not leave his desk unattended – Mr. Ryder would be none too pleased about that no matter how lenient he was with members of staff.

Millicent had looked well enough earlier that morning when both she and Lily had gone out for their lunch break later. They had been chatting away together looking cheerful enough. He suddenly remembered that he had not given Lily a second thought when she had not come back with Millicent. He wondered if they had argued during their lunchbreak and had a slight falling out. It was strange that Lily had,in fact, not returned at all during the whole afternoon after her lunch break. He was at all times very polite with Lily, although she always seemed quite a strange timid young woman and not one easy to get to know. As much as he chatted away quite easily with Millicent and often teased her, Lily was not so forthcoming with any kind of repartee.

Roy was halfway back to his flat when he suddenly remembered that he needed to pick up some food items as instructed by his wife. When he reached into the inside pocket of his jacket for his wallet containing the list that she had given him, there was no sign of his wallet. He stood there frantically going through each pocket realizing to his horror that he had maybe left his wallet on his desk. As the key to his flat was also attached to the wallet, he had no alternative but to turn back to his desk – *maybe he had dropped his wallet and key somewhere around on the floor in the reception area,* he thought as he hurried back.It was just as well that the bunch of keys to the office building were securely attached to a belt that he wore as part of his smart security uniform.

When he reached the building and stood outside the heavy front door, he noticed that it was slightly ajar. Nervously, he stepped inside and closed the door behind him, peering into the dimly lit foyer cautiously. *Who on earth would have left the front door open* – he knew without a doubt that he had left the door securely locked and, being a heavy door, it had to be practically slammed shut before being locked from top to bottom on the outside. Besides which, apart from the office cleaner and of course, Olsten, he was the only person in charge of the complete set of keys to the front door and all the offices in the building.

It was already nearing eight o'clock and he knew that Olsten and his driver had departed at least twenty minutes before he had left and there had been nobody else remaining in the building as far as he was aware – each member of staff had to sign out at the end of the day. He flicked on the switch located by the side of the front door turning on the large chandelier above which flooded the area with bright light.

He stood in the middle of the lobby listening attentively for any noise of somebody else being present in the immediate area of the foyer and when he thought he could hear music coming from one of the offices above, he began to walk up the stairs slowly. He unlocked and checked each office on every level of the building and when he came to the top floor on the fifth level, he unlocked Olsten's office and his conference room and he could hear the music clearly coming from within Olsten's private quarters. As much as he would have liked to have unlocked the area, the only person who had a spare key to Olsten's private quarters was Mrs. Agno Stafros, their much trusted Greek office cleaner, who kept the spacious rooms clean and tidy on a daily basis. Roy knew that it could not possibly be Mrs Stafros this time of the evening as she only cleaned very early mornings and was, in fact, known to be in the building as early as five in the morning, well before anybody else arrived.

Agnos was quite a character and although she was well into her late forties, she was a typical, hardworking Greek woman, always smiling. She was often still in the building when Roy arrived at eight o'clock and she would delight in sitting with him and enjoying a cup of tea before she left the building. Being of the same age, Roy enjoyed her company and he knew her well, as she practically told him all her life story time after time, which he never got tired of hearing. He could see that she had been a beautiful woman in her younger day – and still was, although life had taken it's toll on her appearance, resulting in hard lines on her face. He was always amused how she actually flirted with him and he often told himself that if they were both younger and he was still single, they would have made a perfect couple. Agnos was widowed and lived in a small flat in Soho with her eldest son, who currently worked in a restaurant in the vicinity of Soho.

Roy continued standing outside Olsten's private quarters for a few seconds, listening and then he lightly tapped on the heavy oak door. When there was no answer, he called out and when there was still no answer, he called out again loudly pressing his ear right against the door. The music instantly stopped and there was complete silence. Roy stood back, puzzled, but as he was about to walk away, the door opened and out walked Olsten.

'Is everything alright, Roy?' he said, holding a glass of whisky in his hand.

'Sorry, Mr. Ryder – I came back for something I had left in reception and was surprised to see the front door ajar,' he replied. 'I didn't realize that you were still here considering that you had left earlier with Kyle,' he added.

'Well, I decided to return back here for the night. I have a considerable amount of paperwork to go through and I thought it was just as well to stay here where all my records are at hand.'

'All I can say is that it's lucky I happened to come back – I wouldn't like to think of that front door being left ajar all night,' Roy said, frowning.

'In that case, I'm very glad you did come back, Roy, and please make sure that the door is securily locked on your way back out. I suspect it could have been Kyle rushing out and failing to slam the door security shut. These young men, they are all in such a hurry.'

'Right you are Mr. Ryder – I'll be on my way then and I'll see you tomorrow.'

'Did you find your wallet, by the way.' Olsten called out after Roy as he was about to go through to the stairway.

Before Roy had a chance to answer, Olsten had quickly closed the door leading into his private sitting room but not before Roy heard the tinkling laughter of a female from within.

He turned and quickly ran down the stairs and as soon as he had located his wallet which had fallen underneath his desk, he switched off the chandelier lighting and stepped out of the heavy front door which he slammed securely shut and then locked it from top to bottom on the outside.

It was only after he had walked a few yards away from the building that he frowned, remembering Mr. Ryder had asked him about his wallet. He had not mentioned anything about his wallet. He scratched his head. Mr Ryder couldn't possibly have seen the wallet under the desk.

Chapter Eleven

Millicent arrived at the office the day after her bizarre behaviour; feeling extremely embarrassed to see Olsten and dreading the moment when she had to face him. When he appeared some fifteen minutes later, she need not have worried as he acted as if nothing untoward had happened between them and put her mind at rest immediately saying nothing of what had occurred.

As far as Olsten was concerned the whole matter was best forgotten, as they had more pressing matters to worry about. It was enough that she had obviously been mortified, and for his part he felt it best to completely ignore the whole incident.

He was not to know at the time that the incident was just the beginning of a situation that was going to progress into a nightmare for them all.

Millicent was so relieved that the whole matter was being overlooked. If she had been asked to explain herself, she would not have had the least idea of what to actually say to him in the circumstances; it had all seemed so bizarre to her, and she could not really understand what had made her behave in such a way.

However, more worryingly, Lily had not returned to her workshop the following morning. Millicent called her home, but her mother had seemed to have no idea of her whereabouts and was extremely anxious that her daughter had not returned home the previous evening or, in fact, the whole night. She informed Millicent that she had been worried about her daughter who had been acting extremely strangely and quite out of character during the past week.

Millicent had then asked if she knew of somebody – maybe a boyfriend, who they could contact, who would know where Lily could have gone. Her mother had assured her that Lily would not have gone anywhere without consulting her first. She said that Lily was a most loyal and trustworthy daughter and was certainly not the type to just disappear without any prior warning or explanation. She was also adamant that Lily would definitely not run off with a boyfriend without telling her, especially one who was not particularly honorable, in her opinion.

Millicent had been surprised by that last comment, but it had just reinforced her suspicions that this was exactly what had probably happened. In the past few weeks, she had noticed Lily become more and more withdrawn and it was clear that it all revolved around this man that she had seen during their lunch break together the previous day.

Millicent had a feeling that Lily's mother obviously had some knowledge of this man and his hold on her daughter, but for some reason was not willing to divulge any particular information at this time.

A few days later, when she informed Olsten about Lily's absence, he said he would make some enquiries, although he doubted whether it would be necessary. He was certain that Lily would show up sooner rather than later and insisted that maybe she just needed a few days to herself. He was known to have a kind and benevolent nature and was always very lenient and understanding with his staff when he felt it was necessary. Although he was not aware of the exact circumstances involved, leading to Lily's disappearance, he did not question the whys and wherefores. She was an extremely hard-working young woman and a few days away from her work would not be a problem as far as he was concerned – he knew she would certainly make up for lost time when she returned.

As usual they started off the day with coffee and Danish pastries while going over incoming mail and planned schedules. Olsten was in one of his good-humored, but tormenting moods when he liked to trip her up about her accuracy on recording past events and future events that they needed to plan for. They were laughing together when suddenly they heard a door being slammed so loudly that they both flinched in their seats. Olsten immediately stood up, ready to go out into the hallway to see what all the commotion was about, when Celeste suddenly flounced into the room, waving her arms around and shouting at the top of her voice.

'Take your hands off of me right now – DON'T YOU DARE TOUCH ME. GET AWAY FROM ME OR YOU WILL BE SORRY,' she screamed at Roy as he was trying to restrain her, without much success. He let go of her promptly when she kicked him in the groin with all her strength. He doubled over and moved away from her as far as he could, cursing under his breath.

'That will teach you to manhandle me, you great big obnoxious bastard – tell him. Olsten, that he is not coming near me again or I will call the police,' she said, turning to Olsten.

Oh, here we go again, Millicent thought, as she sat looking on in dismay as she watched Roy hobble as far away from Celeste as he could, looking decidedly uncomfortable and embarrassed. Roy was a gigantic, robust man, towering above most men and had the strength of ten men put together, but he had been unable to restrain Celeste, such was the power of her absolute determination to get to Olsten to vent out her rage on him.

'That woman needs a good hiding and if I was her father, I would have no hesitation whatsoever in taking her over my knee and giving her the thrashing of her life,' Roy mumbled, wincing, as he tried to straighten himself up.

In spite of his angry warning, Roy was a gentle giant, and both Millicent and Olsten knew only too well that he would never lift a finger to any woman not even after being kicked in the groin.

'Thank you, Roy. There's nothing to worry about, just go about your business,' Olsten called after him as he hobbled out of the office.

'Poor man – there was absolutely no need for that, Celeste,' he said, frowning at her.

'Well, the man is a great, big, blundering ox – a buffoon. *I WILL NOT* be manhandled,' she spat out, snarling like a wild cat.

'What can we do for you, Celeste?' Olsten asked, knowing that it was the wrong thing to say to her. They were all so tired of having to deal with her erratic mood swings and trying to deal with her unannounced destructive visits to the office. As much as Olsten tried to be patient with her, he was becoming increasingly frustrated and tired of her behaviour.

'What can you *do for me* - how can you say such a thing to me as if I am just one of your clients. I don't know how you have the nerve to treat me so coldly and with such disregard,' She spluttered, with barely concealed rage.

'I'm sorry, Celeste, you have to understand that we are extremely busy at the moment and need to get on. If you need to talk, I am happy to take you out for lunch later and we can discuss anything you like.'

'Well, now, don't *we* look cozy,' she said sharply, glaring at Millicent menacingly.

'Would you like a cup of tea or coffee, Miss Harrington?' Millicent asked nervously.

'We need to talk, Olsten, and we need to talk NOW,' Celeste shouted at Olsten, as she stood directly in front of him; her hands on her hips, completely ignoring Millicent and her offer of tea or coffee.

'Hold all calls will you, Millicent, until I tell you otherwise,' he said, as he took hold of one of Celeste's wrists, gently pulling her along towards the door leading to his private suite of rooms.

'Oh, darling I've missed you so much,' Celeste said, sarcastically, as she leaned into him, laid her head against his chest and suddenly bit his chin viciously. He quickly drew back, trying to keep her at arm's length whilst still holding tightly onto her wrist.

'I'm so sorry to disturb you during your usual early morning tete-a-tete with *little Miss Perfect* here,' she said, suddenly swiveling her head around like a demon and hissing at Millicent, who stood just outside the door nervously.

'And don't you just look so sweet and neat, Miss Honey Bunch – as if nothing would melt in your mouth,' she added, spitting out her words.

She wrenched herself away from Olsten's grip on her wrist and strutted over to the life-sized doll Olsten kept in his private lounge, put her arm around the doll's neck and leaned into it, making Olsten very nervous that it was going to topple over with her weight against it.

'And as for you, darling girl, what a mystery you are and don't you look like butter wouldn't melt in *your* mouth,' she spat out, scathingly. 'Being as you are made out of *cold clay*, I think you are perfectly suited to our Mr. Ryder here,' she said, grinning at Olsten.

'Please stand away from the doll, Celeste. It is a very expensive model, and I don't want it damaged,' Olsten said, as he walked over to her and again took hold of one of her wrists.

'And who exactly is *this* doll modeled on, may I ask? Could it be your long-lost wife?' she said slyly, looking up into Olsten's face.

'And why may I ask have you removed my lookalike doll from being on display in the reception area?' she demanded. 'That is such a huge insult to me, and I demand that you return it. As your future wife, you should be proud to have it on display for all to see.'

'Could you bring some fresh strong coffee through, Millicent,' Olsten said, by now holding onto Celeste's wrist more tightly. She was wriggling to break free from his hold, spitting like a wild cat and kicking out at his ankles.

Millicent nodded at this request. She couldn't help noticing Celeste's bloodshot eyes. She had obviously been drinking heavily through the previous evening and maybe into the early hours of the morning. Although she was, as usual, dressed in the most fashionable, elegant clothes, they looked somewhat crumpled. There was a strong smell of whisky and stale cigarette smoke on her and her hair and makeup were messed up, mascara smudged around her eyes as if she had just woken up without bothering to freshen herself up. The disheveled appearance seemed to be her usual look these days.

Celeste appeared to calm down as Olsten guided her onto a couch in his private quarters. All the same, when Millicent heard the door close quietly behind them, she had a feeling of dread that something terrible was going to happen. She was quite aware of how dangerously volatile Celeste could be and she suspected that she was at her most explosive, judging by the expression on her face when she first appeared in the office. She was clearly extremely agitated about something and out for somebody's blood - there was absolutely no doubt whatsoever that Olsten was the target of her anger for whatever reason. Millicent believed that whatever those reasons were, they were all in Celeste's head and it was clear that she needed help.

As soon as the door had been closed, Celeste took to pacing around his sitting room and began rifling through some papers laid out on a coffee table, before wandering towards his bedroom.

Olsten stood watching her – he was becoming quite used to this behavior. She had, on numerous occasions, taken it upon herself to go through his wardrobe specifically searching for feminine items and anything else that she could find to give her a reason to berate him with.

Olsten waited patiently for several minutes before following her into the bedroom. She had gone suspiciously quiet, and he wondered what she was up to. He did not want her to go through his personal things, but he dared not say anything to her in case she threw one of her tantrums again.

He found her sitting on the edge of his bed, once again staring at the photograph of a dark-haired woman which he kept on one of his bedside units. After the last time, when she had smashed the same photograph, he realized now that he should not have had it on display again. He made a mental note to himself that he would keep the photograph hidden away in one of his drawers in future.

'Is this your wife, or should I say your late wife that you never talk about? She does look amazingly like the life-sized doll out there in your lounge – how interesting,' she said, sarcastically.

'And may I ask also, who is that small girl that you always seem to be sniffing around? That is also very interesting. Mr. and Mrs. Defoe may be blind and stupid, but I am certainly not. Does it never occur to them to question how you always manage to turn up and save the day when she finds herself in any little would-be calamity? What dirty little secrets are you hiding away, Olsten, darling.' She flicked her hair back from her face dramatically and swayed from side to side with the movement as she attempted to get up from the bed, almost toppling over. Olsten could see that she was either very drunk or under the influence of strong medication.

Not wanting to go over the same subjects again, Olsten ignored the questions and held out his hand to her.

'Come and sit down in the sitting room, Celeste. I need to talk to you and try to clear this whole situation up. I have been so worried about you. I want to know what has happened to you and why you seem to be so unhappy. Of course, I do realize how disappointed you have been about the cancellation of your wedding plans, but I can't help feeling that there is something much more serious happening to you.'

'For your information, it was I who called off the wedding – I couldn't go through marrying the wrong man, as you well know. And why are you bringing all that up now? It is all so long ago, and I am more concerned with the now and I demand to know when you are going to make an honest woman out of me.'

'I have absolutely no idea what you are talking about, Celeste, but I do want to help you – if you could just explain to me exactly what your problem is.'

He started to walk towards her but ducked quickly as she once again threw the picture frame at him, just missing his head as it flew past him, shattering into pieces against the opposite wall.

'Oh, don't you dare patronize me! I am not a child, and I don't appreciate your condescending manner. You are nothing but a pompous, arrogant bastard, full of your own importance. And I can tell you now that I aim to expose you for what you are, and as for that small girl that you seem to persist in stalking - I am going to find out the truth once and for all.'

'Look, Celeste. I've tried to be patient with you, but I can't help you if you refuse to talk to me about your problems. I will listen to whatever you have to say to me except all these constant ludicrous accusations. Let's just go into the sitting room and talk about this calmly. After all, that's why you came here. You said you needed to talk to me, so come on, talk to me.'

Just then there was a knock at the door and Olsten strode through to the sitting room to let Millicent in with a tray of fresh coffee and orange juice. She looked nervous as she passed through the door and walked quickly towards the coffee table to set the tray down. She could not help flinching when she saw Celeste sashay through the door from the bedroom like a panther ready to pounce, staring at her fiercely. She was surprised to see that Celeste was now partially clothed and stood there in her satin underwear with just a silk chiffon scarf around her neck.

'What is she doing here?' Celeste asked tartly, glaring angrily at Millicent.

'Thanks Millicent – no need to pour, I can see to that,' Olsten said, smiling at her.

He could see that she was extremely uneasy, having witnessed too many of Celeste's tantrums on previous occasions, as he was himself, having reached the limit of his patience and endurance.

Millicent swiftly walked back out of the door, quickly closing it and breathing a huge sigh of relief once she was on the other side. She had half expected the pot of hot coffee to be tossed at her head. It was becoming an altogether worrisome habit of Celeste's, to come haring into their offices without any prior warning and although Millicent told herself that she should be used to it by now, she still felt anxious and unprepared for Celeste's wild, impulsive mood swings.

'Come sit down and have some coffee, Celeste. You look as if you need it,' Olsten said as he began to pour the hot coffee, ignoring that she had appeared back out of his bedroom in her underwear.

Surprisingly, she did as she was told and sat next to him and began drinking the coffee slowly. He waited until she had finished and watched her as she sat right back on the sofa and drew her legs up. Curled up like that, she seemed almost childlike as she fidgeted nervously with the scarf around her neck, muttering to herself.

Olsten was completely bewildered now, as she peered around the room in a restless and uneasy manner. She seemed afraid of something only she could see. He sat waiting for her to come out of her trance-like state but suddenly her eyes closed, her head slumped forward, and she appeared to be sleeping, still clutching the scarf around her neck. He reached over to her and carefully removed the scarf.

Back in Millicent's office, all seemed to go quiet now behind the closed door to Olsten's private area. She breathed a sigh of relief and continued typing out some schedules for the forthcoming month. It looked to be another hectic month, but she was at her best when under pressure and looked forward to being busy.

The hours went by, and Olsten and Celeste did not reappear out of his private quarters. Millicent had expected there to be a few more loud crashing sounds and angry raised voices, but all seemed quiet behind the closed door.

Lunchtime came and went and still they had not emerged. At around three in the afternoon, Millicent decided to phone through to check if they would like to have some food ordered and delivered but Olsten declined, saying that he would take Celeste home very shortly after she had rested.

By five, when they had still not emerged, Millicent tidied up her desk and left the office for the day. Not wanting to disturb them again, she instead left a small note for Olsten by her typewriter, informing him that she had completed all her work and had gone home.

She stopped by Roy's reception desk on the ground floor before leaving to inform him that Olsten was still in his private suite of rooms together with Ms. Harrington.

'You may be in for a longer stay this evening, Roy, before locking up. I hope it won't be too long – but you never know,' she said smiling.

Roy rolled his eyes and laughed. 'I'm used to it, Miss, although I don't think the Missus appreciates it when I have to stay later, especially when she is waiting to dish up our evening meal. I think I will be in for some ear bashing when I get back,' he replied.

Roy was a typical Londoner and was what people would describe as the *salt of the earth*. Millicent always found him easy to talk to and often spent a short break drinking a cup of tea with him, listening to his hilarious stories.

'I'm sure you will be able to sweet talk her, Roy, you are good at that,' she said, smiling fondly.

'I'll try, but my sweet talk long ago ran out with her indoors,' he said, laughing before coughing and spluttering.

'You really should give up smoking, Roy – that cough sounds really bad.'

'Couldn't do that Miss. At my age, it's my only enjoyment,' he replied, still spluttering.

'Well, I'll be off now, Roy. I'll see you tomorrow.'

'Mind how you go. Have a good evening, Miss,' Roy said as she stepped out of the front door waving to him.

'You too, Roy – mind you don't bump into any high heels,' she said, laughing.

'I certainly hope not and, in fact, when that lady comes back down, I will either immediately duck underneath the desk here or excuse myself into the gents until she has gone out that door,' he replied, also laughing.

Once outside the door, Millicent stood for a second while she pulled out her purse from her bag to check for some loose change for her bus ride home. On occasions, she was happy to walk back home, although it was quite a trek, but this evening, she felt quite tired. When she looked up, she saw Kyle staring at her, leaning cockily against the front of the limousine car waiting to take Olsten home. He stood up straight and mock saluted her as she walked towards him. She couldn't help thinking that he was one of the most arrogant men that she had ever met – so sure of himself and not in the least likable, as far as she was concerned. His good looks and charm had no effect on her whatsoever, even though he obviously thought of himself as some sort of suave ladies' man.

'Good evening, Miss,' he said, smiling at her.

'Good evening, Kyle. I am not sure how long you will have to wait for Mr. Ryder as he does have a visitor at the moment.'

'In that case, I will go inside and sit with Roy who will hopefully offer me a cuppa while I wait,' he replied, winking at her.

Her face flushed as she turned away, annoyed with herself that he had made her feel slightly flustered. She cursed as she tripped on her own feet in her rush to get as far away from him as she could.

'Oops, mind how you go, Miss, and don't let the bogey man get you,' Kyle called after her in that infuriatingly cocky way of his, followed by that rude clicking sound he made with his tongue.

'You, me – how about it, doll-face,' he said, loud enough for her to hear, again making that clicking sound with his tongue.

She almost felt like turning on her heels, charging back towards him and slapping his face hard. She quickly walked away, but when she turned at the corner of the road, she could see him still watching her with a mocking expression on his face.

She felt so angry that she decided to walk all the way home as it would maybe calm her down. The man was absolutely unbearable and seemed to go out of his way to annoy her. She had the distinct impression that he enjoyed intimidating women and making them squirm when in his presence. She wondered if he was one of those men who had developed a hatred of women from an early age due to a domineering mother. He seemed to have a fixated enjoyment in making women feel degraded, wanting to torment them.

She began to walk faster and faster and although it was still early evening, she couldn't help feeling anxious. As usual, the streets were full of people rushing around, but she still felt nervous and suspicious of any man walking towards her.

It was a time of fear for women in the West End of London as various young wealthy women had gone missing. The bodies of these women had eventually been found laid out in dark alleyways. They had all been strangled, and their faces had been painted to look like a China doll. A single red rose had been strategically placed by the side of the victims.

Back at the office building, Kyle had sauntered into the reception area and promptly sat down, puffing away at his cigarette.

He was feeling quite chuffed that he had obviously ruffled Millicent's feathers.

'Some women are so sensitive - one little wrong word and they get so upset. Don't you think so, Roy?' he asked slyly.

'Oh, I don't know. My Missus is as hard as nails and you would have to go a long way to upset her,' Roy replied, as he began tidying up the reception desk before leaving for the day.

'I'm talking about Mr. Ryder's secretary – she is such a cold-hearted little madam,' Kyle said, rolling his eyes impatiently at Roy's remark about his wife. He was so tired of hearing about Roy's Missus. *She was probably as ugly as sin and as boring as hell - did the man have nothing else to talk about,* he thought.

Roy looked up, his eyes narrowed, mischievously.

'What's the matter, son? Is she not taken in by your irresistible charm?'

Kyle shot him a scathing look, stood up abruptly and walked back out of the door, still puffing angrily at his cigarette.

'I'm going out for a quick cup of coffee, but I will be back later to collect Mr. Ryder,' he said, without a backward glance.

'Goodnight then, son,' Roy called out after him, smiling to himself. He had never particularly taken to the young man; he was far too cocky for his own good.

Chapter Twelve

As Millicent stepped down the narrow stone steps leading to the front door of her tiny basement flat in Great Cumberland Place and let herself in, she sighed with relief and literally kicked her high-heeled shoes from her feet, which were by now throbbing from her long walk from Berkeley Square. She usually took her comfortable walking pumps with her to work but on this day, she had taken the bus in the morning and had not planned to walk back home. In the circumstances, having had that little set-to with Kyle, she had literally stomped all the way back home that evening despite wearing her high heels.

She had calmed down now but still felt rattled about the man's whole attitude; he seemed to go out of his way to offend her. She wondered if Olsten was aware of his rudeness, although she realized Kyle was probably a model of decorum when in Olsten's presence. He was far too cunning to reveal the despicable side that he took delight in exposing when in the company of women.

Although not all women, Millicent suddenly thought as she had noticed on numerous occasions that Kyle seemed to have a high regard for Danielle whenever she came to the office – almost pleading for her approval of him. Danielle, in return, ignored him completely, as if he was invisible. *Maybe that was the secret of how to deal with him*, Millicent continued to ponder.

'Although, why on earth am I wasting my time even thinking about the horrible man,' she said aloud, as she bent down to stroke her cat.

Her white fluffy cat, Tatters, short for Tatiana, had come rushing over to her immediately, winding in and out of her legs and welcoming her back home.

Although her flat was cramped and smelt of damp at times, especially when it rained, she was fairly content living there.

Her neighbours were an interesting group of people ranging from wealthy Jewish families, entertaining artists, models and ladies of the night. Millicent was unaware when she first moved into the bedsit that the previous occupant had obviously been one of those ladies of the night.

It had been a particularly alarming experience to her when coming out of her bathroom the very next morning after she had first moved in, when a man had unlocked the front door and was attempting to enter. Fortunately, Millicent had applied a small chain on the inside of the door and was very thankful that she had this extra protection. She could not help wondering at the time what would have happened if the man had actually been able to freely enter.

'Excuse me – I think you are in the wrong house,' she had called out, while pushing against the door from the inside. The chain was quite thin, and she had been concerned and afraid that it could easily snap any minute. The more she had pushed from the inside, the more he pushed from the outside.

'Hello, my little Delilah – are you busy right now. I can come back a bit later if you would prefer, sweet girl,' he had replied optimistically, although sounding a little intoxicated in spite of it being so early in the morning.

She had peered through the crack in the partially opened door to see the man swaying from side to side, wearing a pin-striped suit although in a dishevelled state, holding his shoes in one hand.

When she had informed him in no uncertain certain terms, that she was not his little Delilah, he had apologized profusely for disturbing her. She had stood there watching him from the front window as he had quickly stumbled back up the narrow steps and was then hopping about on the pavement above making a display of himself, struggling to put his shoes back on.

When he had finally staggered off out of sight, she had sincerely hoped none of her neighbours had observed the scene; she had not met any of them at that time, but if one of them had seen him outside, she suspected that it could not be a very good start for her - they would have probably jumped to the conclusion that she was also a *lady of the night working girl*.

On another occasion, sometime after that particular incident, when she had been laid out on her sofa watching a TV show one evening, she had glanced up at the window when she had heard a light tapping against the glass and there had been a young man waving at her from the outside with a bottle of Champagne and gesturing for her to open the front door. The penny dropped, and she had realized for sure that the previous tenant had obviously entertained various men in the bedsit.

Thank God I insisted that the awful sofa bed was replaced, she had thought, suddenly feeling very itchy.

Her landlord had in turn been horrified when she had mentioned this to him, informing her that he had

had no idea of the goings on before she had moved in, but assured her in no uncertain terms that he would have the front door lock immediately changed for her peace of mind and also arrange to have some iron bars fitted outside the front windows.

She was not in any way offended by the previous tenant's profession, but she certainly did not want any strangers knocking on her door expecting similar favours from her, that was for sure.

Millicent now stepped into the tiny galley kitchen, lit one of the small gas rings on the ancient cooker and placed her kettle over to boil; she was dying for a hot cup of tea to calm her nerves after the day's events.

Later, after Millicent had washed the few dishes and pans that she had used to cook her evening meal, she changed into her dressing gown, switched on her TV, put her feet up and settled comfortably on her sofa to relax for the rest of the evening.

She was awakened suddenly much later when Tatters began to leap about on her lap, she realized that she had nodded off sometime during the evening and when she glanced at her clock placed on top of the TV, she could see that it was already after midnight. She raised herself up to a sitting position on the sofa and gasped when she turned to see a face at the window watching her. She quickly jumped up from the sofa and closed the curtains, wondering how long the intruder had been outside while she had been sleeping. When she heard footsteps running up the stone steps, she nervously peered through a gap at the side of the curtain to make sure that he was gone and, much to her relief, there was now no sign of him.

Feeling very uneasy, she rushed to the front door and pulled the small chain across and then closed the top window securely in her small kitchen. Although she preferred to have some air circulating through the damp bedsit, especially at night, she was far too nervous to leave any windows open now.

Her mind ran riot -she was terrified at the thought that it could have even been the man responsible for all those women found murdered in and around London.

As she was far too tired to open up the sofa bed, she decided to continue sleeping laid out on the top but try as she might, she could not now go back to sleep worrying whether the man who had hovered outside watching her was going to come back. She swung her legs over the sofa, stood up and walked into the kitchen to prepare a cup of hot cocoa with milk, which she hoped would help her to go back to sleep for a few hours at least, before she would have to get herself up and get ready to go to work.

She awoke a few hours later feeling a little more refreshed and relaxed, although she still couldn't help fretting about the man outside her window and wondering if he would return during the forthcoming night again. She quickly took a tepid bath and dressed herself in one of her smart suits, prepared herself some toast, a cup of tea and then, she was out of the door. She had a set routine during the week and could be up, dressed and heading to work within twenty minutes.

As she stepped out of the front door, she frowned when she looked down to see a small note placed under a brick in front of her door. She leaned over and picked up the note, still frowning as she unfolded the note. Her eyes widened as she read the short message, staring fixedly at it for some minutes –before she looked up at the stone steps, fearing that whoever had left the message was waiting for her.

"I know where you live. I will be back to see you again now that I know your secret nocturnal activities. My mission in this life is to clean the streets of sinful women," the note read in straggly, untidy writing and was signed with the letter 'J'.

She stood there transfixed, staring at the note – and placed her hand over her chest, breathing rapidly.

Just then Evelyn, one of her neighbours, together with her man friend who often stayed overnight with her, came tripping down the steps with her daily bag of household garbage to discard in a small cupboard immediately underneath the stone steps by the side of the basement flat.

Evelyn had been a successful model in her younger days and was now an elegant fifty-something-year-old mature lady, always impeccably dressed, and dripping in gold jewellry. Today she wore a Parisian style red beret perched on the side of her head and a belted fashionable leopard patterned, elegant mackintosh. Millicent was always fascinated by all her different outfits, not to mention her jewelry, and the leopard patterned mackintosh was her personal favourite. Evelyn lived in one of the more spacious and plush flats at the back of the house. Millicent smiled at her, now relieved to see a familiar face.

'Good morning, Evelyn,' she said, trying to sound as chirpy as possible in the circumstances.

'Good morning my dear. How are you?' Evelyn trilled cheerfully in return, as she handed over the garbage bag to her man friend to drop in the bin stored in the cupboard.

Before Millicent could answer, she leaned very close to her and grabbed hold of one of her earlobes. Millicent winced in surprise at the slightly aggressive action - she could smell her expensive perfume and the flowery scent of her face powder as she was practically yanked close to her, cheek against cheek.

'Cecelia came to see me this morning, and she is none too pleased with you,' she whispered in Millicent's ear. 'She wants you to know that you must be very careful about what time of the day and night you invite one of your gentlemen regulars around. She says it is not good for the neighborhood and does not set a good example. This is a respectable house, and we do not want it to be tarnished by any kind of ill-repute, now do we, my dear. Cecelia was unpleasantly disturbed early this morning by your unsavory gentleman client leaving the premises making an unholy fracas and if such sordid goings on continue, we will have to take measures to have you removed from the premises —is that abundantly clear, my dear?'

Without waiting for a response from Millicent, she released her hold on her earlobe, and pushed her gently away, smiling sweetly. Then she practically skipped back up the steps, gaily chatting away to her friend all the while yanking him up the stairs behind her. Millicent could hear them laughing loudly as they then walked along the pavement above together.

Millicent stood there stunned, rubbing her throbbing earlobe, a slight feeling of hysteria bubbling up in her throat. She felt like a naughty schoolgirl being reprimanded for behaving badly and she didn't know whether to laugh or cry. How could they just assume that she was entertaining strange gentlemen during the late hours of the night as the previous tenant had? She was mortified at the thought. In fact, she was not only flabbergasted but quite enraged by the very idea and would certainly talk to Cecelia and put her straight on the matter.

Cecelia, who was another former model, lived in a large, expansive maisonette two floors above Millicent's bedsit and kept a vigilant watch over the property and adjoining houses in the area.

Millicent had, on one occasion, witnessed Cecelia hanging out of her front window yelling at a young woman living in the next door basement flat, who worked in a night club as a stripper, informing her in no uncertain terms that her sort was not wanted in a respectable neighborhood and that she would make it her business to see that the she was removed from the area forthwith.

True to her word, the young woman in question was forced to move out shortly after and in her place, another young woman thereafter moved in, who also appeared to have a dubious lifestyle, much to Cecilia's disapproval. She was inevitably also forced to move out of the property.

Millicent couldn't help thinking that it was such a shame– she did not want to fall out with either Cecelia or Evelyn, as the three of them had become such good friends and both had invited her into their flats from time to time, where she had sat with them drinking a glass of Champagne and eating thin slices of brown bread with slithers of salmon sprinkled with lemon juice. She feared that there would be no more glasses of Champagne or slithers of salmon on slices of bread in the future.

In spite of their airs and graces, Millicent found them both fascinating and very funny, although eccentric – they were both typical women of the world and had both travelled extensively in their youth.

Millicent stood for a few minutes, wondering whether or not to confront Cecelia before going to work, but then decided that she would talk to her later. She screwed up the piece of notepaper and tossed it into her bag. She would maybe show it to Roy who could advise her on what to do about the situation.

She sighed as she turned to her front door locking it securely. As she walked up the stone steps, she noticed that Cecelia was by her window watching her and when she smiled and waved, Cecelia immediately turned away without acknowledging her in return.

'I can't be worrying about that now! It's just nonsense and I have far more worrying things to think about,' Millicent muttered to herself as she walked towards Marble Arch to wait for her bus.

What was going on these days – there seemed to be so many little aggravations, not only at work, but now even in her personal life and she was becoming increasingly fed up with it all, she couldn't help thinking, as she hurried along. She felt almost as if there was some kind of mysterious, powerful force out to get her and wear her down although she knew she was being paranoid and over dramatic. She suddenly gulped down a lump in her throat. A feeling of nausea washed over her as a tear trickled down her face. *Paranoid or not, whatever was happening was certainly starting to get to her.*

As she continued to walk towards Marble Arch, deep in thought, she was startled when a loud noise of screeching tires was heard as a car pulled up close to the curb beside her and stopped. The driver honked his horn at her and when she turned and peered into the window, she saw Kyle smiling up at her.

'Want a lift, darling?' he asked.

'No, thank you,' she replied curtly, immediately turning her head away in disgust.

She suddenly felt a sharp pain surge through her head and hoped that she was not getting another one of those terrible headaches. She had never suffered with headaches before and just put it down to the stress of several busy work schedules and deadlines during the past weeks.

'Suit yourself, doll-face,' he replied, followed by that infuriatingly clicking sound he made with his tongue.

The man is despicable, Millicent thought, fuming, as she watched him as he then drove off at high speed recklessly. As she was about to cross over to the other side of the road, she could see her bus pulling up at the bus stop, but by the time she had been able to cross over, it was already pulling out.

'Bollocks – that's all I need,' she cursed loudly, not caring who heard her.

As she looked at her watch, she could see that she was going to be a little late and knew that she would have to wait at least another ten minutes for the next bus. She leaned against the bus stop while she waited. Her head was pounding, and she contemplated going straight back home, but changed her mind when she could see another bus coming along Oxford Street.

As she sat on the bus, she promised herself that she would drop by to see her mother and stepfather after work and sit down for a lovely Italian meal with them. It made her smile to think about their restaurant, as it was quite rowdy and full of life. It was exactly what she needed at the moment to drag her out of this despondent mood that she found herself in.

Although, I doubt very much that it will do my pounding head any good, she thought, sighing loudly.

Chapter Thirteen

He carefully picked the lock to the front door and when the door had clicked slightly ajar, he quietly pushed it wide open and stepped into the darkness of the hallway. Hearing soft music drifting down the stairs from one of the upstairs rooms, he crept silently up the stairs towards a glimmer of light at the far end of the upper hallway.

She was in the bathroom and as he made his way silently towards the open doorway, he could see her soaking in her freestanding, elegant bathtub standing on traditional gold ball and claw feet. There were dozens of candles glowing and flickering around her. Her eyes were closed and she looked relaxed and composed, humming softly to the music playing.

He noticed a strong smell of lavender in the air - obviously the scent of her bath foam, which he observed was almost threatening to overflow from the bathtub. She looked happy. Far too happy, but he was about to change that.

He took his time watching her for several minutes as she languished in the bathtub completely oblivious to an intruder in her house. Stepping forward, he thought how easy it would be to just simply creep up behind her and quickly place the scarf around her neck, squeeze tightly and get it over with – it would be so quick and effortless. But he wanted to relish the thrill of tormenting her, unhurriedly. He shuddered with the excitement of what he was going to do; it was pure gratification for him.

He turned around and walked unhurriedly into her bedroom. He noticed how feminine and orderly she liked to keep her house; everything was perfectly colour coordinated and pristine. He could see that despite being totally out of control of her emotions, she still maintained a particular order in her life and kept her surroundings clean and neat. That habitual side of her personality had not changed during her slow mental and physical decline. But he was going to change that after he had finished his game of pleasure. He would set the scene depicting a woman who had lived the last few weeks of her life in total chaos and wretchedness. He had always despised rigid neatness.

As he wandered through her walk-in wardrobe, he picked up one of her elegant silk chiffon neck scarves and slowly begun to wind it around one of his hands – the softness of the scarf began to arouse his bestial instinct. The scarf would be like a gentle but deadly touch – a loving caress around her neck.

Just then, he heard a movement coming from the bathroom and he quickly walked back towards the door to the bathroom. She had raised herself slightly from the bathtub to take hold of her champagne glass. She took one or two sips of the sparkling drink before placing the glass back down to the side of the bathtub and then sank back down into the scented suds with a contented sigh, still completely oblivious of being watched.

The contented sigh made him feel particularly anxious to finish it - he could sense and plainly see that she was looking somehow refreshed, and it was at that moment he felt his control over her diminishing and becoming less intense.

But all the same, he did not want to spoil his enjoyment. He wanted to take his time and not rush with something that was going to be so deliciously satisfying.

He strolled back down into the lounge where he unwound the scarf from his hand and placed it over a chair as he poured himself a glass of whisky as he casually reclined on one of her sofas with his feet up, taking gulps of the whisky. He smiled to himself at the thought that he could even take a short nap if he felt inclined to do so. He knew that she would possibly fall into a light relaxing slumber herself under the influence of the champagne and no doubt the medication he knew she often took.

When he had drunk some of the whisky, he tossed the half empty glass onto the cream coloured carpet creating a messy stain and, standing up, he slowly walked back up the stairs towards the bathroom, but this time he stood right in the middle of the doorway - stretched out his hand to the side of the wall and flicked the switch to the bright light in the centre of the bathroom on and then off again.

Her eyes snapped wide open, and she gasped at the sight of the figure in the semi darkness standing there watching her from the doorway. She remained quite still, one hand clutching at her throat as he slowly moved closer to her.

'Hello, my darling – are you pleased to see me?' he asked her. 'No, no, don't bother to get up,' he said as she attempted to sit up straight and hoist herself out of the bathtub. But with all the soap suds around her she immediately slipped right back down, and he could see the panic in her eyes as he stood over her smiling evilly.

'How dare you just let yourself into my house – what do you want?' she asked, trembling with fear.

'Is that any way to talk to your beloved future husband – you know you are pleased to see me,' he said, as he stood there re-winding the scarf menacingly around and around his left hand. 'You've been a naughty little girl, and I feel a need - an uncontrollable urge to give you a good spanking,' he told her, smiling and blowing a kiss towards her.

'Why are you tormenting me,' she gasped. 'Please leave me alone and get out,' she pleaded with him all the while watching that scarf being slowly wound around and around his hand. 'All this time you have had a hold on me so powerful that I virtually lost my mind and all self-respect, but this morning when I woke up I suddenly felt free of you and that hold you have had over me has finally begun to weaken and I am going to try to continue with my life as before without your evil dominance over me. So, I am asking you to leave me in peace and don't ever come back – I don't want you in my life anymore.'

'Tut, tut, dear me. What an angry little lady you are on this special day,' he said, giving her another sinister smile.

Her heart began to beat faster, and she began to hyperventilate – spluttering and choking.

'Why I found you so attractive and fascinating, I can't imagine. You enticed me and you are still enticing me with those cold eyes that seem to bore right into my very soul, but I am going to fight against your control over me,' she said, breathlessly.

'Such words of courage, my dear,' he said. 'But you will never be able to escape from my wrath.

She suddenly slumped down feeling that power threatening to engulf her mind and body again.

She lay there trembling and helpless, still watching the scarf being wound around his right hand threateningly - she felt almost mesmerized by the movement.

'Please I'm begging you – I want you to go,' she whimpered, feeling weaker with fear by the second.

He threw his head back and laughed.

'You know you don't mean that, my darling – you know you want me to stay,' he said, leaning right over to her at the side of the tub.

She suddenly screamed, picked up the bottle of champagne at the side of the bathtub and literally swung it against his kneecap with all her strength. He roared like a wild animal and grabbed the bottle from her hand, tossing it over to the other side of the wall where it shattered onto the floor.

She gasped as he grabbed hold of her hair, rendering her unable to move from the bathtub. He knelt right down beside the bathtub gripping her hair tightly and holding her head right back close to his neck. She stared at his neck transfixed by that familiar tattoo of a small crown. With one last feeble attempt to haul herself out of the bath, she clawed at his face - he gritted his teeth as the blood trickled down his cheek.

He began to hold her head under the water until she could no longer breathe. His face was contorted with evil malice.

'Don't hurt me – please,' she spluttered, trying to catch her breath when he dragged her head back up. Again, he plunged her head under the water until she became almost unconscious.

He wound the scarf around her neck - she barely struggled, due to her light headedness at having been submerged under the bathwater and she was hardly fighting him, not able to get out of the slippery bathtub as he pulled the scarf tighter and tighter, until she had gone completely limp and near lifeless. He then loosened the scarf and watched while she slowly recovered, gasping for breath, and then he repeated the strangulation until there was no more breath left in her. When her body slid below the water level, he calmly walked back through to the bedroom to collect a sheet to wrap her body in.

After drying her thoroughly and wrapping her body tightly in a satin sheet, he carried her out to a car and placed her in the boot. He quickly scanned the area to check for any bystander and when he was sure that all was clear, he hurried back up to the open door of her house.

Once back inside he proceeded to trash the house beginning with the lounge, where he tossed every single bottle of alcohol and wine across the carpet making sure to also soil the cushions and curtains by spraying and splattering them with droplets of wine. He continued his mayhem in the bedroom where he urinated all over the bed sheets and finally, into the bathroom creating complete havoc, tossing and smashing everything he could get his hands on.

In the kitchen he found the rubbish bin to be full of slices of dried pizza and other items of half-eaten discarded food, which he scattered all over the floor. He also found various tins of creamed rice in one of the cupboards in the kitchen and decided that it would be perfect to spill the contents all over the bathroom floor and inside the toilet to look like vomit.

To complete his destruction, he grabbed as many of the kitchen pots and pans as he could and tossed them all around the kitchen worktops and sink unit.

After feeling completely satisfied that he had created as much chaos as he possibly could, he stood there smiling – his plan had gone better than he had hoped.

All he needed to do next was to conceal her body in a secret place. He knew exactly where - nobody would ever imagine a body being hidden in such a way – it was a brilliant plan. He smiled - *it was perfect beyond imagination and so ironic in the circumstances – no one would suspect him.* He smiled at the thought of how easy it had been to silence her - she knew far too much. He knew that he had slowly been losing his control over her and the time had come to put an end to her and what could be a better and most fitting way than to encase her in a beautiful ceramic coffin.

Chapter Fourteen

Nancy was just about to call Kyle to join her for their routine lunch break when he marched up the stairs from the basement with a small travel bag slung over his shoulder – he looked uneasy when he saw her. She had the distinct feeling that he had obviously planned to leave the house, hopefully without running into her and thus not having to offer an explanation as to his hasty departure. He put his bag on the floor while he pulled out his set of keys from his pocket.

She was startled when she now noticed that Kyle's hair was a different colour from that dark blackish brown colour slicked back from his forehead, which in her opinion had given him an older and somewhat sinister appearance. His hair was now bleached to a pale cream almost white shade and looked uncombed and messy. What was more surprising was that the colour of his eyes had also changed from a dark brownish black to a piercing blue and his thick, dark brown batwing eyebrows were now also white.

For as long as she had known him, he had always had a healthy tan but now his face looked pale, giving him a washed-out ghostly appearance. He also had a fine, fuzzy pale growth of facial hair covering his cheeks giving him a slightly dishevelled appearance. Those piercing blue eyes seemed to bore right into her soul as he stood there glaring at her.

He ran his fingers through his hair as she stood staring at him fixedly with a puzzled expression on her face. He quickly placed a cap on his head and a pair of sunglasses to cover his eyes. His mouth was now set tight in a grimace – it was evident he was annoyed and impatient to be on his way as soon as possible and the sooner she got out of his way, the better.

That scowl sent a shiver down her backbone. She shuddered and stepped back a little away from him with one hand pressed against her chest.

'You startled me, Kyle – for a minute there I thought it was an intruder in the house.' Nancy said, laughing nervously. 'What on earth have you done to yourself – you look like a completely different person,' she remarked.

The surly expression on his face now changed and he smiled half-heartedly in an attempt to mask his obvious displeasure that his intended hasty departure was being delayed.

'I'm sorry, Nancy. I should have told you earlier that I won't be joining you for lunch as usual today,' he said, ignoring her comment alluding to his altered appearance. 'I received a call from my people to say that I am needed back at my base – I mean my home, to take care of a problem,' he added.

'Oh, I'm sorry to hear that, Kyle. I hope it's not something serious,' Nancy replied, frowning, somewhat baffled by his vague explanation.

'Nothing I can't handle,' he replied, a little too sharply, as he handed over his set of keys.

'Well, that's alright then, Kyle. If there is anything I can help you with, you only have to ask.'

'As I've told you, I have everything under control,' he replied, sternly.

'What about Mr. Ryder - has Millicent made arrangements for another driver to relieve you while you are away?'

'I would imagine that she has, Nancy,' Kyle said, sighing loudly as he picked up his bag and began marching along the hallway leading to the front door.

'Kyle,' she called out. 'Don't you want to keep your keys with you?'

'I would rather you hang on to them until I get back, Nancy – I don't want to end up losing them somewhere along the way,' he replied. She could see by his rigid stance that he was anxious to leave as quickly as possible.

'Look, Kyle. I know you have never liked to talk about yourself, but if you are in any kind of trouble, we can talk about it and maybe I can help in some way. Why don't you come through to the kitchen and we can talk while you eat the sandwiches that I have prepared for you. I really do not like to see you just up and leave like this without giving an explanation to Mr. Ryder. I am sure Mr. Ryder will be very concerned when he finds that you have left so suddenly.'

Kyle hesitated now and she could see that he was thinking about it. He then removed the sunglasses and walked back slowly towards her and for a moment she felt troubled by a certain menacing look in his eyes, although she remained calm.

When he stood facing her, she couldn't help flinching by his nearness and almost stumbled, taking a step backwards.

'I'm sure Mr. Ryder will understand perfectly,' he said, smiling politely.

She sensed that he seemed amused by her obvious discomfort by his closeness.

'I could even pack you some food to eat along the way - I am sure you have a long journey,' she said as she turned and walked through to the kitchen.

'There is no need to worry about me, Nancy. I am not in any kind of trouble; I can assure you. I've told you; I have a personal problem to sort out.'

'Do you have any idea of when you will be back?' she asked him.

'I'm not sure – I can call a bit later and let you know, seeing as you are so *very* concerned about me,' he replied, sarcastically.

'There is no need to be rude, Kyle. I am simply trying to understand why you must leave so suddenly.'

'What is this, a Chinese inquisition?' he asked, raising his voice, suddenly losing his temper as he turned and began to walk away. 'Just mind your own business, Nancy, and let me go on my way.'

There had been times when talking with Kyle that she had felt a chill run down her spine and the hair at the back of her neck rise. It was the strangest feeling, and she could never understand why he made her feel that way. She felt like that now and, also, a little afraid – she could feel the goose bumps creeping all over her arms and she visibly shuddered.

Not wanting to show her fear, Nancy walked back over to him and took hold of one of his arms, gently leading him through to the kitchen, where she told him to sit down while she made him some fresh coffee. Although she half expected him to pull away from her, he seemed resigned to allow her to indulge him and did not seem to put up any kind of resistance at that point.

'Yes, well I could do with some coffee before I go on my way. I really am sorry to be leaving at such short notice, Nancy, but it can't be helped,' he said, a little more kindly.

As they sat there drinking coffee together, Nancy couldn't help feeling that he was hiding some awful secret in his life but try as she might, she could not get him to open up. He did mention that he had important matters to clear up and that it was his duty to sort things out. She thought it strange to talk about duty and important matters to deal with and she couldn't help thinking that he had probably been in the army during some period in his life, although he had never divulged any such information, if that was indeed the case.

As she sat there across the table studying him while he drank his coffee and ate the sandwiches that she had prepared for him, she noticed for the first time a small marking on the side of his neck, she leaned a little closer – it was a small blue crown. She wondered why she had not noticed it before, although she was not in the least surprised that Kyle had such a tattoo as he was just the type to have tattoos and probably had several more all over his body.

When he had finished his coffee and sandwiches, he stood up ready to leave. Nancy had packed him more sandwiches, which she had stuffed into his small bag which was already jam-packed with his items of clothing and a small bag of toiletries.

'I have a very smart suitcase that you could take with you. I am sure you will need to take more of your personal items with you. I trust you to return it,' she said, concerned at how poorly he had crammed everything into the small holdall bag, obviously not bothered to neatly folded anything.

'This will do me fine,' he replied, as he held out his hand to shake hers. 'I want to thank you for all your care and attention while I have been here,' he added, clicking his heels together.

Nancy walked back through to the main hallway with Kyle and watched him as he closed the front door without a backward glance. *Such a strange young man,* she thought as she stood by a front window watching him march off down the street.

Although they had both indulged in the most basic of small talk during their meals together, she had found Kyle to be an unfriendly type of young man who had never opened up to her about his private life. Although he appeared not to have had any male or female friends that he hung around with when off duty – none that she had seen, anyway, he had often gone out alone late at night. Where he had gone, she had no idea.

Later that morning, when stripping the bedding and generally tidying up Kyle's rooms in the small apartment after his departure, Nancy was surprised to find a dark brown wig tossed in the bottom of the now empty clothing cupboard. She also found a small case of several different coloured contact lenses in the bathroom. She was even more startled when she found a large makeup kit complete with facial pan-stick makeup, eye makeup, lipstick and rouge complete with a large tub of what looked like some kind of body balm.

How strange, she thought as she stood there puzzled staring at the items, wondering what on earth he had been up to – he had obviously gone to great efforts to disguise his appearance. Shuddering at the thought that he may very well have been on the run from an illicit past, she was sure now that he clearly had no intention of returning in the circumstances.

This ambiguous and irresponsible behaviour seemed to be a regular way of life for these personal drivers, in her experience. She thought about Demetrius, the previous driver who had left in much the same way, without a word. She had built up a really good relationship with Demetrius, he was a completely different person to Kyle - open and friendly and always had plenty of friends call by to see him. The eventual news of his suicide had saddened and surprised her as he had shown no signs of being depressed at any time.

It all seemed very suspect that Kyle was not who he had appeared to be, and she wondered now what on earth he had been hiding – something serious for sure she now realized.

Surely Olsten knew a little more about him, after all, he had just taken him on without a second thought, but then again, he had been recommended with excellent character references. She decided that when Mr. Lambert passed by the next time to see Olsten, she would mention her concerns. Maybe he could come up with some answers.

Chapter Fifteen

Mrs. Harrington quietly let herself into Celeste's house and gasped in horror at the complete mess she saw before her – it would appear at first sight that the house had been ransacked and probably burgled. There were empty gin and whisky bottles tossed around all over the carpet in the lounge and dining area. Half empty cups with scum gathering on the top of whatever had been in them littered the occasional tables. All her daughter's belongings where haphazardly strewn across the sofa and some were crumpled on the floor. She was stunned and couldn't understand how her daughter could possibly live in such complete filth and chaos.

Celeste had always been incredibly orderly and fussy about not only her appearance but everything around her had to be perfectly colour coordinated and tidy, she could never abide clutter or disorder.

How she had changed over the last year, Mrs. Harrington now thought. She could not begin to understand what had happened to cause her daughter to go through such a complete change of character.

As she wandered from room to room checking to see if anything was missing, she was puzzled that there did not appear to be anything of value taken and she couldn't help wondering who would just break into a house purely to ransack it, unless of course, it was somebody searching for something in particular, like drugs. Her imagination was running riot, and she felt a feeling of pure panic for a moment worrying that the perpetrator was still in the house.

Mrs. Harrington had been so relieved when Celeste had called the day before suggesting that they meet today at her house for a drink, before going out for dinner in the evening. She had sounded so much happier and was enjoying a luxurious perfumed bubble bath at the time which was something that she had always loved. It had given Mrs. Harrington a surge of hope that she was at last on her way back to her previous vivacious self. She had been so happy at the thought of seeing Celeste in such high spirits again. But now, seeing the overall disorganised and dirty state of the house, she suddenly had a feeling of dread wash over her that all was not well, after all.

She called out to her daughter as she walked up the stairs, thinking that she may be in the bathroom, but when there was no answer, she began picking up the clothing scattered all over the floor along the hallway and leading into the bathroom. There was still no sign of Celeste. The bathroom smelt really bad, and she could clearly see that there was dried vomit all around the floor of the toilet and inside the toilet— it looked absolutely disgusting.

When she walked into the bedroom, on close inspection she was shocked to see that she would have to remove all soiled bedding. She held her nose as the strong smell of urine was unbearable. Wishing that she had been more insistent on her daughter returning home, she was amazed that Celeste had sunk so low and now, she was even more determined to forcibly take charge of her daughter, no matter how much she would resist.

'Enough is enough,' she muttered to herself, close to tears as she began angrily pulling off the sodden bed sheets and rolling them up into a ball.

She was saddened and frustrated that Celeste was not at home waiting for her as arranged, and she couldn't help thinking the worst that her daughter had gone off on one of her uncontrollable, self-indulgent alcoholic binges in one of those clubs that she frequented.

She dreaded to think where Celeste could have gone and what state she was in. To go through all the bars around the area would take forever; she could be anywhere in the West End and Mrs. Harrington couldn't help imagining her stumbling along somewhere in a narrow alleyway exposed to all kinds of danger – a walking target.

On one or two occasions when Celeste had stumbled out of a West End night club in one of her drunken states, she had been accosted and robbed of all her jewellery and although her parents berated her for being so irresponsible, they were just so relieved and thankful that she was not physically harmed or worse. Considering that there had been so many young women accosted and murdered in the West End, Mrs. Harrington was terrified at the thought of Celeste being in constant danger – it was just a huge relief that she always had a driver ready to pick her up and take her straight home.

When Mrs. Harrington went back down the stairs and walked into the kitchen area, she nearly passed out with shock. Dried pizza slices were strewn all over the floor and dirty dishes lay in disarray on every work surface; the sink was already overflowing. She steadied herself as she very nearly slipped on a sticky substance all over the floor – there was a sweet rancid smell of fruit juice; she noticed a carton carelessly tossed to one side of the fridge, the obvious source of the stickiness.

She decided that she would call some professional cleaners to go through the whole house and give it a good and thorough going over from top to bottom.

She had felt such hope the day before when Celeste had called to meet, but now she decided that as soon as she came back, whenever she came and whatever condition she was in, she would physically drag her daughter kicking and screaming out of the house and put her straight into a clinic. She wished so much now that she had immediately acted on the decision some time ago instead of leaving her for so long and she hoped that it was not too late. She and Celeste's father had continuously threatened to remove her from the house, but had time and time again backed down, fearing that if they pushed too hard, she would withdraw even more and maybe harm herself as a warning to them to keep away.

Even so, Mrs. Harrington could see now that the situation was far worse than they had ever imagined and cursed herself for allowing her daughter to convince them that she just needed time and space to pull herself together without their interference.

The phone rang, startling her as she stood there thinking what to do next. She rushed to pick up the call, hoping that it was Celeste or her husband with some word of their daughter, but she was disappointed when she recognized the voice of Mr. Ryder.

'I'm sorry, Mr. Ryder, but Celeste is not at home. This is Mrs. Harrington, her mother,' she told him with a definite icy edge to her voice.

'Hello, Mrs. Harrington. I'm sorry to bother you. I just wanted to check on Celeste to see how she was feeling this morning. I don't know whether she has mentioned it to you, but she came to see me a few days ago and appeared to be in a very distressed state of mind. I am sure that, like me, you have been worried sick about her behaviour these last months. I've tried several times over the past few days to call her, but I've not been able to speak to her since she came to see me that last time.'

'Well, of course, we most certainly have been extremely worried about our daughter, as you can well imagine, Mr. Ryder and I don't mind telling you now that I personally hold you responsible. You have a lot to answer for,' she replied, again with that chilling edge to her voice.

Olsten flinched at these words, at the undertone of anger in the tone of her voice. which was unmistakable.

'I can assure you, Mrs. Harrington, I have never harmed your daughter in any way,' he replied. 'I promise you that I have tried my very best to help your daughter whenever I have been able to. She has been here at the office quite a few times in an appalling state, of which I am sure you are aware, and I have always treated her with the upmost care.'

'Yes, I am quite sure you have, Mr. Ryder. Oh, and I am fully aware of the visits to your office, she has told me how you call her at any time of the day and night, sometimes in the early hours of the morning, to instruct her to visit you,' she replied venomously. 'What kind of a man are you?'

Olsten breathed in sharply at these remarks. He was exasperated by the onslaught of her defamatory remarks suggesting improper behaviour on his part and he was so tired of hearing such false accusations of his alleged misconduct made by her daughter, which were completely unfounded.

'That is just not true, Mrs. Harrington. I have called her at times only to check how she is, especially after she has turned up in my office in a distressed state of mind. I have *never, ever* called her during the early hours of the morning to *instruct* her, as you say, to visit me. That is an outrageous accusation', he said indignantly. He could not believe how totally unfair and unreasonable she was behaving towards him.

'After all, you seem to be the cause of most of her problems, Mr. Ryder. I don't mind telling you that I was totally shocked when she decided to cancel her marriage plans to Lewis last year because of your own offer of marriage at that time, which of course, we all know was entirely dishonest on your part. Now she is completely broken hearted and can't seem to pull herself together.'

She continued her barrage of accusations, emphatically refusing to listen to anything he said in defence of himself.

'Mrs. Harrington, I want to make it absolutely clear to you that I had nothing whatsoever to do with your daughter's decision to cancel her marriage plans, *and* I categorically deny any kind of involvement with your daughter other than as a friend to both her and Lewis,' Olsten replied.

Before he could say another word, Mrs. Harrington slammed the handset down. At the other end of the line, Olsten flinched. He immediately redialled the number but there was a constant busy signal. He decided that for now, he would just leave the matter and make a point of visiting Celeste's parent's home sometime during the evening, although he wondered if that was a good idea in the circumstances. He did not want a serious altercation with her father, and it seemed useless trying to explain anything to Mrs. Harrington as she adamantly refused to listen to anything he had to say and had made up her mind that he was entirely responsible for all her daughter's current suffering.

Everything had spiralled out of control, and he felt baffled at what to do about Celeste. He found it completely nerve-racking that she had fabricated so many untruths about him and conjured up a scenario of a doomed romantic liaison between them - all in her own head. And as for calling at all times of the day and night to *instruct* her to visit him! He was baffled by Mrs Harrington's use of the word "instruct."

Back at Celeste's house, Mrs Harrington was on the phone talking to her husband and explaining the situation to him. It was obvious that they would have to have their daughter committed to a rehabilitation clinic as soon as they were able to locate her whereabouts and the sooner the better. Mr. Harrington assured her that he would leave the office immediately and meet her back at their house to make the necessary arrangements.

In some ways Mrs. Harrington also put some blame on her husband – he had thoroughly spoilt Celeste as a child and had never admonished her appropriately when she had done something that they both felt was wrong. She couldn't help feeling that, as her father, Mr. Harrington should have been more forceful at times when dealing with their daughter. She personally felt that he had let *her* down in particular – he was a weak man when it came to any matters concerning Celeste. It was now abundantly clear to them both that she was in a shocking state and needed urgent help.

'We need to call the police and report her as missing! We have given her long enough to sort herself out. We need to take urgent action now,' Mr. Harrington said.

'No, darling, listen! We have to deal with this in our own way for the time being. If we have not had any success finding her by the end of this week, we can then call the police, but for now I don't want it made public,' she replied.

Mr. Harrington sighed loudly down the line. He had never been able to understand his wife's obsession about appearing less than perfect in the public eye. *It was their daughter, for Christ sake! Who cares about the public,* he thought, feeling more frustrated by the second.

'If you think that's for the best, then alright, but I would rather get more help at this stage. The girl is completely out of control,' he replied, feeling completely disheartened. His wife never failed to make him feel not only incapable of making the right decisions, but somehow worthless at times.

After she had finished talking to her husband, Mrs. Harrington dialled Lewis's office number. Maybe he would have some idea of where Celeste could have gone. She had far more faith and confidence in Lewis than her husband. He would know exactly what to do in the circumstances.

It had been a sad state of affairs when Celeste had broken off her engagement with Lewis although the very next day, she had called him and had begged him to forgive her.

At that time, it had been clear to Lewis that she had been going through some sort of emotional crisis. He had even wondered at the time if her obsessive arrangements and wedding plans had been too much of a strain for her. She had been consumed with anything and everything to do with the wedding and he was very aware that she was a perfectionist in everything that she did.

Despite announcing that she had met another man, they had decided to continue living together, while he tried to understand what was troubling her. They had been happy for a very short time, although Celeste had refused to discuss any wedding plans, but as long they were together, Lewis had been content for the time being. But when Celeste had begun to behave totally out of character making their life together intolerable, he had felt that there was no other choice but to move out - hoping all the while that she would eventually come to her senses.

Although she had announced flippantly that she had met somebody else, he had never had any cause to suspect her of carrying on any relationship with another man during the time they were living together. They had been constantly in each other's company and there had never been any calls to the house from another man wanting to talk to her, apart from the odd call from Olsten and of course, her brother Vincent, who at that time was away on business in Singapore.

When Lewis answered the phone in his office, Mrs. Harrington burst into tears and explained that

Celeste was not in her house, and she was frantic with worry about her. Lewis calmed her down, assuring her that he would make enquiries to help them locate Celeste. He had not heard from her for several days, he told her mother now, which had surprised him as she had always insisted on calling him daily whenever he had been away on one of his trips, even if it had only been to say goodnight to him. This had always been a habit for hers during the good days of their relationship and one which she had not been able to let go of. It certainly revealed to Lewis that there was some part of the old Celeste still inside that hysterical, unhinged young woman that she had become. Although he had just got on with his life and was now in another relationship, he never stopped caring about her and whenever she needed any kind of help, he would be right there for her.

After speaking with Mrs. Harrington, he set about calling various places where they had spent time together, including an extremely elite and expensive hotel where they often stayed when in Paris. Having not heard from her for several days, he did wonder now if she had, in fact, packed a suitcase and taken herself off somewhere for peace of mind.

Most of the places he enquired at informed him that they had not had any contact with Ms. Harrington for the past year but would be sure to let him know if they heard from her in the meantime or very near future.

For the next few days, the Harringtons, together with Lewis, persistently searched everywhere hoping for a sighting of Celeste, or at least hoping to hear from her, but when there was no sign or word of her, they became very concerned for her safety. Her brother

Vincent flew back from Singapore and took time off from his business to concentrate on looking for his sister. As the days went by, he grew more and more anxious that maybe she had, in fact, been kidnapped, but when no demand for a ransom came, he then began to search around the back streets of London, fearing the very worst, that she had been stumbling around in a drunken state and attacked somewhere and left for dead.

Although both Vincent and Mrs. Harrington had wanted to immediately report Celeste as missing to the police, Mr. Harrington was still reluctant for the time being to take that action. Mr. Harrington knew that his wife was a stubborn woman, but at the same time he had always known what a snob she was, and how she was always worried about creating a good impression where social gatherings, friends and neighbours were concerned. This particular side of her personality had caused countless arguments, and her justification had always been the same; that she was the strength behind them, and he was the weakest link – meaning that she always knew what to do for the best.

Chapter Sixteen

When it became evident that Lily had disappeared without a trace for a number of days, Lily's mother, Mrs. Reynolds, eventually called the police. Millicent had been beside herself worrying and had visited Lily's mother several times during the days after the young woman had initially gone missing and between them, they had called various people who knew Lily to find out if they had any idea of her whereabouts.

As they sat together drinking tea, Mrs. Reynolds told Millicent she had noticed that Lily took to going out the odd evening during the week and seemed unusually cheerful to begin with and then quite troubled shortly after.

'Lily has always been a secretive girl and keeps all her emotions bottled up. I have been quite concerned about her for some time especially after her relationship with Demetrius ended abruptly. It was such a pity when he left so suddenly and then the news of his suicide was so sad; he seemed such a nice young man and I could see that they were very devoted to each other. She doesn't seem to have any luck with men,' Mrs. Reynolds went on to say.

Millicent was more or less convinced that Lily had been seeing Kyle. *I think she just needs to widen her horizons – I would have thought she had had enough of dating untrustworthy chauffeurs,* Millicent thought, bearing in mind that Demetrius had obviously misled Lily when he had proposed to her, while all the time planning to marry a Greek girl. But she did not want to concern Lily's mother of her suspicions about Kyle and his ambiguous character. She also felt it would be unfair to voice her opinions about Lily's unfortunate lack of taste in men. She knew she was being totally prejudiced about Kyle, but she was not prepared to disclose her thoughts with Mrs. Reynolds about her daughter's probable involvement with him – it would only make her more anxious in the circumstances.

The police searched through Lily's personal belongings in her bedroom for any evidence or clues regarding her whereabouts but were unable to find anything to help their investigation.

When the police turned up at the offices to question Olsten, herself and other members of staff, Olsten informed them that Lily was an extremely level headed young woman who would not have just gone off somewhere on a whim in the circumstances, considering that she had to take care of her mother, who was entirely dependent on her. For her part, Millicent did not feel comfortable mentioning the discussion that they had together in the park the day before Lily had disappeared, especially after her own unexplainable strange behaviour towards Olsten later that same afternoon.

As time went on while enquiries were being made to locate Lily, Mrs. Reynolds went to stay with her sister who lived nearby in a block of flats in Bloomsbury and the flat that she had occupied with Lily in Maida Vale was left empty and locked – or so she thought.

Olsten could not accept that Lily would just disappear without a word to her mother and firmly believed that she must have a very good reason and would return very soon. What concerned him was that his driver Kyle had also disappeared and had left no note requesting leave of absence. There was absolutely no known reason as to why Kyle would just leave his job so suddenly without any explanation. In spite of the fact he had informed Nancy that he was having to deal with some personal problems, Olsten just wished that Kyle had been able to discuss his personal concerns with him beforehand.

During the next weeks of waiting patiently for some word from either Lily or Kyle, Olsten decided to advertise for another permanent driver, although he determined that he would go for an older man this time. Those younger drivers proved to be a bit too unreliable in his experience so far.

To find another such talented, specialty designer like Lily would not be so easy. They had a selection of her designs for the following year, so he was not so concerned about rushing to find a suitable replacement for the time being.

By now Millicent was absolutely certain that Lily and Kyle had gone off together. *But why would they want to keep everything so clandestine,* she wondered. *It all seemed so ridiculous, and she would bet on Kyle running out on Lily sooner than later and Lily returning heartbroken yet again.* Not that Millicent wished heartbreak on Lily again, it was just she felt that Kyle would bring her nothing but trouble – in fact, she was absolutely certain of it.

One early morning following Lily's disappearance, Millicent sat at the conference table quietly going over incoming mail and schedule plans with Olsten, when suddenly four uniformed police officers came marching through the door, cautioning them both to remain seated.

'We have reason to believe that a criminal offence has been committed within these premises, and we need to conduct a search for evidence in connection with the disappearance of Miss Lily Reynolds,' the officer announced, as he held up his identification card.

'On what grounds - don't you need a search warrant?' Olsten asked as he leaned forward peering at the card.

'Not if you freely and voluntarily consent to the search being carried out, and if you have nothing to hide, you have nothing to worry about, do you, Sir? We received an anonymous call alerting us to a crime having been committed here and it is our duty to investigate all such calls,' the officer in charge replied.

Millicent turned and looked at Olsten, a look of shock on her face. She wondered who on earth would make such a malicious call.

'In that case, go right ahead, I have absolutely nothing to hide; we have for the past weeks been more than helpful with your enquiries. We have been waiting for some word from Miss Reynolds but as yet have not had any contact with her whatsoever and we have no idea of her whereabouts at this point in time. I can assure you that if and when we do hear from her, we will contact you immediately. By all means, feel free to search the building, but if you don't mind, my secretary and I will continue with our early morning conference together,' Olsten said calmly.

The police officer in charge nodded to the other officers and they promptly marched through to his private quarters.

Millicent glanced at Olsten. He smiled at her reassuringly and they continued going over schedule planning, although she found it extremely nerve-racking trying to concentrate in the circumstances.

It was when they heard an almighty thunderous crash that they both stood up, startled. Olsten rushed into his private rooms to see what all the commotion was about and when he saw the scene before him, he gasped in horror and disbelief. Millicent had followed right behind him and immediately clamped her hands over her mouth to stop herself from screaming.

Amongst all debris of shattered ceramic pieces, lay the lifeless body of Celeste Harrington - she had been enshrined in the life-sized doll kept in Olsten's private quarters. In her chilling, ceramic coffin she had been preserved with detailed intricate care, her makeup had been applied with care and her hair carefully arranged in an upswept, sophisticated style. She was dressed in satin under garments with just a flimsy silk chiffon scarf tied around her neck. The expression on her face looked to be tranquil, perfectly composed and beautiful. It was a stark contrast to how she had looked during the slow, suffering, chaotic last days of her life.

Millicent stood there motionless with shock, unable to move a single muscle, horror-struck by the scene before her. Shattered parts of the ceramic doll were strewn all over the floor around the stiff body of Celeste; she looked like a mannequin, perfectly and skillfully embalmed. A red rose had been placed inside the porcelain coffin and the petals were now strewn over the carpet.

'Olsten Ryder, I'm placing you under arrest on suspicion of murder. You have the right to remain silent. You do not have to say anything, but it may harm your defence if you do not mention when questioned, something which you may later rely on in court. Anything you do say may be given in evidence. Do you understand?' the arresting officer announced, as two of his officers took hold of Olsten's arms, and one produced a set of handcuffs.

'We now need to place you in our custody for formal questioning; you are entitled to have a solicitor present while you are being detained and questioned,' the officer continued.

Although Olsten appeared to be perfectly composed, Millicent could see that he was inwardly shaken, and she could see fear in his eyes. She went to him to try to hug him, but was pushed back by the other officer, as Olsten's arms were pulled behind his back and handcuffs slipped around his wrists. He winced at their tightness and Millicent began to cry, tears streaming down her face.

'What is going on, Olsten,' she cried almost choking – her throat felt as if it was closing, and she could hardly breathe.

'I'm sorry that you should have to be witness to this, Millicent – please get in touch with James as soon as possible and let him know what has happened here,' Olsten instructed and was then silenced by another body blow from the words of the officer in charge.

'Just a minute, Sir – what have we got here, another hidden body?' The officer in charge stood there, his eyes narrowing in suspicion as he spotted another life-sized doll stored in an open cupboard in the office. He called one of the other police officers and instructed him to smash the model.

'There is absolutely no need to do that! That is a very expensive model and has a great deal of sentimental meaning to me,' Olsten said, as he struggled to break free from the officers holding onto him, although the cuffs made it impossible for him to move.

'Oh, I'm sure it has, Sir,' the officer in charge replied as he nodded to another officer to go ahead to demolish the model. Both Olsten and Millicent shut their eyes and flinched as the officer swung his baton hard against the ceramic model, sending it crashing to the ground in pieces.

The officer in charge looked almost disappointed when this particular model did not conceal another body. 'I'm sure you understand that we had to be absolutely sure – in the circumstances, it was necessary,' he said looking self-satisfied and justified by his order.

'Get onto the station – we need a search warrant to search the whole place with a fine toothcomb especially the loft and basement, who knows how many more life-sized collectable dolls we will find hidden away! Get C.I.D here now, too, and forensics. We will also need to carry out a full search of your private residential home,' he mused, mindful of all the women who had gone missing and were thought to have been lured to their death after partying in various nightclubs in and around the West End of London. He glared at Olsten; feeling absolutely convinced that they had found the man responsible. Some of the victims that had so far been recovered had all been painted and varnished to look like a mannequin with a red rose placed by the side of their body.

Millicent ran over to the shattered model and began to scoop up all the expensive jewelry scattered around in all the broken pieces of ceramic.

'Please do not touch anything, Miss – this area is out of bounds while evidence is collected,' one of the officers told her.

Millicent looked on in dismay as Olsten was then frog-marched out of the office, down the stairs and out into the street where he was to be assisted into one of the patrol cars parked outside the building. She could see that a crowd had gathered outside already, there were even some journalists, and photographers poised to take photographs of Olsten. She wanted to run out and shout at them all to go away and leave them alone. How on earth had they all come to know that this was going to happen, but then she realized that where there were police cars, there would always be crowds of people gathering around to watch – it was like a circus out there.

One individual in particular suddenly caught her attention, lounging against the front of one of the police vehicles. She squinted trying to get a clear view of his face but from her angle she was not able to get a really good look at him, although the sighting troubled her.

One of the officers proceeded to take all personal details of all staff currently on the property and they were all informed that they would be questioned sometime over the next few days and instructed not to leave the country.

'This area is now out of bounds and will be closed while forensic investigations are carried out,' the remaining officer now said. 'This is now an official crime scene, and we have to treat it with caution so as to not contaminate or destroy evidence. We therefore have to establish a perimeter to protect the scene to prevent people from entering the crime scene while forensic evidence is collected. We now request that everyone vacate the building immediately,' he said, looking at Millicent.

Millicent could only nod, her whole body felt numb. She squeezed her eyes shut tightly, wishing that it was all just a bad dream.

'Miss – did you hear what I said,' the officer asked.

Her mind was racing as she slowly and reluctantly turned away from the window to face the officer.

She could only wonder if Olsten had also noticed that the dolls had been switched around. Celeste's life-sized lookalike doll, which had previously been relocated to a storage cupboard, had been moved to his private quarters and his beloved collectable doll had been found in the storage cupboard. But knowing Olsten only too well, she felt sure that he had not missed this fact.

It suddenly occurred to her that whoever switched the dolls around thought it more fitting for Celeste to be specifically enclosed in her own lookalike life-sized doll.

'We will need to question you in due course, so please do not go anywhere in the meantime,' the police officer's words cut into Millicent's thoughts.

She flinched and turned away from the officer to stare out of the window again, paralyzed and horror-struck.

'Yes, I understand,' she replied, wishing that she could fly off as far away as she could at that moment.

Roy, who had followed the police officers up the stairs when they had entered the building, now walked over to Millicent and led her away from the window where she appeared to be transfixed, unable to move. He gently guided her down the stairs to an adjoining kitchen to the reception area and sat her down on one of the seats while he made her a cup of coffee.

She started to shake uncontrollably, unable to comprehend what had just happened, as he handed her a cup of hot, strong coffee.

'It'll be alright, don't you worry Miss. There must be some sort of misunderstanding here, but I'm sure Mr. Lambert will sort it all out,' Roy told her, while he sat down opposite her.

'I need to call James Lambert,' she said, the shaking caused her to slop hot coffee over the rim of the mug she had just been handed.

'Now, don't you worry about that Miss, I've already called him, and he is on his way as we speak to give support to Olsten,' Roy replied, ripping off some kitchen roll and mopping up the spilt coffee from the table.

'How did this happen – it is just the most horrifying thing that I have ever witnessed in my whole life,' she whispered.

Millicent sat there for a few minutes, thinking about the last time she had seen Celeste – her mind racing.

'That day Miss Harrington came by the office that last time,' she asked Roy. 'How did she seem when she left the building?'

'Now let me think. Yes, I remember now, Mr. Ryder called me a little after you left to say that I should go home, and he would lock up. So, I did not actually see them leave. I offered to stay later, but he insisted that I leave, and he would take care of closing up.'

'And, what about Kyle? I do remember that he mentioned that he was going to sit with you inside while he waited for Mr. Ryder.' She shuddered as she thought about Kyle.

'That's right. He did come in for a few minutes after you left but quickly stomped back out quite ruffled by something that I said to him at that time. Strange young man,' he replied.

'And did Kyle go back later to collect Mr. Ryder?' she asked.

'I'm not entirely sure. As far as I remember, he did say he was going to stop off for a coffee somewhere while waiting to pick Mr. Ryder up – I expect he must have returned a little later to wait outside as usual. When I checked the register the next day, Mr. Ryder had signed out at around ten thirty that same evening.'

Millicent sat there slowly drinking her cup of coffee, puzzling over why Celeste had remained in Olsten's private rooms the whole day and why Olsten had himself not come back out at any time during that afternoon. *What on earth had been going on in there,* she couldn't help wondering.

Although not wishing to pry at the time, she wished now that she had said something the next day when sitting with Olsten in his office. She had been dying to say something about the situation but had not dared in the circumstances. As usual, Olsten had not made any reference to any such disturbance in the office caused by Miss Harrington. Millicent had felt that it was as if he had not wanted to show any disrespect towards her by discussing her with anybody, especially not his secretary. All the same, she could not help thinking that the subject of his alleged relationship with Miss Harrington was something that he did not wish to make known to anybody. It was obviously a well-kept secret.

All other members of staff were politely ordered to vacate the building and informed not to return until further notice once the forensic investigations were completed. Before leaving they were all advised that they would all need to be questioned in due course. They all filed out of the building as instructed, looking totally confused, not knowing any details of what had transpired leading up to the arrest of Olsten in his office.

Shortly after the staff had left, several plain clothed police officers, obviously C.I.D. and higher up than the truncheon wielding uniformed officers arrived, together with a pathologist and a team of forensic scientists, all dressed up in their papery, disposable protective body suits made from highly dense polyethylene to prevent contamination at the crime scene.

The pathologist concluded that the young woman had been strangled with her own scarf, which was still loosely tied around her neck, but could not determine the actual time of death until a postmortem was carried out at the mortuary.

Upon arriving at the crime scene, after conducting an analysis of the area and taking photographs, the lead investigator, who introduced himself as a detective inspector, made sure the crime scene area was safeguarded and barricaded with police tape to prevent unauthorized people from entering the scene thereafter.

Once Millicent had quickly returned to her office to collect her coat and bag, Roy took her to the nearest café for more coffee. She was glad of the company as she did not want to go straight home; she needed somebody to talk to. Roy talked on and on about anything and everything to take her mind off of the scene she had just witnessed. During the next two hours she learnt more about Roy that she had known since working with him for the past five years. Although he always seemed to be a fairly gruff type of man, she now realized what a lovely and funny person he actually was and felt so thankful for his company in the circumstances.

His stories about his younger days working in the night club scene as a security man, or bouncer, fraternizing with notorious gangsters, fascinated her no end and she never tired of listening to his gruesome tales of the murderous mobsters that he came into contact with. How he had not ended up cut to pieces in some dark alleyway, she couldn't imagine. Although in the circumstances, it was perhaps not the ideal time to share such memories with her. It did, all the same, take her mind off the awful scene that she had just witnessed.

Before they eventually emerged from the café, Roy made Millicent promise that she would visit him and his wife for dinner sometime over the next week and although she cried off initially, he would not let her go home until she assured him that she would accept his offer.

Feeling very protective of her, Roy decided that he would personally escort her back to her flat and although she declined his offer, he insisted and linked his arm into hers as they walked together.

Chapter Seventeen

Olsten observed one man, in particular, amongst the crowd of spectators outside his office building, lounging against the waiting police car, who was watching him closely as he was being led outside following his arrest for the suspected murder of Celeste Harrington.

'Please move away from the car, sir,' one of the officers told the man sternly, before opening the door ready for Olsten to be assisted inside.

As the man took a step back from the car, he looked straight into Olsten's eyes, his mouth twisted into a malicious grin as he deliberately nudged against him with his elbow causing him to trip backwards against the car.

'Good morning, *your majesty* – not doing so good today, I see,' the man said, sarcastically.

Olsten flinched at the obvious hostile action, his eyes narrowing. When he fell against the man, in an attempt not to fall over, his sense of awareness told him that the scent of his body in close proximity was distinctive and instantly recognizable.

'Is there anything you want me to do, *your highness*?' the man then asked in a mocking tone, as he pushed Olsten away from his arm aggressively.

'No, there is nothing you can do. Do I know you?' Olsten asked. His eyes narrowing again as he continued to stare into the man's eyes.

The man then leaned over to Olsten, and he whispered in his ear. 'Don't you recognise me? I am your worst enemy. There is nothing anybody can do for you now.'

'Please sir, step aside,' the police officer repeated as he nudged the man out of the way while he assisted Olsten into the back seat of the police car.

As Olsten sat between two officers in the back of the police car he leaned forward and strained to look up at the window of his private quarters. He could see her standing there watching him – she looked like an angel in that flowing white gown – he blinked and then she disappeared from the window.

By now, there was a huge crowd gathering outside Olsten's business building and as he sat there in the police vehicle, he felt trapped like a wild animal in a cage in a circus.

When Olsten looked again for the man who he was now convinced was a face from an earlier period in his life, he had disappeared from the area. He sat there racking his memory, trying to think where he had seen that face before and then it suddenly came to him. There was no mistaking that distinct body odour.

'That man I was just talking to – you need to apprehend him and question him in connection with this matter. I have reason to believe that he is connected to what has happened here,' Olsten said, turning from one police officer to the other.

'What man are you talking about, sir?' one of the police officers replied.

'The man who was just leaning against your police vehicle. Did you get a good look at him?' Olsten asked.

'Just settle down, sir – he was just one of the onlookers that hang around such scenes. I don't know why people pay such attention and revel in somebody's misfortune. It seems to be a way of life that people want to sensationalize all badness in this world, and we certainly have enough of that. The values of society are certainly diminishing all the time,' the officer said.

Olsten turned away feeling that it was pointless talking to the police officers in the circumstances; the man had simply vanished from the scene, anyway. Being seated between the two officers made him feel quite unpleasantly confined in a cramped space and he made a sudden movement to edge slightly forward to give himself a little more space to breathe, but one of the officers yanked him back aggressively.

'Just settle down, sir,' the officer told him, one hand on his shoulder to keep him still. Olsten struggled for a moment or two and then, he leant back into his seat and sighed deeply. There was no point in struggling, no point in sharing his knowledge of who the other man may be or why he felt he was significant to the investigation. From the circumstantial evidence, the police had already got their man. He needed to talk to James.

As the car slowly pulled out from the curb and sped off, the loud siren nearly deafening him, Olsten sat there wondering how on earth he had not been able to sense what had been happening around him for so long, leading up to this moment.

His mind was racing now, and he was anxious to speak to James to alert him to take care of that one person who he suspected could be the next victim. He needed to urge James to ensure that no danger was to befall her.

The image of Celeste lying amongst all the broken ceramic pieces was still so vivid in Olsten's mind. He realized how guilty he must have looked to Millicent, and he could not get that look of pure horror on her face out of his mind. The expression on her face had gone from shock, absolute disbelief and finally to horror as she had stood there facing him. He could actually read the doubt in her mind as she had stood there, struggling with her conflicting emotions while the tears had streamed down her face.

He hoped that she would get through all this; he would instruct James to take absolute care of everything in his absence. He trusted James to organise matters financially and see that all employees were taken care of while they all looked for alternative employment.

While he sat there despondent, with his head down, he felt desperately wretched that so many lives around him had been disrupted or destroyed unnecessarily. He promised himself that when all had been put right and he was able to resume his life as before, he would ensure that those unfortunate people would be exonerated in more ways than one, especially poor Celeste. He knew that no matter how badly she had behaved over the past months, she was not to blame or guilty of any wrongdoing – she had not been in control of herself. He would hunt down the despicable culprit who was responsible for all the mishaps that had been deliberately inflicted on them all, if it was the last thing he would do. They were all not to know that such a dominant and controlling power had been amid their lives to render havoc all around.

He could not stop thinking how Celeste had looked, so serene amongst all the rubble. Her body had been so well preserved; her makeup and hair had been done with such care and precision in a very professional way. Only a person with a special skill and knowledge could have achieved that finish to a corpse.

Olsten's head drooped down again, and the officers suddenly felt his body go slack as he appeared to go into a state of unconsciousness. They had to shake him back to wakefulness, although he seemed distant, dislocated from reality almost. It wouldn't do for them to present an unconscious suspect at the police station.

Olsten was remanded in custody after being formally charged with the murder of Celeste Harrington. His application for bail was refused, given the charges and the fact that the police continued to investigate other murders which they felt they might be able to lay at Olsten's feet. Further charges seemed inevitable given that Celeste's body and those of other murdered women bore significant similarities. The police had their man, or so they thought.

'How long might I be here?' Olsten asked of James one afternoon when James had been granted permission to attend a meeting Olsten had requested whilst in prison on remand.

James looked carefully at his friend, his client, and shook his head.

'I really can't say, Olsten. Weeks at best, maybe months before your case is heard in the Crown Court. Until then, you'll have to keep your chin up. The police will be investigating the other murders, for which they think you are responsible, but whist they are doing that, I will be preparing your defence argument.'

'But I am innocent, James!' cried Olsten, and one of the prison guards gave him a warning look. 'I can't stay here for weeks, months, for something I didn't do! I'm not staying here. I'm not.'

James looked at him, at the high colour and the irritated expression on a somewhat noble face. He shrugged at his friend, not knowing what to say. 'I'm sorry, Olsten,' was what he eventually settled for as he nodded to the guard, indicating that his interview with his client was over. 'I'm afraid you'll have to.'

Olsten Ryder, however, had other ideas.

Following his interview with his solicitor, he seemed to deteriorate. He stopped eating the slop that passed for food, and he did not participate in any form of exercise when he was allowed out into the prison yard for an hour. When he began to show signs of low blood pressure and an almost catatonic state, the prison doctor was summoned to his cell and declared that Olsten would need transporting to the hospital wing of the prison.

'He's got such a low blood pressure,' the doctor said. 'It's a wonder he's still alive. Organise to get him over to the hospital straight away. Let me know when he's been admitted.'

The prison guards sighed and moaned about the extra work they would have to do, grumbling amongst themselves when they returned to an empty cell. Olsten was gone.

The prison was placed under full lockdown, inmates returned and locked in their cells and all privileges suspended whilst the whole building was searched from top to bottom. Inmates in the immediate cells both next to and opposite Olsten where questioned vociferously, but no-one had seen or heard anything untoward. According to them, all they had seen was the doctor leaving, and their fellow inmate laid on the bed looking dreadfully pale and sickly. After a thorough search and investigation, the prison governor was told that Olsten Ryder had disappeared into thin air.

Neither James nor Millicent had been able to contact him at his home in London or any other place that he had been known to frequent. It was well known amongst all members of his staff that he had a property in Italy where he would sometimes spend his weekends, but the property had been closed up and he could not be located anywhere in and around the area.

James sat in his office completely at a loss as to what to do. He had tried contacting Olsten everywhere he thought he could be found but without success. He knew that apart from his property in Italy, he had many contacts in New York but again, all his enquiries as to Olsten's whereabouts proved fruitless. He frowned now as he read the news in the Evening Standard.

"Olsten Ryder (39) who was remanded in custody after being charged with the murder of socialite Celeste Harrington (20) has since disappeared without a trace. If anybody has any information as to Mr. Olsten Ryder's whereabouts, please contact the Marylebone Police Station immediately. All informants will be afforded complete anonymity and any information provided will be held in the strictest of confidence. Mr. Ryder is thought to be a dangerous predator and should be approached with caution. His trial date has not yet been set, and police believe his disappearance to be an attempt to avoid the course of justice."

In the years that James had known Olsten he had never seriously questioned him in detail about his private life, and he did not even know if he had any relatives. He couldn't recall Olsten talking of them, and he had never volunteered any other information about his past.

Now, as James tried to delve into his background and past, he could find no information whatsoever and suddenly had an awful thought that Olsten had been hiding something terrible from his past. Even when he contacted the Parsons School of Design in New York, there was no record of his ever having been there. James was totally perplexed and after spending weeks trying to track Olsten down, he was no nearer to finding any leads.

Although Millicent never discussed with anyone in precise details about the incident in Olsten's private quarters, when she had last seen Celeste having yet another tantrum, she often thought about that afternoon and what may have happened when she had gone home leaving them together uninterrupted. How she wished she had gone straight in to offer more coffee or make some excuse to see what was going on at that time. She couldn't help feeling baffled when she had returned to her office the next day when Olsten had made no reference at all to the incident. Even though she had been particularly concerned about some deep scratches on the side of his face, she still had not questioned him.

But now Millicent wondered what exactly had gone on inside that room behind the closed door on that fateful afternoon. She went over and over it in her mind but could not remember anything to have given her cause for concern that something serious had been happening behind the closed door. After Celeste's initial outbursts, there had been no raised voices or any other loud suspicious sounds to give her any worry or cause to intervene. Although now, when she really thought about it, maybe the fact that it had gone deathly quiet had been a definite cause for concern.

Chapter Eighteen

When Millicent arrived back to her flat accompanied by Roy after Olsten had been arrested, she rolled her eyes with exasperation when she immediately spotted Cecelia peering out from her window watching them closely. As she stood there for a few minutes with Roy, he put his arm around her fondly while they stood there talking.

'Now look, don't be a stranger, Miss. if you need anything at all, I will be right here for you, and you must promise to visit me and the Missus from time to time. I will be working in a nearby nightclub for the time being until something is sorted out. I'm sure we will be back in the office working together before you know it, so keep your chin up,' he said, giving her a bear hug.

Millicent could see the intense disapproval in Cecelia's pinched face, her eyes narrowing as she continued peering out of the window at them.

Oh, that's all I need – she probably thinks that Roy is one of my callers, Millicent thought. She knew that Roy would find the whole situation hilarious, and it would have lightened up the whole situation at the time, but she was not about to cause any further friction with Cecelia. She decided to ignore her in the circumstances. She could clearly see from Cecelia's expression she was infuriated that Millicent *was* openly conducting her *business* in broad daylight.

Let her think what she likes – I really couldn't care less, Millicent thought as she said cheerio and waved to Roy before unlocking her front door and stepping inside.

Before walking away, Roy stood outside watching her while she let herself in and did not move until she had closed her door and was safely inside her flat. He was concerned to notice that although it was still the middle of the day, Millicent had gone immediately to the front window and closed the curtains as if trying to shut out the awful thing that had happened.

Although he had not reacted at the time, while standing outside with Millicent, Roy had been aware of that neighbour watching them with a scathing expression on her face. The woman looked decidedly stern and annoyed as she continued to glare at him. As he turned to walk away, he couldn't resist waving at her and blowing a kiss in her direction. She immediately turned her face away in obvious disgust, her nose in the air, and he chuckled as he walked away. Although he was not the type of man to behave so crudely to women, and in fact always disliked men who behaved in such a loutish way, in the circumstances he thought the nosey old bat deserved it.

Cecelia was outraged and immediately stormed out of her apartment, marched out through the main door and down the stone steps leading to Millicent's basement flat door. She was livid and was intent on informing her young neighbour that she was an undesirable resident who would have to go.

After closing her front door and pulling her curtains closed, Millicent was just about to put the kettle on when she heard footsteps clattering down the stone steps and then a sharp ratter-tat-tat on the glass panel of her front door. When she walked back through the small sitting room towards the front door, she could see the tall rigid shape of Cecelia standing there through the glass panel. When she opened the door Cecelia stood there glaring at her with her hands on her hips. Her stiff stance and stern expression clearly indicating that she was determined to launch into a serious verbal confrontation.

'Well now, Twinkle, are you not going to ask me in — we need to have a *serious little chat*,' she said, through clenched teeth.

Millicent smiled politely and stood aside as Cecelia walked past her, with a haughty expression on her face, through to the small living room and literally threw herself down on a small sofa.

That pet name "*Twinkle*" had often amused Millicent, although she had always had the distinct impression that it was not particularly flattering. She had come to know that Cecelia gave little nicknames to almost everybody she knew. She even called her long-time boyfriend, by the name of "*Passion*" which had also been a source of great amusement to Millicent as she suspected that it really described the opposite of his sexual prowess.

In all the time that Millicent had lived in the house and known them both, she had never known Cecelia to give Evelyn any such nickname. Millicent was sure that she did have a very special little nickname for Evelyn – although maybe not a particularly flattering one, she suspected. They were quite openly seriously competitive towards each other. Cecelia constantly complained that Evelyn used people whenever and however she could, whether to gain profit or absolute control over them - or in most cases both.

Although they were both wealthy in their own right by inheriting money from parents and relatives, Evelyn was by far the most affluent and had even inherited a considerable amount of money from a former boyfriend.

Standing at around six foot tall, Cecelia towered above Millicent, making her feel slightly small and insignificant when in her presence. Being a former model, with her razor edged, chiselled jaw line and high cheekbones, Cecelia was always impeccably dressed, with an eye for clothes; even when wearing a shirt and blue jeans, she still looked incredibly elegant. Millicent guessed that she was in her early sixties, but she was still very attractive and seemed to be full of life and involved in several society functions.

'Would you like to have a cup of tea?' Millicent asked her, wanting to be polite even though she could clearly see by Cecelia's face that it was not going to be an entirely pleasant social visit.

'Well, yes, thank you my dear, that would be very nice as long as it is Earl Grey– as you know I drink nothing substandard when it comes to tea,' she replied, in that snobbish way of hers.

As Millicent walked back in the kitchen to make the tea, she could hear Cecelia sitting there tutting loudly. She had always known from the start that both Cecelia and Evelyn looked down their noses at her and considered her social status much lower than theirs.

Compared to their flats, which were incredibly expansive and filled with elegant furnishings and antique pieces, her flat was miniscule but comfortably furnished and although she did tidy it up from time to time, it always appeared to be cluttered, untidy and full of cat fur. Millicent had been amused when one previous work colleague had referred to the bedsit as "*Millicent's humble abode*".

When Millicent came back through to the sitting room with two cups of tea, Cecelia was standing frantically brushing off the cat hair covering her backside. Millicent gasped when she could see her black jeans literally covered in white fur.

'Oh, my goodness, just look at my jeans, they are ruined! Would you please get me a hairbrush. Or, better still, if you have some cellotape, I can brush off the hairs just as effectively,' Cecelia said, looking more agitated by the second – her face a picture of fury.

After she had been able to clear her jeans of all the white hairs, she asked Millicent to place a clean towel over the sofa before she sat down again, although she perched herself on the very edge of the sofa with a strained look on her face. She then launched into the reason for her visit while Millicent sat there listening calmly. Millicent had, of course, guessed what her reason was for visiting her.

'Now listen – let's get right to the point, Twinkle. Evelyn, I *and* the other occupants in this house have had a meeting and we regret that due to certain activities of yours - which I won't discuss at this moment, we would like you to move. We have all found your antics while living here unnerving to say the least and although we do not wish to embarrass you in any way, we do find it a little distasteful to have such goings-on in our neighbourhood and we will not tolerate it. After today's little show of disrespect for your fellow residents, I suggest you pack up immediately, without delay.'

Millicent gasped in dismay and although she tried to assure Cecelia that it had not been her fault about the various men who had called by the flat from time to time, Cecelia refused to listen or be convinced otherwise.

'And as for that, that, despicable individual who has just left,' she stuttered in anger. 'I can't tell you how embarrassed I was when he had the audacity to blow a kiss at me. I will not tolerate such disgusting behaviour. Why, the man probably thinks that I am in a similar debasing profession as you.'

Millicent turned her face away at that point. She found it almost impossible to suppress her amusement and as she felt a bubble of laughter threatening to erupt from her throat, she began to hiccup loudly much to the distaste of Cecelia, whose face was a picture of twitching rage, seeming to get redder and redder by the minute in spite of her carefully applied very pale face powder.

Millicent knew that she was being painted as a scarlet woman as far as Cecelia and Evelyn were concerned and there was absolutely nothing that she could do about it. She steadfastly and persistently insisted, apart from Roy, she had not known any of those men loitering around outside her flat and guessed that they had obviously been known to the previous occupant living in the flat.

According to Cecelia, one man had rung her bell enquiring about Millicent by name and thereafter apologised for ringing the wrong bell. Cecelia explained that it was very late on the night in question; in fact, it was during the early hours of the morning when the man had disturbed her. She said that she had asked the man who he was expecting to receive him, and he had been very specific when he had answered that he had an appointment with Miss

Millicent Bradford, alias Delilah, for services rendered.

Millicent was amazed at this and no matter how much she continued to deny that she had anything at all to do with the man in question or any other man turning up for *services rendered*, Cecelia was adamant the man had specifically enquired about her.

'He also told me that you had promised to provide him with such an excellent service, it would entice him to come back for more,' Cecelia informed her, her manner becoming more prickly by the second.

At that stage, Millicent again did not know whether to laugh or cry and in the circumstances, she had to stifle her amusement. Even in her current downtrodden mood, she found the situation hilarious.

'Well – I'm so glad to see that you find it all so amusing, my dear, and I am sorry to say that we have no other choice but to insist that you move out of the house as soon as possible,' Cecelia told her triumphantly.

In the meantime, Roy set off, retracing his steps, and slowly walked through the busy streets of London to his own flat, all the while thinking about Millicent being on her own. He hoped that she had some close friends and kindly neighbours to keep her company – well, apart from the nosy neighbour that he had just seen who had looked anything but kindly. At least he had his wife to go home to.

He then thought about the prospect of finding other means of work in the circumstances. His wife would not feel very happy about the prospect of him going back, although temporarily, to his old job in one of the busy and popular nightclubs where they had met. She had been delighted when he had accepted the regular day job with Mr. Ryder, as it had meant that they would spend more time together. In the club, he would generally work from ten at night right through till six o'clock the next morning and then spend most of the day sleeping.

Still, he thought as he strolled along, *at least I will have no trouble getting back my old job.* Even though quite some time had passed since he had seen any of the old faces from the past, he knew that they were all still around. Going back to that work would do until such time as he could find something less dangerous, or hopefully when everything had settled down, he could return to his reception duty with all the old faces that he had become so fond of.

When he had left his previous position as a bouncer, he had been told that anytime he wanted to go back he would be welcomed with open arms. He had always been a reliable and trustworthy young man who had kept his mouth shut and got on with any task that was given to him in those days. The only problem was that it was a dangerous environment with the usual cluster of London's notorious thugs and gangsters, but Roy had never gotten involved with any of the rough stuff.

At the age of eighteen, Roy had been offered work doing odd jobs at the *Cromwellian,* a very popular society club that attracted a variety of clientele. Since he towered over most men, being just over six feet and two inches tall with a very robust and powerful build, he had soon been offered a promotion to the position of security man or bouncer. He was perfect for dealing with unreasonable and awkward clientele. Although the other bouncers secretly called him a gentle giant because of his very polite and affable manner, when he needed to put on a tough and brawny act, he could manage quite well and only had to glare at a person being difficult and they would back-off, which was just as well as he hated using brute force.

Roy's wife, Doreen, had constantly nagged him to find alternative employment at that time. She would be horrified now at the thought of him going back to his previous job with all those rough sorts, as she called them, especially as he was older and not so fit now. In his younger day, working in a night club, rubbing shoulders with the likes of some of the most fearsome gangsters was exciting, but now he was not so sure that he wanted to go back to those days. Doreen had seen a lot of unpleasant scenes while working in the club herself as a croupier and when she had married Roy, she had been more than happy when he had asked her to quit her job.

Like Roy, those days had been exciting to her as a young eighteen-year-old and she could have easily followed some of the other girls and been drawn into the more dangerous and sleazy side of the job. It was important that working as a croupier, all the girls had to have a beautiful face and a fabulous figure to fit into the skimpy costumes and while Roy was not the jealous type, he was forever worried about her safety amongst some of the more dubious clientele who spent time at the club. So, he had also been glad when those days had ended with their marriage beginning, and when he had eventually gotten the day job with Mr. Ryder, he had never imagined having to go back. Only now he might have to.

He was therefore quite pleased that night to be saved from having to discuss the matter with his wife because a desperate Millicent had turned up on his doorstep, asking if she could stay with him until she could find a new flat. Roy had not hesitated, and Doreen had clucked like a mother hen over the distressed Millicent, making up the spare room for her and then preparing supper for them all during which time, Millicent's dilemma took precedence over his own, for which Roy was very grateful.   In the circumstance, for now, she was reluctant to bother her mother who would no doubt confront Cecelia, insist that she move back home, and Millicent did not want any more drama at this time.

Later the following day, Millicent discussed her situation more fully with Roy, who had been astounded by the ignorance of Millicent's neighbours, and he offered to find her alternative accommodation as soon as possible. He assured her that he had good connections in certain areas, although they may not be described as what Millicent might call 'highly desirable. 'True to his word he was able to find her a lovely one-bedroom flat in one of the Peabody Housing Trust buildings in Green Park, very near to where he was living with his wife. With the help of Roy and a couple of his friends, Millicent was able to move into the new, fully furnished flat, the following week.

The new flat was so much better than the previous tiny basement flat in Great Cumberland Place and although she was now in a high rise building and had to take a lift to the third floor, she was delighted that the flat was smart and newly decorated and was free of musty dampness. Most of all she felt far safer, as the flat had its very own intercom system and there would be no more unwelcome guests turning up at her door.

Why had she not thought about moving much sooner; it would have been so much easier getting to work and she would have only had to take a ten-minute stroll to work every day. But what was the point of thinking about such a thing now, she told herself. She no longer had her job in Berkeley Square. How she would miss it and how she would desperately miss Olsten and all the other faces that she had been seeing on a daily basis.

Even so, Millicent had been absolutely delighted during the process of moving; it kept her mind busy and away from the awful events that had been taking place over the past few weeks. Although she had never liked the idea of living in a high-rise building, she quickly got used to the environment and always seemed to bump into somebody different whenever she went in and out of the lift or took the stairs.

Having been so unceremoniously dumped and asked to leave immediately, Millicent had been surprised when Cecelia and Evelyn had arranged a little soiree for her in the small garden at the back of the house in Great Cumberland Place, to celebrate her move. They held it on the day she had told Cecelia she would be returning to collect the few belongings that were still at her old flat and she was even more surprised to see tears in Evelyn's eyes as she had hugged her and had presented her with a small gift.

'Now my dear, do be careful in that area,' she had told her. 'You will meet some undesirable types especially if you continue with your extracurricular activities – *nocturnal creature* that you are,' she had said laughing and patting Millicent's cheek a little too aggressively.

'Yes Twinkle, we must keep in touch - you know you are always welcome to visit us back here from time to time,' Cecelia had told her smiling sweetly and then winking at Evelyn.

Chapter Nineteen

Shortly after Olsten had been arrested and had subsequently disappeared; Lily had eventually been found wandering along Waterloo Bridge, having no recollection of how she had got there. She was found by a woman passing by who stated that Lily had approached her in a dream-like state, confused and disorientated, repeatedly asking bizarre questions about what planet she was on and what year it was. She had then literally keeled over, collapsing at the woman's feet. When an ambulance had been called and Lily had been transported to the nearest hospital, she had been diagnosed with complete exhaustion and transient global amnesia, a sudden but temporary episode of memory loss.

Although Lily complained of a pulsating headache and slight visual impairment, there were no evident signs of any serious physical injury apart from bruising to her wrists and a visible small puncture mark on the side of her forehead. Whilst she did not have any past history of migraines or any history of seizure disorder, a neurological examination was carried out which revealed that although her mental status was fairly stable and her long-term memory seemed to be intact, her short-term memory was impaired, and she had no recollection of any recent events leading up to her being picked up on Waterloo Bridge. In spite of her disheveled appearance and being in need of a shower, she showed no signs of malnourishment or being seriously mishandled.

When her mother had been informed that Lily had been found safe and was in hospital, she was immediately rushed to the hospital in a police car.

Lily instantly burst into tears when her mother sat by the side of her hospital bed. Although she initially claimed that she could not recall anything at all that had happened to her over the past weeks, she confided in her mother that she had been abducted by an alien and had been subjected to mind probing procedures.

Although Mrs. Reynolds was shocked by Lily's revelation, she tried not to show any sign of being alarmed by this information. In the circumstances, she felt that Lily was completely disoriented and was not entirely in control of any rational thought process.

'I just thank God to see you back safe and sound, Lily – we have all been so worried about you. Over the past weeks I couldn't help thinking the very worst and now, I know that you have gone through a traumatic time but at least you are back and can come home soon. I don't want you to worry about anything at the moment,' she said, as she clasped both Lily's hands in her own.

'There is absolutely no need for your daughter to worry about anything Mrs. Reynolds,' said a female police officer standing by. 'Your daughter will only be detained here in hospital for another day during which time we will need to question her more regarding her whereabouts these past weeks.'

'I absolutely insist that I am allowed to stay with my daughter until she is discharged,' Mrs. Reynolds said.

'That's perfectly alright, Mrs. Reynolds, as long as you understand that we have to carry out a forensic medical examination on your daughter and she will be visited by a psychologist to assess her current mental and emotional condition before she is released.'

Mrs. Reynolds looked shocked as she glanced back at Lily. She was especially concerned that she would repeat her claim that she had been abducted by an alien.

'Why would she need a forensic examination?' she asked looking back at the female police officer. 'She hasn't committed any crime.'

'This is just a general official procedure to determine whether or not an assault has taken place while your daughter was abducted. We want to resolve this matter for you in order that your daughter can return home as soon as possible.'

'But I was not abducted – I just simply went away for a short holiday,' Lily said, as she raised herself to a sitting position in the bed. 'Tell them, Mother – I only went away for a few days.'

Mrs. Reynolds glanced at the female officer who shook her head. 'You have been away for some time, my dear,' she said to Lily, as she watched her daughter becoming more confused by the minute. She gripped Lily's hands more tightly in an effort to comfort her.

'Look dear, you are tired, and you need to sleep. We can talk about this when you feel able to remember all facts of the matter more clearly,' she said as she turned around to look at the female officer, who was standing by with the intent of emphasizing what the young woman's mother had just said.

'We have every reason to believe that you were abducted, Miss Reynolds. You have bruising around your wrists, indicating that you were maybe bound in some kind of tight rope while you were incarcerated and you have an unusual marking on the side of your forehead – a small puncture, all signs of mistreatment. You disappeared without even telling your mother where you were or taking leave from your job. You have been missing for weeks, believed to have been taken against your will. You can decide at any stage if you prefer not to have a forensic medical examination – nobody can force you, but it can provide useful evidence if the case goes to court. The sooner an examination takes place, the more chance of collecting evidence. The examination will be carried out by a doctor or nurse specially trained in these cases.'

The female police officer looked from Lily and then to Mrs. Reynolds. 'Is that all understood?'

Mrs. Reynolds again grasped Lily's hands tightly when she noticed that she had begun to visibly shake.

'I don't want an examination– I just want to go home,' Lily said as she pressed her cheek against her mother's hands.

'Is that absolutely necessary?' Mrs. Reynolds asked.

'There is no need for concern, Ma'am; your daughter will be treated with the upmost care and every effort will be made to ensure that she is comfortable and not made to feel uneasy in any way. The doctor or nurse will just need to ask any relevant health questions about the alleged assault or any recent sexual activity. They will take samples, such as swabs and also urine and blood samples.'

'But I did not say that I was assaulted – I really cannot remember anything,' Lily insisted, looking at her mother nervously, tears streaming down her face.

'Miss Reynolds, you were reported missing to the police and any forensic medical evidence that's collected is important to our investigation. As I said a police officer specially trained in supporting victims of assault will talk to you and help you to understand what's going on at each stage. If you wish, an advocate will also offer practical and emotional support. You must allow us to do our job.'

'Oh, for goodness' sake – please just get on with it, the sooner the better and then my daughter can come back home, and we can both try to forget all about this terrible experience,' Mrs. Reynolds said, sighing loudly, exasperated by the whole situation. She leaned over from her wheelchair to hug Lily.

'I just wished that you had just come straight back home, my dear, and there would be no need for all this fuss,' she whispered in Lily's ear. She tried not to feel too disturbed about her daughter's mental state of mind for the time being, she just hoped it was a temporary condition.

Lily resigned herself to a forensic medical examination and when it was over, she lay back on her bed feeling emotionally drained. Her mother had told her that she would return later that day and bring her a change of clothing as Lily had said that she wanted to go home the very next day.

Fortunately, as the examination did not reveal any evidence of sexual assault, the doctor agreed that she would be better off at home with her mother. In the meantime, the doctor told her that they would arrange for her to attend counseling sessions to assess the overall condition of her short-term memory loss and her emotional wellbeing. She also agreed to answer some more questions if and when she remembered anything that had happened to her during her disappearance.

Lily could not express the total shock and bewilderment that she felt when she learned of what had happened to Celeste Harrington and that Olsten had been accused of her murder, which had allegedly taken place in her house and later her body had allegedly been moved to his office.

Shortly after she returned home, two police officers attended at their home to question her about Olsten, and she answered all their questions to the best of her ability and informed them that she barely knew any details about Olsten's personal life and certainly did not know where he was at the present time. She now realized why she was being especially pressed to answer numerous questions in relation to her workplace, and it explained why there had been a police officer standing by whilst she was in hospital. The police obviously thought Olsten may also somehow have been involved in her disappearance.

She had been looking forward to going straight back to work but after talking to her mother, who attempted to bring her up to date with what had been happening in her absence, she tried to call Millicent only to be told by her mother that in the meantime she had gone to Italy.

She desperately missed Millicent and had been anxious to see her and talk to her. Millicent would have been a great comfort to her as she always felt that she could confide in her.

As Lily and her mother were sitting together the evening after she had been allowed to go home, her mother mentioned that according to Millicent, she had been extremely upset during their lunch break just before she had disappeared.

'I was so worried when you did not come back home after work that day or the whole night. I called Millicent the next day to ask her if she had any idea of where you could have gone. She said that you had not reported for work that morning. She told me that you had a lunch break together the day before and that you had become upset sometime during that time and she assumed that you had gone straight home. She asked me if I had any idea about a new man in your life as she believed that you may have run off together. It was the only explanation she could think of in the circumstances. Was that the case? Did you run off with a boyfriend? You can tell me – I will not be upset. I just want to know what happened and if he hurt you in any way.'

Lily sat there, puzzled by what her mother was saying and then she closed her eyes tightly trying desperately to remember what had happened that particular day during the lunch break with Millicent. She could vaguely recall falling to her knees after being surrounded by a bright flashing light and then being aware of being lifted up in the arms of a strange alien figure and being carried away. Her eyes snapped open, and she averted her face away from her mother, not wanting to repeat her previous admission – it was too bizarre to think about for the moment.

On top of everything else, she was told by James sometime later that Kyle Fenton had also gone missing shortly after she had disappeared, and he wanted to know if there was any link between the two of them. Lily was shocked and assured him that she had no idea of Kyle's whereabouts - she insisted that she had hardly ever spoken to him at work. She told James that Kyle had always been very polite to her, and she was puzzled why James would think that she had been involved with him.

Although James had heard a different account of Kyle's manner from Millicent who had told him how offensive he was to her, he did not press Lily too much on the matter – *for the time being anyway.*

'Look dear, try not to worry about all this for now,' her mother comforted her. 'You will remember everything eventually and then you can get on with your life again. But in the meantime, forget about rushing back to work - you can just take it easy. You can't go back to work for Olsten Ryder at the moment anyway, because the operation and trading of the business has temporarily been closed until further notice and any access to the premises has been denied. According to Mr. Lambert, the business may close down permanently if he is unable to contact Mr. Ryder.'

Lily leaned over and hugged her mother – she felt safe being with her and decided that while she was at home she would maybe do some decorating in the flat; after all it was a long time coming and it would be a de-stressing exercise for her and maybe she would slowly forget her strange experience in time.

While she tried to settle back into a routine with her mother who was a great comfort to her, she often woke up shaking from a repetitive dream of a sinister face looming over her constantly tormenting her.

At the same time her mother had been puzzled when they had returned home – there were obvious signs that somebody had been staying there in their absence. In spite of her having emptied out the cupboards of food items before leaving to stay with her sister, she was surprised to find the cupboards had been restocked with food. She also noticed that her daughter's bed had been slept in recently; she was certain that she had stripped the bed before leaving.

Chapter Twenty

After the disappearance of Olsten, James and Danielle began to spend more and more time together and eventually realized that they had fallen in love and wanted to spend their life together. It came as a surprise to Danielle as it had been far from her mind to enter into a serious relationship, let alone marry again especially during the current disruption in their lives.

James made her incredibly happy and that inner loneliness that she had experienced for the longest of time and which she had been unable to completely deny in her subconscious mind, gradually left her and she embraced her newfound happiness.

Danielle had dreamed of becoming a fashion designer from the age of six, when she began to dress up her dolls with her mother's cast-off clothes, beads and baubles. Her mother spent a great deal of time with her, cutting up her old dresses and sewing little miniature outfits for her daughter's dolls. Her mother had been a seamstress as a young woman and still enjoyed making her own clothes and bed linen.

Her mother, Elise, had married a French man named Franchot Dupont, who came from a family of farmers and together they built up a vineyard, which through the years had bought them great wealth and comfort. They lived in Aix-de-Province, in a converted farmhouse and Danielle and Leon, her younger brother, were raised in a lively country house where food, love, music and enjoyment were ever-present.

By the time Danielle was twelve years old, she was a whirlwind of fashion ideas; whatever clothes her mother bought for her, she soon made certain changes of her own and became a fashion icon with her school friends and they all began to copy her fashion dress sense. She excelled in her arts and craft lessons at school and by the time she reached the age of sixteen she had already talked her parents into allowing her to go to the Parsons School of Design, in Paris.

Thereafter Danielle was so thrilled to have been selected out of six other applicants to work in one of the most prestigious fashion houses in Paris. It was all much more than she could possibly have hoped and worked for over the years, realizing a long-held dream of becoming a couturier with the masters of fashion. She was brimming with creative ideas and eager to introduce her designs.

It was not so long after that Danielle became interested in historic French fashion dolls. She painstakingly began making doll's clothes in her own time. She was able to copy life-sized patterns which she would then reproduce to the size of eighteen-inch doll-sized patterns. She studied the miniature fashion dolls of the nineteen century that were made from alabaster and China. They were exquisite and represented the style of fashion and trimmings in that period.

Her dream had been to build herself up as a top designer of collectable miniature doll costumes and she was determined to have her very own boutique. It was when she came across several of Olsten Ryder's collectable doll creations, which were added to the permanent collection of the Louvre Museum of Decorative Arts in Paris, that she was determined to accomplish her ambition and work with him. She first established herself by freelancing as a feature animation costume artist/designer for Walt Disney Studios, DreamWorks, Sony Pictures, Art Centre in Pasadena, Cal Arts, and many other prestigious organizations before finally working with Olsten as his collectable doll dress designer.

Danielle had married Arnoud De La Fontaine, during her busy years pursuing her career and for a short while had been happy. They had both been thrilled when they had a baby daughter Sophie. One Sunday, during torrential rain, when Arnoud was making his way home from visiting his aged mother, his car had spun out of control and both he and their baby daughter Sophie were killed instantly.

Danielle and Olsten worked well together and whenever Danielle was in London, they would socialize together and attend the various functions to promote their business. Olsten realized that it was almost like a tonic for Danielle when she was in London. She was, of course, very businesslike in her own eccentric French manner and gradually began to recover from her tragic loss as much as she could.

James had found Danielle just at the right time. They were both at an age when they knew what they were looking for in a partner and how to successfully divide their time between their private life together and their business life - compromise was the secret ingredient sprinkled with lots of love, respect and loyalty.

He was a typical masculine and ultra egotistical type of character, the type of man that Danielle ordinarily loathed but at the same time, his arrogant and at times warped sense of humour attracted her. What she had never realized before was that he was a good hearted and loyal person underneath the bombastic persona which he displayed to most people.

James had been a constant irritation to her at first and she had made numerous excuses whenever he invited her out for dinner when she was in London or when he was in France, and she invariably tried to avoid him as much as she could.

When they both became embroiled in a desperate search for Olsten and found themselves seeking out each other's company more and more, Danielle began to feel differently about James.

Although James had been divorced some time ago and was still very close to his ex-wife, Felicity, she had, in the meantime, remarried and now had a child with her new husband. During her marriage with James, they had both desperately wanted children and when Felicity first announced that she was pregnant, James had been ecstatic. Very soon after, she had a miscarriage. She had been inconsolable and had blamed James for his constant trips away and neglecting her. Although James tried to comfort her as much as he could, their relationship seemed to become more and more strained to such an extent that living together became impossible.

Felicity was a very earthy and sweet woman, and he missed her for the longest of time after the divorce. He had felt certain that with a child they could have made their marriage work. As a busy mother Felicity would have been totally committed to the caring of the baby and his constant absence from the home would have been more acceptable. It was not to be though, and their parting had been inevitable.

James soon after settled back into a bachelor's life and had been happy enough welcoming a life of work and more work after his divorce. After having countless short-term dalliances and having a reputation as a serial womaniser, he had decided that he was through with women - until he met Danielle.

Danielle was his new beginning, and it was the right time for them to come together. She was his type of woman, and he was her type of man -both independent but loyal to a fault.

Chapter Twenty-One

Millicent slipped into an emotional crisis, that overwhelmed her senses, and she spent day after day slumped in front of her TV watching movies and day-time soap opera after soap opera. She became lost in a world of make believe - completely losing track of time, barely having the energy or inclination to even take a daily shower, such was the extent of her shock after what had happened.

A whole six months had gone by since the disappearance of Olsten and she felt lost and confused; he had never once tried to contact her or James. She did not want to believe that he was guilty – she refused to believe that he would do such a terrible thing. She wondered where he could possibly have gone into hiding - she realized that he could be anywhere as he was an incredibly wealthy man with money in Swiss bank accounts and owning various properties all over the world.

When she received a jumbo-sized box of rich, dark chocolates and a single rose delivered to her door one day, she had been certain that they were from Olsten, and this reinforced her hope that he was nearby and watching out for her. The chocolates were delicious although after eating one, she always developed a blinding headache and felt an enormous feeling of melancholy, but she could not resist them.

Each morning after literally hauling herself out of bed, she would drag herself to the kitchen to prepare a pot of coffee and then slump on the sofa in front of her TV where she would remain for most of the day. Sometimes she just fell asleep on the sofa at the end of the day or other times she managed to stumble back into her eternally crumpled unmade bed.

Her mother called daily and begged her to go into the restaurant business with her and Roberto, but Millicent insisted that she needed time to think things over and decide what she wanted to do.

As Millicent sat at her kitchen table late morning sipping her strong black coffee, the phone rang – she hesitated for a moment knowing that it was her mother calling as usual. She hauled herself out of the chair and reluctantly padded over to the phone preparing herself for yet another lecture of the day.

'I worry about you, Millicent,' her mother said. 'You need a good talking to. You are not taking care of yourself. It's not doing you any good shutting yourself up like this all day and every day,' she sighed in exasperation. 'I've never known you to be as bad as this, Millicent; why don't you just come over to the restaurant and help us out every now and again, just until you find yourself another job. It would be far better for you than sitting alone every day in your apartment. I'm not suggesting that you come back home permanently because I know you love your independence and I'm glad that you are settled and happy in your new flat'.

Millicent rolled her eyes and started laughing although the shrill sound of her laughter made her cringe – she knew she sounded a little hysterical.

'Listen Mother, I'm alright. My break to Italy was the first holiday I'd taken for years, so I like sitting at home and relaxing. It's not as if I'm going to make a habit out of it. It's just that I feel so exhausted at the moment, and I just want to be on my own and have time to think'.

'It's just not healthy for you, cooped up in your flat like that not seeing a single person from day to day,' her mother said. 'I'm really losing patience with you now, Millicent. If you could just help out in the restaurant now and again, it would bring you out of yourself - you know how much you enjoy all the customers milling around over here every day.'

'MOTHER,' Millicent almost yelled down the phone, although not meaning to. She winced at the sound of her own shrill voice which seemed to vibrate right through to her tired brain. 'You don't need help in the restaurant. I don't know why you are making such a fuss about this - I'm perfectly fine. It's not as if I'm losing my mind - I'm just enjoying myself and relaxing for a few weeks.'

'A FEW WEEKS,' her mother screamed down the line. 'Now you listen to me, my girl, either you get your sorry self over here or I'll come over there and drag you out of the flat myself. I'm sick and tired of calling you every single day and begging you to come and see us. I'm coming over there right now and I am not going to take no for an answer.' She paused. 'Hah, enjoying yourself – my foot!'

'MOTHER,' Millicent shouted down the line, suddenly sounding desperate, 'I promise I will come over next week. Please, just give me time. I've booked myself a hair appointment today and it will make me feel much better. I've not been sleeping very well lately - I just need a little more time to myself'. Millicent suddenly burst into tears, sobbing loudly down the line.

'Alright, Milly dear,' her mother said, in a soft cajoling voice. 'Don't cry, dear - I know I am being very pushy, but I don't know what else to do. You go get your hair done today and next week we can go out for lunch together, it doesn't have to be here – we can go somewhere else completely different and eat something else other than Italian food. I'm getting tired of eating pasta anyway. We could even go to the theatre to see one of those period costume dramas that you love so much,' she said in the hope of tempting Millicent to leave her flat. 'What do you think of that dear?' she asked

. 'That sounds fine to me, Mother,' Millicent said in between her sobs. 'I'm so tired, Mother, I'll talk to you later - is that OK,' she replied almost begging.

'I only wish that kind Mr. Ryder was around to talk some sense into you,' her mother said. 'I'm sure you would soon jump to attention. I don't know - I really don't,' she said in an exasperated tone as if she was gritting her teeth while talking.

'I'm telling you, Millicent, if you don't pull yourself together, I swear I will put an advertisement in one of the newspapers for that man to see - I'm sure he would somehow come to your rescue'.

'Yes, I'm sure he would, Mother,' Millicent now said as she blew her nose rather loudly. 'I only wish he would get in touch with me, just once so that I can stop worrying about him. If only I knew that he was safe, wherever he is, I could then just get myself together.'

'Alright, dear,' her mother said. 'I'll leave you alone for now. I'm telling you though, we will definitely go out to dinner and then to the theatre next week, and if I have to come over there and drag you out by your hair, I will, and you can be sure of that, my girl'.

She was determined not to be too indulgent with her daughter especially after hearing about that poor

Mrs. Harrington who had berated herself for not acting much sooner with Celeste.

'It's a deal, Mother,' Millicent said as she hung up and replaced the handset.

She wiped her eyes with the back of her hand and walked towards her bathroom to take a shower and get dressed ready to go out for her hairdressing appointment. After showering and dressing she quickly checked her food cupboard and fridge to see what she would need to buy as she was getting low on essentials. She had been living on cornflakes, soup and beans on toast for the past few weeks and decided that she needed to visit a local food store. Although she had promised to visit Roy and his wife for the odd dinner invitation, she always cried off when they called, making excuses that she was spending the evening with her parents. She hated to fob Roy off like that, but she felt that seeing him would bring back memories of happier times that were now lost and she couldn't bear thinking about them.

Later that evening she heard her doorbell ringing and when she hurried over and picked up her security intercom phone, she heard the voice of her previous boyfriend, Gian. He announced that he had been ringing her office and could not get hold of her, so he decided to pay her a visit.

One side of Millicent was wary of the thought of Gian appearing back into her life, but the other side cried out to be comforted. Although she did not question how he knew where she was now living, she pressed the release button to open the downstairs main door.

When she opened her apartment door and peered out into the dim lighted corridor, she suddenly let out a gasp when she saw Olsten standing there, smiling at her. Everything in front of her eyes went black and she collapsed to the ground.

He lifted her up and carried her through to her lounge area. He laid her down on her couch and covered her with a blanket that she had carelessly tossed onto the floor when she had leapt up to answer the intercom. He gently stroked her hair back from her swollen face, wet with tears.

'Come on now, Millicent, I'm surprised at you,' he said softly. 'Everything is going to be alright - you are not to worry about me. It's important to me that you take care of yourself. I will be very disappointed if you continue to bury yourself day after day in your flat. You have a wonderful life ahead of you. There is so much time for you to enjoy and cherish - you must always seize the moment before the moment is gone and believe me, it is gone so quickly my dear. Life is like a game of chess - you make all the moves, sometimes you make the right moves and sometimes you make the wrong moves.'

Millicent gazed up at him through a swirling mist. She attempted to lift herself up from the sofa, but he gently pushed her back.

Just you rest for now. I want you to give Danielle a call tomorrow and accept her invitation to Paris. She cares about you and wants you to work with her over there. Here is a return flight ticket and I've taken the liberty of ordering you a car tomorrow afternoon to pick you up at four thirty. You need to let Danielle know the flight details – she'll meet you at the airport. There is no chance of you saying no in this matter, Millicent - I insist that you go and that is the end of it'.

'And by the way, stay away from those chocolates,' he then added, picking up the half-eaten box by the side of the couch and tossing them into a small trash bin.

Millicent lay there in a daze nodding her head still staring up into his face, the tears streaming down her face – she would do anything that he told her to do. He gently wiped her face with a tissue, stroked her hair back out of her eyes and then he was gone.

'MILLY, MILLICENT,' Gian was yelling. 'Are you alright?'

Millicent looked up at him rubbing her eyes. 'What are you doing here, Gian? Where is Olsten?' She tried to get up from the sofa, but Gian held her down.

'When you answered the door, you passed out and I carried you in and threw you on the sofa,' Gian told her, looking concerned but slightly amused. 'I quite understand, of course, I've known for years that I have this effect on women - I mean you've either got it, or you haven't, and I've always been aware that I make women swoon at the very sight of my handsome face.'

Although Gian was behaving flippantly, he felt quite alarmed at her appearance. 'I heard that you were in a bad way, but I didn't expect to see you looking so haggard – you look like you are about a hundred years old,' Gian said as he sat by her side, hugging her to his chest.

At this comment, Millicent abruptly pulled away, she had momentarily forgotten how so insensitive Gian could be. She turned away, wiped the tears from her eyes and started to laugh. In a way, it cheered her up and bought her back down to earth.

'Who the hell is Olsten anyway? Oh, now I remember, he's your notorious ex-boss accused of murder, isn't he? You gave me such a scare passing out like that and calling out his name. Are you going crazy or what? Your mother called me this afternoon and asked me to drop by. I've tried to call you several times, but you never answer your phone except obviously when you are expecting a call from your mother. It's no good burying yourself up here and feeling sorry for yourself – after all he was only your boss or was there something going on between the two of you,' he added, wiggling his eyebrows up and down in mock concern.

It wasn't so much that she had been feeling sorry for herself - that was not the reason at all for her gradual withdrawal from people and the outside world. It was more a case of utter heartbreak and disappointment of being forcibly wrenched from a life that she had become so passionate about and that small group of people who meant so much to her.

Gian had always been insensitive and careless in his whole way of dealing with people, especially women. He had never seemed to be able to see or feel the other persons' needs or try to understand anything that he did not remotely relate to.

Millicent had spent month after month giving and giving to this man who had given her absolutely nothing back of himself in return. She did not expect flowers, jewellery or chocolates every time they met; all she had ever wanted was for him to have met her halfway and treat her with affection and respect - the way she had treated him.

Their relationship had been purely a physical attraction at first, but then Millicent's total commitment and soft-hearted way of subconsciously making excuses for a hopeless match carried the union on until she had exhausted herself and had finally made the decision to finish the slow tortuous habit that she had acquired against her better judgement.

When she had first met him, her impression of him was how cocky he behaved. As she spent more time with him, she saw through his steely confidence and although he was inconsiderate and completely absorbed in himself most of the time, she found a hint of sincerity hidden in the deep layers of self-seeking concentrated persona and discovered that he actually craved approval.

But now, as she looked up at Gian, she told herself that every girl needs this type of man just once in a lifetime to warn her off from the type of man she doesn't want to spend the rest of her life with. This reflection made her smile, and she couldn't help feeling grateful to Gian for teaching her a valuable lesson in life about men. He was not a bad man but all the same, she realized that he was totally irresponsible and would probably never change. At that moment she thanked God that she had not married him.

Her mind went back to that evening in the restaurant when she had been helping her mother out. The restaurant had been full of Italian families that evening celebrating one young man's birthday at one of the tables. Gian, the birthday-boy in question, seemed to be a very arrogant young man and sat at the table as if he owned it with his arm slung around the shoulders of a very beautiful young girl's shoulders. During the evening, he had got very drunk.

The more intoxicated he became, the more flirtatious be began to act with Millicent. At first, she felt extremely annoyed that every time she stood over the table, his drunken banter reduced her to a flustered

red-faced spluttering idiot but eventually she had to laugh with him.

After that he came often to the restaurant and although he always came with friends or with a girlfriend, he was always very polite and finally asked her out as he was leaving the restaurant with some friends one evening.

She accepted much to her own surprise but realized much later that the physical attraction between them had been so overpowering to her at the time, that she could not possibly reject his invitation. She would always remember that first kiss they had together; it was smouldering, and her lips had been burning from that first contact.

The problem with that relationship became all too obvious to her when she slowly began to realize that Gian loved women of all types and sizes.

One evening when she let herself into her apartment, she had discovered him in her bed with one of their close female friends. In spite of the fact that he had previously proposed to her, and they had been planning their wedding, she finally admitted to herself that he had to go.

She had felt so betrayed and angry at that time and had gone to work the next day like a bear with a sore head. Olsten had been considerably kind to her that day and had insisted on taking her out to dinner that evening for her birthday. It had been a lovely evening, and he had even bought her a beautiful gift. Remembering Olsten's kind and generous heart now made her feel suddenly happy and renewed – she would pull herself together and get on with her life.

After sitting with Gian for an hour and convincing him that she was feeling much better, she finally pushed him out of the door promising to call him sometime later. When she locked the door behind him, she wrapped her dressing gown snuggly around herself and marched into her kitchen to pour herself a glass of wine to celebrate her newfound sense of a bright new beginning in her life.

Gian had insisted that he wait while she got ready to go out to dinner with him, but she had been adamant that she was feeling fine and needed to make a very important call.

She went back into her lounge with her glass of wine and sank back down onto her sofa. She let out a huge sigh of relief - she was going to be okay. She leaned over to put her wine glass on a side table and that's when she saw the airline ticket. She jumped up from the sofa and picked up the ticket - it was a first-class ticket to Paris in her name.

'I must be imagining this,' she spoke out loud to herself

She rushed over to the telephone and immediately called her mother. Her mother was delighted to hear the excitement in Millicent's voice. She was a little afraid that Millicent would be annoyed that she had interfered by calling Gian in the first place, but she seemed not to be in the least bothered, which was a relief in the circumstances.

'Did he mention anything about an invitation to Paris,' Millicent said breathlessly. 'I've just found a first-class air-line ticket.

'He may have, dear. I'm not sure now – I mentioned that you needed to get out with your friends again. Why? Have you both decided to get back together again and have a romantic trip to Paris? I hope so, dear, that would be wonderful for you.'

'No, no, Mother – nothing like that,' she shuddered at the very thought of it - not that Gian was so very repulsive.

'Why don't you go off and visit your French lady friend - I recall you telling me that she invited you to work with her – that would be a wonderful experience for you.'

'I know, Mother, I know,' Millicent said excitedly, 'But I don't speak a word of French'.

'Why worry about a small detail like that,' her mother laughed down the phone. Go take some French lessons.'

'I really do not have time, Mother, I'm leaving tomorrow afternoon'.

'WHAT!' screamed her mother down the line. 'What on earth are you talking about? Whatever Gian said to you, it certainly worked. I can't tell you how happy I am that you are back to your old self, my dear. I'll come over there first thing tomorrow morning and help you pack. I'm beside myself with excitement now. Let me go and tell Roberto the good news,' she then said as she blew a kiss down the line and hung up.

Millicent replaced the handset and smiled to herself. 'I can hardly believe that Gian would do something like that,' she whispered to herself as she looked at the ticket she had been clutching to her chest as if it had been a million-dollar cheque.

She ran into her bedroom and pulled a suitcase down from her closet. 'I've got so much to do,' she said, excitedly. 'I'm so glad I had my hair done today; at least I will look presentable when I get on the flight tomorrow.'

She then ran back into the lounge to make another call and started dialling the number of Danielle's chateau in Paris.

When she heard Danielle's voice, she immediately felt so full of optimism.

'Danielle,' she gasped down the line. 'I fainted, and Olsten picked me up and carried me to my sofa - he told me that I should accept your offer of employment and then he was gone. He left me a first-class ticket to Paris'.

She heard Danielle shrieking with laughter on the other end of the line.

'Hells bells, Millicent, what are you babbling about. It's so wonderful to hear you back to your normal scatterbrained self. Have you been on the Tequilas, my dear? It's really great to hear your voice. Pack all your glad rags and get your derriere over here prompt. I'm going to take you dancing and prancing,' she said laughing. 'But hold on a minute, did you say Olsten, darling,' Danielle sounded puzzled. 'What's going on over there now?'

'No, no Danielle, I meant Gian, a previous boyfriend. I can hardly believe it myself. He must have had an attack of a guilty conscience after his despicable treatment of me. I don't think I ever told you about him – the cheating swine slept with one of my best friends. But anyway, he has made all the arrangements, bought the ticket and has even booked a taxi for four thirty tomorrow afternoon to take me to the airport,' she said, hardly taking a breath.

Later that night, after Millicent had neatly packed some outfits in her smartest suitcase, she took a shower and collapsed into her bed. She immediately fell into a deep sleep and dreamed of Olsten - they were walking up an aisle together and when they reached the end, he took her hand and kissed it.

'You will make a beautiful bride, Millicent,' he said as he joined her hand with that of her future husband's.

Chapter Twenty-Two

Danielle ran over to Millicent as soon as she saw her head bobbing amongst all the other passengers walking through the arrival lounge in the Charles de Gaulle Airport. They ran into each other's arms and hugged.

'Oh, Ma Cherie,' Danielle said, as she kissed each side of Millicent's face. 'It's so good to see you at last,' she said, as she then gave her a gentle playful slap across one side of her cheek.

'You naughty girl, you can't imagine how worried I've been about you sitting back there in your apartment alone staring at the walls.'

As Danielle and Millicent walked out of the airport with arms around each other, both talking non-stop at the same time, a very handsome debonair young man had taken hold of Millicent's airport trolley containing her suitcase and hand luggage and marched in front of them.

Once outside the airport, the young man placed the baggage in the trunk of a car and opened the car door for them. Danielle then linked her arm through the man's arm and pulled Millicent towards them both.

'This is my handsome baby brother Leon - he has been simply dying to meet you,' she said in her usual gushing way and winking.

Millicent's heart skipped a few beats as she stood facing Danielle's brother Leon. He had taken hold of her hand and as she looked into his eyes, she felt light-headed. Leon's eyes were the most beautiful rich amber colour she had ever seen. Her cheeks suddenly became quite flushed, and her knees felt like they were going to give way under her. He then leaned across and kissed her on both cheeks – she felt a delicious tingle all over her body. She wondered why Danielle had not mentioned before how charming and handsome her brother was.

'It's a pleasure to meet you Millicent – Danielle has talked non-stop about you. You must be exhausted,' he said. 'Please just sit back and relax - it's a long ride to the chateau.'

'Danielle and I have planned quite a schedule for you during the next two weeks touring around,' Leon continued. 'But for this evening, you and Danielle are going to have a cosy dinner together, just the two of you to catch up on all your news. You must get a good night's rest after before the onslaught of the next two weeks generally touring around.'

'Thank you so much, Leon,' Millicent said with her hand still in his. 'I'm so happy to be here and I can't wait to see Paris and the Chateau de Versailles and the Louvre Museum and the Rodin Museum, and so many other places that I've heard about in your beautiful country.'

When Danielle and Millicent were both comfortably seated in the back of the car, Leon started the engine and slowly drove out of the parking area. It was a beautiful but cool climate.

'Well then, my dear, you are certainly in for a treat – we have so much to show you,' Danielle said. 'I have taken a short leave from work so that we can spend plenty of time together seeing the sights.

'I feel so happy to be here with you,' Millicent said again leaning across to hug Danielle again.

Leon, who had been quietly driving along, started laughing.

'Well Millicent, my sister is a mine of information and is determined to show you around every little niche and bend of Paris.'

'Yes, my dear,' Danielle said, 'I've already bought museum passes for us. With the museum pass, there's no admission charge, no waiting in lines and no limit to the number of times you can visit more than seventy museums and monuments in Paris and in the Paris region. We can go to the arts museums including the Louvre Museum and Rodin Museum - the whole lot if you like.'

'How does it sound so far,' Leon asked Millicent. 'We are now on our way to my place where you will be my guest for this evening, or as long as you like, but you must promise to try all my special wines.'

Millicent knew that Leon had carried on the vineyard after their parents had died and as much as Danielle had loved the country estate and was tempted to stay on with Leon, she also knew that Danielle was not a country girl at heart; she loved the city life and preferred to explore her life as a fashion designer travelling around.

As they drove out through the streets, heading towards the outskirts of Paris, Danielle chatted non-stop, and Millicent sat back feeling perfectly contented sitting and listening.

'We have planned out the perfect combination of Paris sightseeing and wine country touring. You'll see the best of the *City of Light* with a cruise down the Seine River and a great wine tasting dinner. We will visit Versailles and Giverny, just outside of Paris and explore the Champagne and Loire Valley regions and their fine wines. This includes beautiful 4-star hotels and gourmet meals. We've actually set out a 7-day itinerary,' Danielle told Millicent as she dug into her huge handbag and pulled out a notebook including some pages from a tour brochure.

'And here is your Itinerary. On day one, we'll meet our guide, Bridgett Bonnet, at 3:00 pm outside the Hotel Bedford, located just behind the Place de la Madeleine, close to a number of beautiful restaurants and wonderful shops. We begin with a city orientation tour to see the beautiful and major sights of Paris. We then return to the hotel and enjoy an introduction to wine tasting taught for beginners - you, not us, we are certainly not beginners of wine tasting, are we?' She said looking across at Leon's reflection in the rear-view mirror. 'We are practically veterans in the art of wine tasting – positively alcoholics,' she said as she threw her head back and laughed out loud.

'But anyway,' she continued. 'Then, we'll head out for a welcome cruise, where you'll enjoy a delicious dinner with wine on this elegant cruise, accompanied by live music and dancing as we cruise by the city's greatest monuments, illuminated against the night sky – a positive feast of entertainment,' she said with an exaggerated flourish of arm movement, inadvertently nearly hitting Millicent in the face. Millicent had quickly ducked with a smile on her face.

'Oops, I'm so sorry my dear. I'm getting quite caught up by the moment. I'm also getting quite panic stricken at the thought of seeing James again - he's going to join us for a couple of days.

He was absolutely over the moon when he heard that you had decided to come here after all. He said that he had tried to call you on numerous occasions, but you never answered your telephone'. At this, Danielle then turned and gave Millicent another playful slap.

'You are a naughty, naughty girl,' she said, again laughing.

Millicent sat there with a dazed expression on her face, not from the slap she received, but from the excitement of listening to Danielle.

'I'm looking forward to seeing James again too, Danielle, I do feel awful now that I've worried you all so much – what would I do without you all. My poor mother has been beside herself over the last few months. I must call her before I go to sleep this evening. I must tell her how much I love her.'

Millicent had tears in her eyes at that point and when she looked up at the rear-view mirror, Leon winked at her reassuringly

'But, what about the job, Danielle, I need to get right into my work with you. I'm raring to go with assisting you with new designs and fabric selections. This is going to be the most exciting thing for me. Olsten always told me that the design side of the company was more suitable to me than being his secretary.'

'I know, ma Cherie – all in good time, but first you need to see our beautiful country here. I will show you around the first week but after I will need to go back to work and Leon will continue the rest of your tour around Paris and other places of interest. You will absolutely love it, and you certainly need to see lots and lots of different faces for the sake of your sanity,' she said as she playfully put her hands around Millicent's neck in mock strangulation.

'After all the time you've spent sitting alone, we just think it will do you the world of good to get out and about before starting your new job. So, as I was saying,' she then resumed reading from the tour brochure papers. 'On the second day of our tour, we will head to a Champagne exhibition and during the 2-hour drive, our tour guide Brigitte will provide an introduction to this region and its wines. You'll visit the famous house of Veuve Clicquot in Reims for a tour of their vast and beautiful cellars, ending with a tasting of the deliciously brewed wines. Afterward, you'll see the spectacular Reims Cathedral, where all the kings of France were crowned, followed by a luncheon with regional wines, of course, at the elegant Millénaire restaurant. We will then move on to Epernay in the Côte des Blancs and the renowned house of Moet et Chandon for a tour and another tasting. And, then back to Paris and a glorious dinner with yours truly and that rascal Mr. Lambert who will honor us with his magnificent company,' she said with a tell-tale twinkle in her eyes.

Millicent started laughing, she was going cross-eyed with all the information she was hearing, and her head was spinning, in a good way.

'You know, I'm going to be falling around drunk the whole time,' she said as she again looked at Leon's reflection in the rear-view mirror.

'No, don't worry Millicent, you will learn to just take a sip, swill it around your mouth and spit it out. Champagne tasting can be a little different - you can sip and swallow if you like,' he told her as he winked at her again.

'As I was saying, before I was rudely interrupted,' Danielle said as she continued, again, reading from the tour brochure.

'On the third day, we start the morning with a short drive to the Chateau of Versailles, the extravagant palace built by King Louis XIV. You'll have a guided tour of the State Apartments, including the famous

Hall of Mirrors, followed by lunch at the La Flotille Restaurant right on the Grand Canal. We will then go on to Normandy and see the beautiful home and gardens of the famous impressionist painter Claude Monet at Giverny. We will then return to Paris, for another evening at one of the fabulous restaurants. The following day is a free day to enjoy the sights and soak in the Parisian atmosphere. We can maybe take a short walk to Bistro du Sommelier, owned by one of France's biggest names in wine, which will include a visit to his personal cellar, with its many rare and very old bottles'. Danielle suddenly paused and took a deep breath before continuing.

'The next day we will leave Paris for a two-day excursion to the Loire Valley, which takes approximately a two-hour drive. We'll visit the Chateau of Chenonceau, probably the most famous of the Loire Valley castles. The chateau is also a producer of fine wines, and we'll stop for a tasting of their AOC Touraine wines. Lunch will be served at the Chateau's own elegant Orangerie restaurant. This will be followed in the afternoon by a visit to another great winery in Vouvray. The day after that, we will taste wines of the Anjou region; but first, a stop along the way to see the lovely Chateau of Azay-le-Rideau. Our very next stop is quite unique - it's the Cave aux Moines; a cave cut deep into the hillside along the Loire River. We'll tour the cave to see their production of mushrooms and snails, which are specialties of this region, before lunch in their restaurant in the middle of the cave! Now won't that be exciting,' she said as she stopped to take a sip from a bottle of water.

'We will then go on to visit the Chateau de Fesles and taste wines of appellations Coteaux de Layon, Quarts de Chaume, Savennières and Anjou. If you are still standing on the last day after breakfast, we'll return to Paris in our wonderful chauffeur driven car, driven by our very own handsome and debonair chauffeur.'

'Wow,' Millicent said as she clapped her hands, applauding Danielle and her wonderfully lengthy detailed description of the fantastic tour planned for her, although nearly going cross-eyed with all the information which had gone into one ear and out of the other. She was beyond excited and leaned across to kiss Danielle.

'You two are the best, I'm going to have a wonderful time; I'm definitely going to become an alcoholic – that's for sure, but that's okay,' she said, laughing.

Sunny skies greeted them as Millicent and Leon joined the other participants on a circuit to explore the worlds of coffee, cheese and bread a week later. They first visited the coffee and tea shop Verlet, located on rue Saint-Honoré. The family-run establishment had sold coffees, teas and gourmet food since its creation in 1880, Leon explained to Millicent.

The owner gave them a glorious presentation of the history, cultivation, and harvesting of coffee, and provided samples of three different coffees for tasting. He then led them to Verlet's coffee roasting facility, where he demonstrated the roasting process.

Leon glanced across at Millicent's lovely face; she had acquired a faint tan since touring around and now looked refreshed and healthy. She no longer had the dark shadows under her eyes or the tired weary expression that he had noticed when they had picked her up from the airport.

He had taken the liberty of leading her around holding tightly onto her hand and she seemed to have no objection to this. To all the other participants, they looked like a young couple in love.

They had spent the first week with Danielle and it had been full of exciting days and evenings spent eating superb food and wine tasting. Throughout the whole time, Millicent had felt quite tipsy and lightheaded - she was not entirely sure if it was the effect of the wine tasting or Leon's presence making her feel like that.

Although she missed having Danielle around them, she couldn't help feeling thrilled that she had Leon all to herself now. The following days were full of excitement, peppered with romance and her whole body tingled with anticipation from one day to the next.

Leon was likewise mesmerized with her, unable to drag himself away for even a second and she certainly felt the same.

After a tiring but exhilarating day of constantly traipsing around sightseeing, Millicent welcomed a relaxing evening in a restaurant dimly lit with romantic candlelight.

She sat on the opposite side of the table gazing into Leon's eyes enjoying the good food and wine but most of all his company. It was a wonderful evening, and she knew then that she was going to marry him.

Chapter Twenty-Three

Olsten was never traced following his disappearance. In spite of making extensive investigations in London, Paris and New York, no trace of him was ever found. It was as if he had never existed - he had vanished from the face of the earth. There were times when James thought he saw that familiar face watching him from a distance in a busy airport or as he was driving through the streets of London but then as quickly as the face had appeared, it quickly vanished from his view.

James took charge of dealing with the company and the assets and as he believed that Olsten would wish for the company to go on in his absence, he turned over the business to Danielle on the understanding that if they were able to track Olsten down eventually, the business settlement would have to be reassessed.

Various investigations had been carried out by the Police and all staff had been questioned thoroughly. What James had not been aware of before Olsten's disappearance, is that Olsten had yet again come to the rescue of Amitola shortly before Celeste had been murdered, which had inevitably been tied in with the outcome of Celeste's demise as far as the investigation was concerned.

It had later transpired that Celeste had followed Amitola one evening as she had left a party and had attempted to seize the young girl and carry her off to a car by the side of the road where a man sat waiting to drive them away.

When Olsten had appeared suddenly and had quickly taken hold of Celeste, pulling her away from

Amitola, she had clawed at his face leaving deep scratches. These scratches on his face were still visible when he had been arrested and when particles of skin had been found in Celeste's fingernails shortly after her body had been recovered, they were immediately tested and evidently proven to be Olsten's, which was further damning evidence against him.

James and Danielle went over and over the facts leading up to when Olsten had been arrested and although Danielle could not believe that Olsten could do such a thing, James was still completely mystified about certain things that had happened during the time he had known Olsten. He certainly did not believe that he could harm anybody but had been puzzled all the same at times by Olsten's odd and suspicious actions.

'It did all seem to evolve around Amitola and Celeste was determined to find out exactly what the connection was - she had become totally obsessed and preoccupied with delving into Olsten's past,' James said, rubbing his chin.

'Whatever happened to that driver - what was his name Carl or something similar sounding?' Danielle asked. 'Surely he would know something – after all he saw Olsten practically every day.'

'In the circumstances it had not been possible to question Kyle at that time as he had also disappeared. What is going on with these people – if they are not losing their memory, they are disappearing. Such complete madness and mayhem,' James said, frowning.

'But what exactly was Celeste's interest in Amitola and what business was it of hers anyway?' Danielle asked.

'Who knows what was going on in her mind; it seems she had become obsessed with her belief that Amitola was his secret daughter. She obviously wanted to get back at Olsten with some scandal to shame him for rejecting her. Even Mr. and Mrs. Defoe, through the years, suspected that he was her benefactor, but it had not occurred to them that he could have been related to her. Even so, although they did not question the fact that he was always right there when Amitola had been involved in various accidents throughout her childhood years, they were astonished all the same. Who could blame them -it was completely unbelievable.'

'But why would he feel shame anyway -I just don't understand. Surely having a child from a past relationship is nothing to hide or feel disgraced about.'

'It wasn't as simple as that and while we all suspected that Olsten had, in fact, been married at some stage and that his wife had consequently mysteriously disappeared, Celeste actually implied that Olsten had murdered her. So many crazy ideas had been pouring through Celeste's mind - she had slowly been driving herself demented. But apart from all that, Mrs. Defoe believes that Amitola is actually related to royalty and that the knowledge of her birth out of wedlock had been kept a closely guarded secret so as not to cause a huge scandal in the circumstances.'

'Do you mean that Olsten had a child out of wedlock with a woman of royal birth? I find that a bit fanciful and I'm sure a lot of foster parents want to believe that the child they are caring for is of royal birthright' Danielle said, laughing.

'Maybe it does sound farfetched, but Amitola was, after all, born in Italy, supposedly to a young unmarried girl of a noble background, and the family did not want to be dishonoured by such knowledge being known,' James replied.

'But why was Celeste so convinced that Olsten had murdered a previous wife? Surely if she was so convinced of that, why was she so madly in love with him? That would be enough to put me off wanting to marry a man. I didn't even know that Olsten was involved with Celeste romantically anyway - I thought she was due to marry somebody else. I did meet her once or twice at some function or other and she seemed such a lovely young girl, full of the joys of spring. Whatever happened to her to become so deranged like that?' Danielle then asked.

'Who knows, although I did have my suspicions that she was taking medications that did not agree with her. In fact, it had been revealed that she had been prescribed diet pills, and I do know that they were Amphetamines, and those pills are well known to cause paranoia and other unpleasant side effects.'

'I just find it so shocking that her body was hidden in that life-sized doll, I mean how bizarre is that? That is so creepy and only a sick mind could think of that. After a short time that body would have started to really reek filling the whole building with a foul smell,' Danielle continued, grimacing.

'Whoever placed the body into that ceramic doll mould, made sure that it was professionally embalmed with a preservative varnish substance in order to stop it from decaying. It had to be somebody who knew exactly what they were doing. But anyway, if that police officer had not inadvertently knocked the thing over the body would never have been discovered. I mean, in different circumstances, what a clumsy thing to do and he would certainly have been made to pay for that expensive broken doll. I am sure Olsten never imagined that such a thing would happen like that - who would guess that a body could be hidden in such a way. Such a shame and a sad end - she was a beautiful young woman.'

'Well – after all, it's not such an original idea, is it? The ancient Egyptian's did it all the time. I must say I find it rather romantic to be laid to rest in such a way – especially in satin underwear,' Danielle said.

'Well, I'm sure that can be arranged, my lady, if that is your wish,' James replied, laughing to lighten the mood.

'I hope that Olsten knows what he is doing though, going on the run like that. I just feel that it is all so unbelievable that such a horrifying thing like this could happen to him,' Danielle said.

'I have a feeling that Olsten knows exactly what he is doing, he just needs to stay as far away as possible to bide his time while he investigates the whole situation – he would want full control of the situation without any interference from the police. Don't forget I've known him for a number of years - we actually knew each other in New York before both travelling back to the UK. Knowing him as well as I do, I suspect he will find out exactly who and what is behind all this eventually. I never knew such a man before as Olsten. At times I felt as if he could predict what was going to happen next, almost as if he could read minds,' James said, suddenly putting his hand up knowing what Danielle was obviously going to say next.

'He certainly did not predict what did happen in the end though, did he?'

'I think he was somehow blind-sighted along the way and didn't want to believe such a thing would ultimately happen - I think he was unwilling to believe that Celeste's bizarre and unreasonable behaviour would lead to such a tragic end. Maybe it was beyond his control at the time, and he probably found it impossible to deal with her in the end, and … who knows, he may have completely lost his patience with her.'

'What *are* you saying?' Daniele asked, feeling shocked by what James was insinuating – it was just too incredulous to believe.

'You do seem to contradict yourself. When you say that knowing Olsten as well as you do, that you suspect he will find out exactly who and what is behind all this eventually - do you actually have any idea of who else could be held accountable other than Olsten?' she asked.

'Yes, I think I do,' James replied.

'Well - are you going to share it with me?' Danielle asked, laughing, but feeling a little irritable by his answer all the same.

'Nothing would convince me to believe that he could be responsible for such hideous crimes against women. But let's just say that Olsten had been too secretive for his own good and I can hardly believe now that I did not really know the man – not as well as I thought I knew him anyway,' James replied pensively.

'So, you *are* saying now that you suspect Olsten after all – make up your mind,' Danielle said, irritably.

'No, absolutely not, but I often wondered about so many things that happened in the past. I found it not in the least strange when I happened to relocate from New York around the same time as Olsten and we both continued our business connection exactly the same as when we met in New York. Now, tell me why I did not find that in the least odd. Or was it just coincidence?'

'When you say connection, what exactly do you mean?' Danielle asked.

'The connection between Olsten and Mr. and Mrs. Defoe and myself -we all seemed to relocate from New York at the precise same time.'

'Yes, I see what you mean – but what has that got to do with anything?' Danielle replied.

'Thinking back now, I do question the events leading up to the unfortunate end for Celeste and somehow, they do seem to add up and do not appear to look good for Olsten at all. Although Olsten had continually denied that there had ever been anything between them, I just can't help thinking that she was not entirely guilty of fabricating the whole situation. I did happen to witness one conspicuous scene where the two of them were seen together in a compromising situation. Mrs. Harrington never doubted that there was something going on between them and although Lewis had always been a gentleman and never confronted Olsten, they both blamed Olsten for her mental breakdown, especially Lewis, at the end.'

'Well, of course he would, James – he must have found it extremely hard to watch her go from a happy young woman all set to marry him and then within a day changed so completely. He must have been so shocked when she called him in Paris that day to announce that she was in love with another man and no longer wanted to marry him. But nothing explains why Olsten would kill her, though, and I wonder now if they charged the wrong man with murder. I would think it quite obvious in the circumstances. Although Lewis was perfectly composed and calm on the outside, well to some extent, when Celeste announced that she was in love with Olsten - he could have been secretly enraged and lost control one evening. He probably asked her to join him for dinner one evening for old time's sake and then lost control,' Danielle replied.

'What? And do you also actually think he had gone on a rampage killing all those other women all around London because of being rejected by Celeste, I don't think so.' James replied.

'Oh yes, I forgot about all the other bodies. How gruesome is that, though - that their faces were all painted and varnished to look like a doll,' Danielle said, frowning at the thought. Horrific images were flashing through her mind.

'But think about it, Danielle - Celeste's body was found encased in that ceramic doll inside Olsten's private quarters and it was evident that he had been the last person to see her. Who else would have had the knowledge and skill to actually place a body inside a ceramic mould?'

'Yes, but apart from all that, Roy said that Olsten's driver could have been the last person to see her although he may well have driven her to be with Lewis. According to her mother, Celeste had been seeing Lewis again from time to time even though he was practically engaged to another woman. Lewis had never stopped loving her and wanted to be right there for her when she needed him. So, I think that he may well have been the last person to see Celeste. I still believe that he could very well have snapped eventually. It seems she had taken it upon herself to call Kyle at all times of the day and night to pick her up and chauffeur her anywhere she wanted. Tough for a fiancé to take. She should have been phoning Lewis, although…'

'No, I don't believe for one minute that Lewis has anything to do with this, it just does not add up,' James said, rubbing his chin again.

'Add up to what?' Danielle asked.

'It doesn't add up to how she ended up encased in that collectable doll in Olsten's private quarters,' James answered, trying not to sound irritable. 'Well let's just leave it at that for now, this is all so exhausting trying to figure it out.' James said putting his arms around her, hugging her close to him protectively and once again feeling incredibly lucky to have her in his life.

Part Two
1972 – Time Release

Chapter Twenty-Four

There was five years difference in age between the two brothers and the oldest, Orbido, had always felt fiercely protective of his younger brother Jud, at all times. As a small boy, Jud had worshipped Orbido and had followed him everywhere he could with fanatical devotion. They were as different as chalk and cheese. As dark-haired as Orbido was, with his warm, engaging brown eyes, Jud, in contrast, had white hair and steely blue eyes - he was an albino, and he had hated it when he was old enough to realize that he was different. He had wanted desperately to look like his brother Orbido, who had been everything that he wished that he could be - he had been his hero.

For a time, it had been an idyllic childhood for the two boys, and they had enjoyed all the comforts of a loving environment with caring parents who gave them not only all the materialistic possessions that all small boys craved for, but also all the love and affection that they could possibly give them without any preference afforded to one over the other. Their privileged life was ordained for them by the long line of their ancestry and birthright of royalty within their sphere.

Being of an imperial background, they were both trained from an early age to follow in their father's footsteps to rule the kingdom after his demise, although as the second son Jud was assumed as the spare. Orbido, in particular, was groomed specifically, as it was deemed that he would inevitably replace their father as the supreme leader unless he himself either failed in his duty as the next in line or met his own demise in the meantime.

Childhood life was good for the two brothers until it became increasingly noticeable that as Jud grew older, he began to show signs of behavioral problems, and it gradually became clear that these behavioral and learning difficulties caused him to progressively withdraw into himself and his mental health problems became a great concern to his parents.

After recovering from a fall from his beloved horse and being left with a limp, Jud became even more and more disconsolate and no encouragement and support from his parents or older brother could comfort him. He especially became jealous and competitive towards Orbido in all aspects of their daily life, and he felt that Orbido was being given more affection from their parents. Jud resented this favouritism, and he began to hate his brother to the point of obsession. His mother watched in horror at times when her youngest son slowly began to spiral out of control, becoming more and more aggressive to his older brother.

In spite of all the high technology machinery that was available for their reconstruction of mind and body in their scientifically and technically advanced realm, Jud had refused as a young boy to be subjected to such trials and every time he was prepared to go through the glass compartments for body and mind corrective procedures, he would go into convulsions. It was thought that due to the lack of pigmentation in his skin, his body rejected the treatments. After one such treatment there appeared to be great prominent blue veins branching out all over his body and although they slowly disappeared over time, it was thought not safe to put him through another session.

As a teenager, he then began to exhibit signs of disaffection and antisocial behaviour towards all members of his family and there were periods when his discontented existence caused him to create as much chaos as he could to gain more and more attention. The more destructive he became, the more his parents became intolerant of his behaviour, and they finally made the decision to place him into a strictly supervised special treatment centre for disturbed minds, hoping to give him time and space to develop his emotional and social skills and to acquire a greater level of self-control.

Sadly, during the short time that Jud was in the treatment centre, he became dangerously uncontrollable and plunged more and more into a downward spiral of teenage disaffection, completely distancing himself from family and friends.

Finally, when he reached his eighteenth birthday, much to the relief of his parents, he slowly began to calm down and they hoped that at last he had changed for the better and would once again revert to that lovable individual that he had once been as a small boy. But once again, when his older brother then announced his intention to marry the one girl Jud had secretly adored since boyhood, he then progressively began to plunge into that darkness of his mind again.

It was ordained that the marriage take place as soon as possible before the demise of their father. It had been observed that their father's health had been slowly deteriorating at that time and despite having regular rejuvenating sessions, his body was slowly rejecting them. It had been his last wish that he see his oldest son married before his body gave out on him. For a time, life went on as before until the death of their father soon after the wedding, and it was during this period of time that Jud began to plan his ultimate revenge against Orbido as the new supreme leader, becoming more and more resentful of the authority he now had over him.

Jud thereafter became manically obsessed with the thought of overthrowing Orbido from his supremacy and spent all his days planning and scheming to remove his brother from his position of power.

After the death of her husband King Shia, their mother Aria spent less and less time with her two boys and grew increasingly neglectful of her duties to give them her full support. It was this failure to provide her full support and attention, where her oldest son was concerned, that gave Jud hope of being able to influence and turn her against Orbido. From the onset of the forthcoming wedding between Orbido and his beautiful bride-to-be, Jud had continually tried to convince his mother that Orbido had actually stolen the affections of his bride-to-be by force and thereby causing her to reject him as a potential suitor.

Being well aware of his jealousy of Orbido, Aria was not misled by Jud's attempts to manipulate her to support him over his older brother. Aria immediately summoned Orbido to discuss the ongoing problem of her youngest son and his obsessive jealousy.

It was decided that he should be enlisted in their imperial militia and undergo specialized training in environmental and intergalactic psychology, hoping that it would give him insight and understanding of his own mental state and thereby strengthening it. After initially refusing to be banished in this way, Jud finally agreed to accept this enlistment which would take him away for a two-year period.

A careful watch over Jud had been maintained at all times on the order of Orbido to monitor his progress. Jud had observed this close attention to his every move, and it had just spurred him on to prove to both his mother and brother that he could succeed. But most importantly, it gave him time to scheme against his brother and his new bride.

After a short period of time Jud surprised his mother by becoming a respected member of the militia and he was then presented with an honourable promotion and given the title of Doctor Jud Durand, making both his mother and brother very proud of him. But what they both did not realise, and suspect, was that Jud had been biding his time and through the intense training that he had been receiving, he was now able to develop his mind to such an extent that he could alter another person's personality to his own wish and thereby dominate an individual to carry out his command at will through them.

It was with this particular skill that he was ultimately able to drastically change the life of his brother and thereby set the wheels of destruction into motion - his heart was filled with such hatred and malice towards his brother.

He intended to carry out this newfound skill of complete mind control on his brother's new wife in order that he could cause a rift between them and ultimately separate them forever. He had been shamed by her rejection of him and over time he had developed a ferocious need to vent his rage on all females.

While in the army Jud had also developed his physicality and after all the intensive training over the last two years, he now no longer had that debilitating limp which had haunted him in his younger years and made him feel awkward and unattractive. Jud had grown into a very attractive young man and with his thick white curly hair and hypnotic steely blue eyes; he finally felt confident that he could stand beside his brother without that feeling of being inferior in mind and body.

In the meantime, he was getting ready to put his destructive plan into operation against his brother and his bride and had taken to disappearing from their realm for months at a time. So, when he was then placed under surveillance, they were horrified to discover that Jud had been visiting other realms and causing chaos and destruction wherever he went.

He was immediately placed into a closed and secured environment where he could not escape, but he was in full control of his ability to interfere with the minds of others and before long he had contrived his own escape with the help of the guards watching over him. What his mother and the people of their sphere did not realise was that he had been slowly gathering information and experience in preparation to carry out a plan to overthrow his brother from his leadership. But worst of all he had developed a blood curdling thirst for seducing young women and stealing their minds, thereby rendering them helpless and ultimately becoming the victims of his hatred and absolute loathing towards all females. This festering hatred had led him on a killing spree.

The day came when Jud could finally put the plan for his brother and sister-in-law into action to change their lives forever and it was during the scheduled rejuvenation procedure for his brother's bride that he saw a perfect opportunity to banish her and his brother out of the kingdom for all eternity. It was a simple scheme and one that would only require the touch of a switch, to complete the task.

Orbido had been unaware of the extent of his brother's pure hatred and resentment of him and had been unprepared for the onslaught of his brother's terrible wrath - a fanatical rage and a desire for revenge and destruction. He was completely oblivious of the fact that Jud had wanted to wreak mayhem and punish Orbido and his bride – he wanted to blast them out of the kingdom forever, never to return. He wanted to ensure that his brother's bride completely dissolved into space - lost forever without a trace.

Once the deed was successfully executed, Jud's ferocious need to punish and take control of any female connected with Orbido, thereafter beginning to spiral out of control as he closely followed his brother's long and patient journey to be reunited with his lost love.

Chapter Twenty-Five
The Present Day

Eight years had passed since the disappearance of Olsten and everybody who had worked closely by his side had moved on with their lives although each and every one thought of him often and sincerely hoped that he would reappear one day back in their lives.

They had all been invited to celebrate Amitola's twenty-first coming of age birthday party at Mr. and Mrs. Defoe's home and to meet her fiancé who was going to announce their engagement.

They were all looking forward to not only attending this happy occasion but to actually seeing each other again after such a long period of time since that terrible day when Olsten had been arrested. Although they had all kept in touch throughout the years often by phone or the usual Christmas card, this was going to be the very first time that they were all going to be together enjoying each other's company. It had been a long time since they had all been in the same country let alone in the same room.

Each and every one of them secretly hoped that Olsten was going to suddenly walk into that room laughing and greeting them all like he used to.

Millicent had married Leon and moved permanently to France where she had given birth to a baby boy. Their life together was everything that Millicent could have wished for and although she sometimes missed her busy and somewhat interesting days living in

London, she was completely content with her life in France with her husband and child.

She often thought about Olsten and hoped one day to see him again -she was sure that he would turn up out of the blue to surprise them all. In the meantime, through a lot of hard work and ambition, she had slowly developed her dream of becoming a collectable doll dress designer and with the help of Danielle, she became quite successful in her own right and enjoyed working freelance, designing period doll costumes which had been her vision and preference. Her Edwardian era design trends were especially successful, and she was quite proud of herself. She hoped that Olsten would be proud of her achievement, wherever he was.

Lily had recovered from her ordeal and although she had never been able to remember the exact details of her own disappearance all those years ago, she often had flashbacks and nightmares of a sinister face standing over her controlling her mind. She was now working as a freelance jewellry designer, regularly visiting Paris and working with Danielle in between her assignments in London.

As for Danielle, her previous heartbreak and lonely days following the death of her first husband and her baby daughter all seemed so far away now as she sat at her dresser dabbing her *Chanel No. 5* behind her ears. So much had happened during the last eight years but somehow everything had worked out very well for her in the circumstances. As she thought back to past years, she felt a great sense of pride in how ambitious and dedicated she had been as far as her business was concerned. Although she realised that she had put so much of her personal life on hold and sometimes regretted not paying enough attention to the people around who meant more to her than her work, she could not dwell on past mistakes now. She felt happier now than she had ever felt and was thankful that she had so much more to look forward to.

She smiled as she picked up the wedding photograph on her bedside unit – they had both beamed with happiness on their special day in front of the camera. Their wedding reception had been held in the William Kent House, where they had posed for their wedding photos - It had been a perfect location.

She had been sad that Olsten had not been present, but they had all thought about him and at some point during the celebration in the evening, she could have sworn that she caught sight of his face smiling at her somewhere at the back of the opulent grand hall - she had smiled and waved frantically across the crowded room, but as quickly as that face had appeared, it disappeared.

James had looked so handsome and debonair on that day although he had been a nervous wreck, rushing around like a lunatic making sure that all arrangements were finalised and more importantly that Danielle did not run away at the last moment and leave him at the altar.

He had told her later that this had been his biggest fear. During the two years that they spent together before their marriage, he took to calling her his very own elusive butterfly and free spirit, because she was so very self-regulating, and he would invariably have to track her down. During those times she had consciously put up a guard to protect herself from becoming too hopeful of a true trusting and enduring relationship.

She had been determined to be a little bit out of reach and mysterious with James at the beginning. All that had changed when they were married. She hated to be apart from him for any long period of time, and they scheduled their business as much as they could just to be together as much as possible. If she had business in Paris, he would fly over with her and if he had business in London, she would immediately alter her schedule to be with him. They had bought a wonderful home in a secluded area of France where they loved to spend time together as much as they could.

As Danielle now began to dress for Amitola's party, she looked down at her stomach where her dress was just a little too tight. She had not announced the news to James yet - she didn't want him to get too excited or distracted during the evening. When she had called her doctor's office that morning, the news had been confirmed - she was three months pregnant. She was elated at the news and could hardly contain herself from opening her window and shouting out the news to all who happened to pass by.

She had not even told Millicent the news yet. Of course, she wanted James to be the first to know in any case. She was the godmother to Millicent and Leon's first-born son, Aaron, who they all absolutely adored, and Danielle could not wait to have a child of her own again.

She still felt the pangs of heartbreak at the loss of her husband Arnoud and baby daughter Sophie - the thought of the wonderful times they had together as a family would never leave her.

She heard James calling her then and he came bounding up the stairs and into their bedroom in his usual strident fashion. He looked so handsome in his tuxedo and as she stood there in front of him straightening his bow tie, she couldn't help laughing; he could never keep still for a single second and always reminded her of a mischievous fidgeting schoolboy.

'Could you just keep still for a moment,' she said, laughing as he began to kiss and nuzzle her neck.

'No, I can't,' he replied breathlessly, mockingly. 'Not when I'm around you, I could just eat you, right here and now,' he continued, suddenly howling like a wolf and then panting with his tongue hanging out.

'I swear that you get crazier by the day. I hope you are going to behave yourself this evening and not shame me completely with your wild and reckless ways.'

'I'm going to do exactly that. There is no stopping me, born wild and reckless, that's me,' James said as he picked her up and threw himself and her onto their bed. Danielle let out shrieks as he showered her with kisses all over her face, neck and throat.

'Would you get off, you great big buffoon, you are going to ruin my dress and makeup,' Danielle said, still laughing.

Although he had pinned her down on the bed, Danielle was able to raise her knee against his stomach and send him spinning off the bed onto the floor.

'Okay, now you have asked for it, woman,' he said as he bounced back up, but as fast as he tried to stop her from springing off the bed, Danielle was quicker and had run out of the bedroom and down the stairs before he could grab hold of her.

'You are not going to get your wicked way with me,' she said, shrieking with laughter as he bounded down the stairs after her.

Their maid Carla had heard all the commotion and had come running out of the kitchen and as Danielle ran past her, James came charging down the last few steps of the winding stairway and literally slammed straight into her knocking her backwards, causing her to fall on her backside.

'My goodness, Mr. Lambert,' she said breathlessly, 'you have knocked the wind right out of me.' James bent over, took her hand and pulled her up and as she sprang back on her feet, he planted a big playful wet kiss on her cheek.

'Mrs. Lambert,' she shouted out to Danielle, 'you will have to take your husband into hand; he is acting completely crazy today'. She pushed him away, laughing as she wiped her cheek with her apron.

James ignored her comment as he resumed his chase after Danielle, howling like a wolf. Carla rolled her eyes upwards and walked up the stairs to continue her chores. She was sure that he would be even more out of control when he heard the good news. She would not admit to Danielle that she knew about her condition, but she had noticed all the symptoms – she had no intention of spoiling Danielle's surprise before she told her husband.

Chapter Twenty-Six

Through the years, Roy had often thought of Olsten and wondered where he had been hiding. From time to time, he noticed an article in one of the financial papers and in the background of a particular photograph, he felt quite sure that it was Olsten standing way back inconspicuously. At times when he would stroll around the semi darkened great opulent lobby of the night club where he was currently working, he felt sure that a figure of a man striding in front of him and out of the main door was Olsten, but whenever he rushed out behind him, he had gone out of sight.

What he could not understand was why Olsten had never come back. His name had ultimately been cleared after a thorough investigation had been carried out, which had revealed and proved that he was innocent of the crime he had been accused of.

After meticulous forensic tests had been finalised, it had revealed that skin particles underneath the victim's fingernails were not from Olsten after all. It was determined that the skin particles were absent of any natural pigmentation, indicating that there had been some similarity of DNA which had puzzled the forensic team at the time.

Although some suspicious items had been found by Olsten's personal housekeeper, including a wig, contact lenses and some pancake make-up, which proved to be probative value of evidence, the wig was found to contain white hairs within the scalp-cap netting, possibly belonging to that of a person with a hereditary condition of albinism. It had become clear that all the evidence gathered together had ultimately ruled out Olsten as the main suspect.

When Nancy had been questioned about the items left behind by Olsten's driver at that time, she had told the Officer in charge of the investigation that she had suspected that Kyle had been hiding something strange in his past. She had felt sure that he had possibly been in some kind of dilemma with the army and believed that he had maybe been dishonorably discharged due to some kind of serious misconduct, but the Police were never able to track Kyle down for questioning.

Thinking back now, Roy couldn't help berating himself for not insisting on speaking to Olsten about the particular evening when he had gone back to the building and had found the main front door ajar. But because of the sound of female laughter coming from within Olsten's private rooms, he had felt a little awkward to broach the subject. It had also not escaped his attention when he had left the building that Olsten's limousine had been parked a short distance away that evening, although there had been no sign of Kyle waiting in the vehicle for him.

He had fully expected to be called to Olsten's office the next day for instructions to arrange to have all locks changed as a security measure in the circumstances, but there had been no mention on the subject.

The next day he had spoken to Mrs. Stafros; he had made sure to arrive well before anybody else in order to be able to talk to her in the strictest of confidence. He had explained to her that he suspected that there had been an intruder in the building the evening before. She had informed him that when she had gone into Olsten's private quarters earlier that morning to carry out her usual cleaning, she had found a handbag left in the bathroom.

As much as she was extremely reluctant to involve herself in any such invasion of Olsten's privacy, Roy persuaded her to hand over the handbag and found it contained several items including a badge confirming that the owner of the bag was a young hostess working in the Ritz gambling casino.

Roy convinced her that they should not mention this item to Mr. Ryder and that he would himself return the bag to its rightful owner. He explained that he felt, in the circumstances, it would be more discreet to simply remove the handbag from Olsten's bathroom and save him any kind of embarrassment, if any. The cleaner did not agree with this as she made it very clear to Roy that it was absolutely none of their business - she thought he was meddling in something that had nothing to do with him, although she had been concerned that the handbag belonged to a hostess working in a nightclub.

Roy had been determined to find out who had been in the building after hours with Olsten. He had thereafter visited the premises to inquire about the young woman in question named on the card found in the handbag. He had been informed that the particular hostess in question had abruptly left her position in the gambling casino and had consequently disappeared. He had also been informed that this had not been a one-off occurrence as several other young hostesses had disappeared without giving notice to quit their jobs. The Manager had told him that it had been becoming a problem in his club and one which he had been very concerned about.

The bodies of the missing young hostesses were eventually found dumped in various alleyways around the Mayfair and Belgravia areas dressed and made up to look like dolls - each and every one of them was made-up to look identical with a long flowing black wig, huge, feathered lashes, lips painted bright red and wearing a long flowing white gown.

Never discussing this with anyone, Roy had put it out of his mind and continued to work for Mr. Ryder until that fateful day. After what had happened, Roy had settled back into his life as a security man in Annabel's nightclub in Berkeley Square in the centre of London's exclusive Mayfair district, which attracted all the top models, rock stars and celebrities of the time. Although Roy enjoyed his work to a certain extent and basically looked upon it as being a social whirl, as he was invited to all the parties by certain members of the club, his wife still worried about him, especially as he was not getting any younger and she hoped that he would eventually find a day job. To work in such a prestigious place suited Roy though, as he had met some very affluent people through the years and knew that if ever he needed anything, they were more than willing and available to give him assistance.

One evening, a set of keys to a luxurious mews house in Little Chester Street in Belgravia Square was handed over to Roy as a personal gift to him. Roy's wife had been ecstatic although a little worried about what he had done to deserve such an extravagant gift. Although he was not absolutely sure of who had donated this extremely generous gift, he felt in his heart that it was Olsten still thinking about the people who had been closest to him and looking after them all.

Everyone who had worked with Olsten before his disappearance had also received such a gift in and around the Belgravia area. Nancy had been left a small but luxurious flat in Sloane Square, as were Lily and her mother and also Mrs. Agno Stafros and her younger son.

Roy was looking forward to meeting all the old faces at the birthday party - it would be interesting to see how they were all doing. From time to time, he had kept in touch with Millicent, who had all the news about James and Danielle, but he had lost touch with the others and was looking forward to catching up with them all. He was still hopeful that they would all be working together eventually again one day.

His wife Doreen had been delighted when they had received an invitation to Amitola's party and although neither of them had ever met Amitola before, she had heard so much about the young girl that Olsten had appeared to have taken under his protective wing during those previous years.

Roy wondered if Olsten indeed knew of the impending celebration – *surely, he would not want to miss it.*

Chapter Twenty-Seven

It was a glorious morning - a sunny golden day and the birds were singing loudly outside Amitola's bedroom window, almost deafening her. She leapt out of bed and skipped across to the French doors, which opened onto a balcony over the terrace of the ancient manor house where they lived. She stepped out of the doors and stretched her arms high above her head, breathing in the fresh air.

Today was her twenty-first birthday and she was feeling happy and at peace with the world. She felt different somehow, as if she was about to step into a new life and world -a life that she seemed to have been long awaiting and one that had been waiting for her. She closed her eyes and in the centre of her consciousness she saw a figure standing by her side in another place - a faraway place which she felt was familiar to her.

She was suddenly startled when a small bird flew onto her shoulder tweeting loudly in her ear - her eyes flew open at that moment and the picture in her mind faded. She sat down on the edge of the small wooden bench on the balcony and gazed across the vast, green lawns spread out from the house below, which were bordered by rows and rows of flowerbeds filled with a colourful array of beautiful flowers. This had been her home for most of her life and she suddenly felt a feeling of sadness that she was soon to leave it for another life.

Her parents had organized this huge party to celebrate her birthday, and she was planning to tell them and her friends about her impending engagement to Orbido. She was so happy - it was as if she had been waiting for this day all her life and now that the day had finally arrived, she wanted it to be perfect.

From that very first moment of meeting Orbido, she could not get over the feeling that she had met him somewhere before; he reminded her so much of someone, she was not sure who, but someone she had known before. At the time, she had told herself that it would come to her eventually; maybe it was someone from her past life she jokingly told herself. Orbido was the most gentle and kindest man she had ever met and apart from her father, the man she could most trust.

She suddenly thought of Mr. Ryder then and remembered all the times that he had protected her when she had had all those childhood accidents. He had always been there for her, and she had always trusted him to watch over her.

When he had disappeared, she had missed him so much, but when Orbido had come into her life, it was as if he had somehow replaced Mr. Ryder as her guardian angel -always looking out for her wellbeing.

Thinking about Orbido, it occurred to her how very much he reminded her of Olsten and how similar their personalities and appearance were. The two faces began to flash in her mind until they became as one.

She shook her head to clear her mind and tears slowly trickled down her face at the realization of her very true existence. Her dreams as a small girl had terrified her as she had seen herself spinning around in a dark, never-ending tunnel but now she thought that maybe it had been a premonition of a journey in her life and a forewarning of what was to come at the end of her passage in time. Those constant dreams throughout the years had puzzled her and even now as those dreams had begun to creep into her daydreams she also felt a surge of excitement.

After she had showered and dressed, Amitola ran down the stairs to join her parents outside on the veranda having breakfast. She sat down and sipped a glass of freshly squeezed orange juice. Her mother then dished up some eggs, small sausages and hash browns with toast and placed the plate in front her which she immediately tucked into. Mrs. Defoe smiled as she watched her daughter enjoying her breakfast - she had always had a good appetite.

'I envy you, dear,' she said. 'I don't know how you can eat so much and stay so slim.'

'You used to be exactly the same when you were that age,' Mr. Defoe said. 'But now, of course, you have what is known as the middle-aged spread.'

'Nonsense, I'll have you know that I do not class myself as middle-aged yet,' she replied, smiling and winking at Amitola.

Her father had been reading his usual morning paper but laid it down on top of the table when Amitola had finished her juice and sat looking at her. She looked from one face to the other and started laughing as she then continued to tuck into her food.

'Goodness, you both look so serious,' she said as she looked up, chewing a mouthful of food. 'Mm, mm, this is delicious, Mother – I could eat a horse, I'm so hungry.'

'Happy Birthday darling, your father and I have a special gift which we would like you to have now. We have several gifts for you, but they can wait until later this afternoon.

Her mother stood up from the table, hugged, and kissed Amitola and then handed her a large leather box with her name engraved on the top in gold letters. When she opened the box, she gasped when she found the most beautiful set of emerald jewellery including a necklace, earrings and bracelet.

'Oh, such beautiful jewellery; emeralds are my absolute favourite,' she said, as she flipped the lid back down and traced her fingers over the gold lettering on the top. As her fingers touched the lettering small sparks began to emit from the box and she blinked and quickly turned to see if this had been seen by her parents, but they both appeared not to have noticed.

Her father who had also stood up from the table, took her head in his hands and lovingly kissed her first on her forehead and then on the tip of her nose.

'Amitola,' he said very seriously, 'your mother and I have something very important to tell you. It is something that we always believed that we should have told you a long time ago, but it was stipulated that this information was only to be passed to you on your twenty-first birthday. Your mother insisted that it was your right to know some time ago, but I want you to understand that we have always been so afraid that we would lose you'.

'What is it, Dad – you will never lose me; I love you both so much and I could not have wished for better parents.'

Mrs Defoe poured some fresh coffee and as she handed Amitola's cup to her, she leant across and kissed her forehead.

'And we could not have wished for a more perfect, loving and considerate daughter,' she said as she sat down at the table. 'We always wanted a large family, but it was not meant to be. You see, Amitola, we are your foster parents and took you under our care from a convent orphanage when you were a newborn. We were so happy at the time and did not care if we were given a boy or a girl. When we first set eyes on you, we both fell madly in love with you; it was as if we were especially chosen for you as you were for us.'

Mrs. Defoe paused as she took a paper napkin from the table to dab the tears in her eyes and blow her nose.

'When we brought you home with us,' she continued, 'it was as if you were our own and right from the very start you were so perfect, such a happy special baby. So, let us tell you more about what was in the official papers. An anonymous businessperson left a very generous and substantial amount of money in trust for you. It is believed that this is the same person who delivered you to the convent orphanage, mysterious as it may sound. I must admit I absolutely loved the idea of how you were found outside a convent. Imagine all the mystery surrounding you, although some may think tragic, I thought it was so romantic.'

Mr. Defoe rolled his eyes at this last comment. 'She has always been an incurable romantic, although not so much where I am concerned,' he said, laughing, before his face became quite serious again.

'There has been quite a lot of controversy surrounding this whole situation for several years, but it appears that this anonymous person has securely protected your personal interests and wellbeing throughout your whole life. The package of papers that we were left also enclosed a gold band on a chain with instructions that you should wear the ring on your twenty-first birthday.' Mrs. Defoe said, as she handed the ring to Amitola. When she placed the ring on the index finger of her left hand, it began to radiate warmth throughout her whole body.

She sat looking at both her parents with a smile on her face.

'I have known this for a long time now. Do you remember the psychoanalyst I was seeing after I was attacked in the park that evening coming back from a friend's party? Of course, you do - how could we ever forget that part of my life. I can talk about it without my whole body shaking now. At the time I was so terrified at what could have happened if that very kind Mr. Ryder had not been in the area at that particular time. Although I never wondered how Mr. Ryder was always around to rescue me from general childhood accidents, I did finally realize in later years that he was a very special person who had come into my life.'

Mr. and Mrs. Defoe glanced across the table at each other when Amitola mentioned the incident in the park which seemed so long ago now. During those times, Mr Ryder had always seemed to be around to protect Amitola and his doing so had baffled them for the longest time, to the extent that they were determined to discover the truth as to the exact connection between Olsten and their daughter. That said, they had both been afraid of delving too much into something that they could not fully comprehend.

It had been such a sad loss to them when he had disappeared so suddenly – it was as if some strange powerful force had surrounded Olsten and was out to ruin him after that last incident in the park. They had heard days later that he had been arrested and charged and arrested for the murder of a wealthy young woman, the very young woman who had attacked Amitola in the park.

Olsten's reputation and business had come crashing down around him. The press had attacked his credibility from every angle, making him appear like some demonic, evil monster. The whole affair had spiralled out of control beyond belief.

'I know what you are thinking, Dad,' Amitola said, as she sat watching him. 'I never believed anything bad that was said about Mr. Ryder - he is a kind and wonderful man. He always seemed to be there for me, and I felt safe with him. I often wonder where he is now. I do miss him terribly.'

'Listen, let's not go into this today,' Mr. Defoe said. 'We have a wonderful party organized for you this evening Amitola, and we want you to have a fantastic time. We love you very much and want the very best for you. Orbido tells us that he has a surprise announcement to make, and we can guess what that surprise is going to be.'

Amitola started to laugh. 'Don't spoil it now, Dad, I know you know what Orbido is planning to announce.'

'Anyway,' Mrs. Defoe said, as she stood up from the table. 'I'm going to call the florists now and make sure that all the flowers are delivered on time. I have left more of your gifts on your dresser for you, Amitola, we hope you like them.'

Mrs. Defoe had tears in her eyes as she turned to walk away through the French doors back inside the house. She had not realized just how completely stable and mature their daughter was and she felt that they were so lucky. She had often worried through the years what sort of woman Amitola's real mother was; did Amitola have bad genes; would she inherit bad flaws in her character. She knew that all these fears were natural when fostering a baby of unknown origin.

There were so many things that Mrs. Defoe had been afraid of during the earlier years. Now she could relax, as she believed that this had been the ultimate test of Amitola's character. On hearing this news, she could have quite easily exploded, demanding to know the whereabouts of her real parents and then go off searching for them.

Amitola suddenly appeared behind her and linked arms with her mother and said, laughingly, 'I can't take all the credit for my sound and secure character, your loving upbringing has a lot to do with it, you know'

'Oh,' Mrs. Defoe said, 'you startled me, Amitola. There you go again, reading my mind.'

'Come on, Mother, you were thinking out loud, you often do that, you know. It's no wonder I always know what's on your mind, it's not difficult,' Amitola said, playfully. Then her voice became serious as she continued.

'Yes, of course I wondered what could have happened to my real mother and what kind of woman she was to have just abandoned me like that outside a nunnery, but I just feel so thankful that I was rescued by two wonderful people like you. You are the only mother and father that I know and love, I don't need anybody else. I feel so lucky and blessed to have you both'.

Mrs. Defoe turned and kissed Amitola again and stood watching her as she went skipping up the wide stairway to her bedroom. She stood there for a few seconds thinking about the box of beautiful jewellery that she had handed to Amitola – *what a lucky girl to have been left such a wonderful gift to be worn on such a special day.*

'I just love the set of emerald jewellery that has been gifted to me, Mother,' Amitola called down from the top of the stairs. 'It will, of course, be perfect with my white satin dress'.

'I told you – you are doing it again, reading my mind, but I can't take credit for choosing the jewellery. That was left for you a very long time ago.' Mrs. Defoe replied smiling to herself as she walked on through to their study to check on delivery services.

Constance Defoe sat down at her desk and picked up a photograph of Amitola that had just been taken the week before, she looked so stunning. She was just about to set the photograph back down on the desk when, for a second, she thought she had clearly seen a shadow of a person standing directly behind Amitola embracing her.

She blinked her eyes and looked more closely at the photograph again, but it was almost as if the shadow had faded as quickly as it had appeared - a ghostly shadow of a tall man. She leant across the desk and pulled out a piece of tissue paper from its box to wipe over the glass covering on the picture frame.

'I must have imagined it in this lighting,' she told herself, frowning. It had looked so clear for that split second.

So much mystery had surrounded Amitola throughout her life and although sometimes it had alarmed her, well, frightened her if she was completely honest, through the years she had become more and more used to all the odd and unusual occurrences. Although Mr. Defoe never seemed to question any of the events, he always especially had his suspicions about Olsten being constantly around monitoring their daily life with Amitola.

Mrs. Defoe had noticed that Amitola, right from an early age, was special and, in particular, had been able to read her mind. It had astonished and alarmed her at first that Amitola always seemed to know exactly what she was thinking - it was as if she was able to read a person's innermost secrets. She felt sure that her daughter was possibly psychic; this was another romantic notion of hers. She had discussed it with her husband who had always laughed off any such notions. It had puzzled Mrs. Defoe all the same.

Mr. Defoe had remained seated at the breakfast table after his wife and Amitola had gone back into the house. His mind went back to that whole episode seven years ago. It seemed such a long time for the facts to remain in his memory like little crystal daggers stabbing away at his heart.

The headline in the London Times had read: "SUCCESSFUL BUSINESSMAN CHARGED WITH MURDER".

The full story went into details about past incidents leading up to the present-day event; for all intents and purposes, the accused looked guilty before even going before a court of law.

He remembered Mr. Ryder's face so clearly on that day when he had called by to see them a short time after his arrest. Olsten had informed them that he was going away for a long time but that he wanted them not to worry and that he would be in touch with them at a later time. They had not been aware at that time that he had absconded from a prison cell.

Mr. Defoe lit a cigarette and sat back in the chair. It had been a huge relief to him and his wife when Amitola had met Orbido, and she seemed so happy and contented these days. She had met Orbido by chance in a library after her fifteenth birthday and he had approached her and had introduced himself as her new guardian angel. She had laughed at him thinking that it was quite a unique introduction, but it had certainly attracted her attention at the time.

Amitola had told them excitedly later that evening that she had met a most unusual boy. They began seeing each other on a regular basis and she had soon after invited him to meet her parents. Mr. and Mrs. Defoe had liked him from the very start, and he soon became a regular guest at their house. At such a young age he seemed a forceful young boy but with an extremely calm temperament. He also seemed to be exceptionally mature beyond his years and Mr. Defoe felt that it was for this reason that his wife liked him so much; she had great confidence in him and felt comfortable and secure in the knowledge that he took care of their daughter. As the years went by and the relationship matured and grew serious, Mr. Defoe could see very clearly that they had become soul mates and were inseparable. The only thing that puzzled him and his wife was the fact that Orbido did not freely offer any information about his lineage, and he was, in fact, very reluctant to talk about anything to do with any immediate family members or relatives. As far as they were led to believe, his family came from a very long line of wealthy ancestors. It had all sounded a little vague to them at the time but quickly became of little importance in the face of their daughter's happiness.

Chapter Twenty-Eight

As Mrs. Defoe was about to lift the handset to call the florists, the doorbell rang. She walked through to the hallway and called out to her husband that she was going to answer the door. Opening the door, she felt a rush of warmth in her veins when she saw Millicent standing there.

Millicent had kept in touch throughout the past years, and they had developed a close friendship. She had married a short time after the tragic events concerning Mr. Ryder and had just recently had a baby boy. Mrs. Defoe had been delighted when she had heard that Millicent had met Danielle's brother in Paris, and they had fallen madly in love almost at first sight. Of course, according to one of Millicent's earlier letters to Mrs. Defoe, Danielle had conspired in this meeting and had been elated when her brother and dear friend not only got on so well with each other but were a perfect match.

Mrs. Defoe took Millicent's hand and pulled her inside. Millicent laughed; she was so happy to see her old friend, and flung herself into her arms, giving her a bear hug.

'It's so lovely to see you, Millicent, you look wonderful. How is little Aaron doing? I bet he has taken over your life completely.'

'He has the lungs of a lion; he literally roars when he needs feeding. I never get any time for myself since he turned up and I could just die for a whole night's sleep. Leon is good though; he does make an effort to get up during the night when he knows that

I am just too exhausted to move. Several friends assure me that this is just temporary and that after a few months they start to calm down. I can't wait and the thought of being able to sleep peacefully through a whole night just excites me more than I can tell you.'

'It just depends on the baby,' Mrs. Defoe said, as she steered Millicent into the kitchen. 'Some babies just get louder and louder and never stop crying from the minute they wake up to the time they go back to sleep; whenever you can actually get them to go back to sleep.'

Millicent hurled herself down on a chair in the kitchen suddenly looking completely and utterly deflated.

'Oh, please don't tell me that, I am going to age before my time,' she said in mock desperation as she slumped dramatically on the tabletop. 'I just hope I can get rid of this extra weight that I put on during my pregnancy and I want to cut off all my frizzy hair. I swear my freckles multiplied by the hundreds and literally blended together during those nine months of pregnancy,' she said, sighing hopelessly.

'My goodness, you look gorgeous and positively glowing, Millicent. I can't think what mirror you have taken to looking into, but I can tell you now that you are looking radiant,' Mrs. Defoe said, laughing. 'Do you want a good strong hot cup of coffee, iced tea or some wine,' she added, as she turned to open the fridge.

'Oh, a strong cup of coffee is good for me to begin with and then I may just have a glass or two of wine later,' Millicent said as she lit up a cigarette, winking at Mrs. Defoe.

'My two vices at the moment, or should I say, the two redeeming factors in my life: my cigs and wine. No, I am only kidding; Leon and Aaron are the most precious gifts that I could ever wish for. Leon happened to me at a time when I most needed him and we are truly and completely happy together. He not only brought romance and sophistication to my life but total and complete stability. That day when everything changed so drastically seems like a hundred years ago now, don't you think, Constance?'

Mrs. Defoe poured some coffee and handed the cup to Millicent.

'We all seem to be thinking of the same thing today. We had to speak to Amitola today about the official papers outlining our foster care legal rights. She said she had known ever since the attack in the park before Olsten was arrested. I have somehow always dreaded that she would become hysterical and demand the identity of her real mother. But she just kind of smiled at us in that serene way of hers. And, of course, it has bought all those memories of the attack flooding back to us today. I have always felt that poor Mr. Ryder was just as much a victim of the tragedy as poor Celeste was; of course, not in the same sense, but he was after all destroyed completely. That whole affair with Celeste Harrington was so terrible and I can't imagine what possessed him to kill her in the circumstances.'

'Oh, come on, Constance,' Millicent said. 'We have been over this again and again. You don't honestly believe that he killed her. He was a wonderful, charming and gentle man, who would never harm anybody. I know there had been evidence of a struggle with Olsten when Celeste had literally attacked him during that evening when she had tried to abduct poor little Amitola. He told me that she had appeared either drunk or high on some illegal substance and had become hysterical and had literally scratched his face and neck to shreds. He had said on many occasions that the poor woman had been slowly becoming completely demented and he worried about her safety and hinted at his concern that she would inevitably come to some serious harm. Besides which, after Olsten's disappearance, he was cleared of all charges because of the forensic evidence.'

'Yes, my dear, but it came out later that the poor girl had absolutely no history of taking illegal substances. Her mother categorically denied that there was any truth in those allegations of drug addiction. She was adamant in her belief that Olsten had killed her daughter to keep her quiet about certain knowledge that she had about his past personal history.'

'Yes, it was a terrible thing to happen to Celeste but it's ridiculous that Mrs. Harrington believed that Olsten killed her daughter to keep her quiet. Mind you, I could never understand her fixation where Amitola was concerned; after all, it really was no business of hers to go raking into Olsten's personal life as if he was keeping secrets from her. Believe me, I was right there when she came into Olsten's office on several occasions behaving completely irrational under the influence of either drink or drugs and making all kinds of accusations against Olsten.'

Millicent paused as she took a gulp of the hot coffee. 'This is so good, Constance. I must admit, I do miss a good hot cup of Colombian coffee although I do love the fruity flavours of the French coffee. Leon tells me that I drink far too much of the stuff and actually claims that this is probably the reason why I can't sleep at night.'

'In some ways,' she continued, as she set her cup down on the table, 'Olsten was quite a mysterious character, but I never tried to probe into his personal life. I believe he had been married before although he would never, ever speak about it. He kept a picture of a woman in his private quarters adjacent to his office. The woman was quite beautiful with long dark hair, and he was standing behind her with his arms around her in the picture. Whenever I questioned him about it, he just kind of brushed it aside and said he preferred not to talk about it.'

'But anyway,' she continued, picking up her cup again and taking another gulp of her coffee, 'that last particular time when he had seen Celeste, he said that she had been out of control and was consumed with rage and jealousy. When the police were going through his belongings in his office, the picture of Olsten and his wife was found shattered on the floor, almost as if someone had thrown it to the floor in a fury and ground the heel of his or her shoe on the glass. Celeste had on a previous occasion hurled the picture at Olsten after going into a rage at seeing the photograph. She took to snooping around his office and private quarters on many occasions. It was so strange when her body had later been found enclosed in that life size ceramic doll. Of course, not long after that, as we all know, Olsten went missing which the police took to be obvious proof of his guilt. I still refuse to believe that the whole sequence of events had anything to do with Olsten. I was so horrified at the discovery of the body, and I do understand that it all seemed to point a finger towards Olsten. But the Olsten I knew would never, ever harm a fly and I will never be convinced otherwise.'

Those memories came flooding back and her eyes began to tear up. Constance couldn't help noticing that Millicent's hand began to shake when she took out another cigarette and lit it.

Constance moved her chair right next to Millicent and put her arm around her shoulder hugging her close. Millicent quickly took out a tissue from her handbag to blow her nose which she realised with embarrassment was beginning to drip.

'But Millicent, you said yourself at the time that you became more and more apprehensive and puzzled at Olsten's integrity each time he popped up in Amitola's life when he felt that she was in danger. Didn't you think it strange when he always just happened to be around whenever Amitola seemed to be in some kind of peril? It was just too much of a coincidence that he always just happened to be in the same area at the same time. There were so many incidents over the years, and we were just completely amazed when Mr. Ryder always showed up at the scene. Of course, we never said anything at the time, but we were not blind and naturally at the back of our minds we knew that there had to be a connection.'

'Yes, I always wondered about that. There were so many times I wanted to ask him how and why, but I just backed off every time as he emphatically refused to discuss his personal life. I always suspected that his wife died in very tragic circumstances. At times, I noticed a deep sadness in Olsten, and I began to wonder if his wife had maybe died in childbirth, and he could only cope by watching over an orphaned child. He was not the type of person who would reveal his most innermost feelings, so I really tried not to probe too much.'

'Well, I don't know about you two,' Mr. Defoe said as he strolled into the kitchen, 'but I am going to take a swim before all the action starts around here. How are you, Millicent?' he asked, as he marched over to where she was sitting and kissed her on her forehead.

'I am certainly looking forward to all this action, George,' Millicent said, laughing. 'I told Leon this morning that it will be the first time that I have left the house without that little bundle of joy that we have created together, forever attached to my person. I am a little bit nervous about being away from him, but Mrs Belleau, our nanny, assures me that I have nothing to worry about. She tells me that she has seen ten children of her own grow up to be adults under her care and she is still happy to take care of more babies. God, the very thought of having ten screaming babies to bring up horrifies me.'

'I'm sure you will want another one sometime later in the future, Millicent, maybe a little sister for Aaron to have fun with and play the big brother to protect her at school,' Constance said with a grin.

'At the moment I am quite happy with just the one baby for now but when the memories of sleepless nights and constant feedings begin to slowly recede from my mind, maybe I will think about another one. But, for now, absolutely not – no, thank you very much.'

'I wish you would come and stay with us,' Mrs. Defoe said, 'instead of staying in that hotel. We would be more than happy to put you and Leon up here, wouldn't we, George? This house has fifteen bedrooms and eight bathrooms you know – positively fit for a rock star and we would really love to have you join us. Honestly, we would really enjoy having you here with us, Millicent, and so would Amitola; not that she would notice who was actually staying with us at the moment, her mind seems to be miles away these days.'

'We absolutely insist that you stay here with us. I'm sure you know how much we have missed you and have been waiting so long to see you and catch up on all your news,' Mr. Defoe said.

'I don't know,' Millicent said. 'You will already have a house full of guests over the next few days.'

'Millicent, dear, you know that I would much rather you stay here than in a hotel, even though you have a suite of rooms - it's still so impersonal. Please say that you will think about it.'

'You know, I think I would like that,' Millicent told her. 'Besides it would be good for us all to be together like this. I know that Leon would much prefer to be here especially with your huge garden grounds - it would make him feel less homesick.'

'That's settled, then,' Mr. Defoe said, leaning over and hugging them both.

'Right then, who's ready for a lovely glass of white wine?' Mrs. Defoe asked.

'Yes, please,' Millicent replied, jumping up to get some glasses.

Chapter Twenty-Nine

Later that afternoon Amitola stood in front of her dresser mirror admiring the emerald jewellery that her mother and father had given her earlier that day. The earrings and necklace looked stunning and perfectly suited the white satin dress that she had chosen to wear for her birthday celebration. She held out her hand to admire the beautiful ring that her mother had also given to her and blinked as the red stones suddenly seemed to transmit rays that had a strange hypnotic effect on her.

She looked up and stepped into the mirror as if in a trance and there he was waiting for her, those penetrating dark brown eyes gazing into her eyes. He took her hand and kissed it as he smiled at her and held out a beautiful red rose. As she bent over to smell the rose, he drew her closer to him. When she looked up again, she gasped when she looked into his face – it was a ghostly white face with steely blue eyes. She could feel his eyes boring right into her soul, and she grimaced as a sharp bolt of pain suddenly tore through her brain.

She began to struggle and wrenched herself away from him and then he seemed to spin away from her like a tornado - his loud manic laughter ringing in her ears. She looked down at the rose that she had clasped tightly in her hand and dropped it as it withered before her very eyes. The thorns of the stem had pierced her fingers, and she looked in horror as the blood trickled onto the carpet creating a bright red stain.

Amitola shuddered as she stood there peering closely into the mirror. She knew that she had just had one of her glimmers into the unknown, as she always called them. But this time she had felt a force so strong, penetrating right into her mind and for a second or two she had to really struggle to pull herself out of the feeling of being wrenched out of her body to a dark place. That face had frightened her, and she knew that it was an angry force and one that wanted to harm her or destroy her even. She glanced down at the carpet and was relieved to see that there was no bright red stain.

She picked up the photograph of Orbido on her dresser and traced a finger over the image of his smiling face and felt calm again just looking into those kind brown eyes. She had taken the photograph of him some time ago and had it framed especially to keep close to her in her bedroom. Whenever she awoke from one of those reoccurring dreams that she still occasionally had from her childhood years, of tumbling endlessly through open space, she would reach out for the photograph and hug it close to her chest to stop her hammering heart.

Just at that moment the telephone rang on her bedside table and even before picking it up she knew that it was Orbido. When she heard that soft, calming voice she relaxed immediately, and her hammering heart quietened. Since the very first day she had met him, he had had a calming effect on her and always seemed to know when she needed him.

Downstairs, Mrs. Defoe was busy with the hired helpers who were finalising the preparation of the food and finishing all the flower arrangements. There was a young band of musicians rehearsing outside and that reminded her to take out some food and drink for them as it was going to be a long afternoon and evening. There were quite a number of guests invited and most of them had sent over the gifts for their daughter, which she carefully placed in a storage cupboard.

Mrs. Defoe then thought about the doll that Mr. Ryder had given to Amitola many years ago as a birthday gift.

On that thought, she almost jumped out of her skin when her daughter suddenly appeared behind her and whispered softy in her ear,

'Do you remember this doll, Mother?' Amitola asked, as she tenderly traced the features of the doll's face with her finger. 'All this time and her beautifully painted features have never faded. Her dress is still as beautiful as when I first received her. Did you know that the jewellery is real diamonds and emeralds?'

Mrs. Defoe looked at the doll sadly as if it bought sad memories flooding back that she did not want to think about. 'Did you know that you used to sleep with this doll and hold on to it tightly through the night and if I tried to take it away from you, you cried out in your sleep?'

'I know,' Amitola said. 'I always felt so safe sleeping with this doll; I couldn't sleep without her even though she was so hard and dug into my neck.'

'Do you remember when you received the doll? It was so kind of Mr. Ryder to send it to you after your accident outside the library that time. Millicent had it delivered for you with some candy and flowers. It's so strange when you think about those times; it's almost as if you and Mr. Ryder were exactly on the same wavelength and your thoughts and his were connected, he always seemed to sense when you were in danger.'

Amitola smiled. 'Mother, you always were melodramatic, and you will never change, but I do love you so very much,' she said, as she turned away to go back to her room.

'By the way, dear,' Mrs. Defoe shouted after her, 'you look absolutely beautiful in that white dress and the emeralds suit you so much'.

'Thank you, Mother,' Amitola yelled back. 'I can't wait to see you in that red dress you are planning to wear this evening'.

'There she goes again,' Mrs. Defoe whispered to herself. She had originally planned to wear a black dress but had second thoughts as black had always made her look so drab. She had picked out the red dress only this morning and had not even mentioned it to Amitola.

Later that afternoon at precisely four o'clock when all the guests were mingling around in the vast garden drinking champagne, Mr. Defoe lightly tapped the side of his glass with a spoon for their attention, ready to make an announcement.

'As you know, we are all here to celebrate the twenty-first birthday of our dear daughter, Amitola,' he said, as he stood there with his arm around Amitola, his voice breaking slightly with emotion. 'And we are also here to announce her engagement to Orbido, the love of her life,' he said extending his hand out to the young man to join them.

Orbido walked across to Amitola, who had tears pouring down her cheeks. She held her hands out to him and when their hands clasped, there was suddenly a blinding flash of light and a loud whooshing sound and then they both vanished. The entire scene around them also completely fragmented, dissolving into nothingness at the same time – as if it had never existed.

Chapter Thirty

The journey had been long and time consuming and Jud had been satisfied that at long last he would finally be accepted as the supreme vanquisher and all would rightly be his. The victory over his enemy had been so gratifying. He would have ultimate power and control over their entire nation.

He was confident that he could now return to his realm as the proud successor, and she would ultimately have no other choice but to accept him as the new heir on her return. After all, he was willing to forgive her for her betrayal and for humiliating him by her rejection of him and choosing another over him. He could now claim her as his Queen and then he would punish her, just as he had punished all the other foolish and fickle hearted women.

He felt no pity now for all the women that he had punished, and he smiled at the thought that the one person he hated the most had been held accountable for his crimes. After he had gone on a rampage in the West End of London abusing, torturing and eventually killing all those rich spoilt creatures, he had felt a surge of power each time.

As he sat waiting to be transported to his final destination, he thought how effortless it had all been to mislead all those ignorant woman, especially the two most vulnerable women whose minds had been particularly easy to bend and control – he had enjoyed it immensely. His first mission had been to wheedle his way into Olsten's little empire by replacing his driver Demetrius, who he had callously removed out of the way. Thinking back now, although he had wanted to disrupt the whole running of Olsten's business and influence as many of his female key staff members as he could; poor broken-hearted Lily had proved to be of no real value to his plan in the end and he had decided to return her unharmed – after all, she was not immoral like all the others.

He had hoped that her disappearance would completely disrupt Olsten's business beyond repair, but it had turned out that business had gone on as usual. Nevertheless, he found it quite amusing that he had actually kept her hidden in her very own flat the whole time right under her own mother's nose.

Millicent had been comparatively untouchable. Her dislike and indifference to him had blocked his ability to delve fully into her sub-conscious mind to control her, although he had gradually been able to stab at her wellbeing and cause her to feel deep depression and worthlessness after Olsten had disappeared. He smiled to himself when he thought of her scoffing those contaminated chocolates, all the while being unaware that they had been laced with a strong depressive substance.

The most important cog in the wheel of Olsten's business had been Danielle, but she had also been impossible to manipulate and control. As Olsten's dress designer for the dolls, she would have been the perfect victim in order to destroy the business and bring it crashing down around him. But again, like Millicent, her obvious apathy towards him blocked his ability to even attempt to read her mind. She was a very strong-minded woman, and he found he had no hope of reaching her psyche in an attempt to control her.

His prime victim, though not involved in the business, had been perfect for the purpose of ultimately destroying Olsten's reputation and his whole life. Celeste had turned out to be not only extremely easy to gain control of, but fun for him to mould and manipulate which he had enjoyed immensely – after all she had been one of those immoral woman.

From that very first evening, disguised as his imaginary brother, when he had picked her up and taken her to Olsten's business office for the promised dinner date, she had been a perfect target. In ordinary circumstances he would have loved to have spent time with such a beautiful charming young woman; she had been putty in his hands and had succumbed to his charm immediately. But he had not been interested in ordinary circumstances. He had picked her out specifically to torment Olsten.

The scene had been set – Olsten had been away on business, and he had complete freedom of movement with no commitment to his usual duties. His exterior, of course, had been altered – he was able to change his outward appearance to suit a situation at all times.

When he had pulled up outside Celeste's house that evening to pick her up on the pretext of joining Olsten for dinner, she had come through her front door looking like an angel and he had decided then and there to have some fun with her. When she had climbed in the limousine ready to be taken to Olsten's office building, he had immediately detected that she felt a strong attraction to him, which had made it all the easier for him; such a fickle-hearted, immoral woman.

Being always of a flirtatious nature, Celeste had been quite dazzled by his good looks. He had been able to read her mind as she had sat in the back seat gazing at the back of his head thinking how lovely it would be to run her fingers through his thick black hair. She would have been mortified if she had known that he had been able to read every thought going through her mind at that time.

Such was the power of his ability to reach the centre of her consciousness, he had known it was going to be so easy to alter her emotions and seduce her. He was going to change her entire thought process - changing the storage of her knowledge and memories of her current existence. He had been completely confident that he could transform her whole personality ready to put his plan into action to ultimately destroy Olsten's reputation beyond repair.

She had been like a lamb to the slaughter when he had led her into the opulent lounge where Olsten usually entertained his guests. She had stood there peering around at the lavishness of the grand room, wondering why she had never been invited before, but at the same time wondering where all the other guests were.

'Such a beautiful woman should not have to be shared. I am sure Mr. Ryder wishes to have you all to himself without any interruptions,' he had said, reading her mind.

'Now let me take your coat and I will prepare you a drink that will knock your head off,' he added, smiling seductively.

'So, where is the beguiling Mr. Ryder – it's quite rude of him not to be waiting for me,' she had said, sitting down on one of the plush velvet sofas.

'He is going to be slightly delayed but has instructed me to take care of you in the meantime, which I fully intend to do,' he had replied, smoothly.

'Oh, I see and how do you intend to take care of me, precisely?' She had answered flirtatiously. 'After all, I don't even know your name.'

'Names are of no importance,' he had replied, winking at her.

She had sat there in excited anticipation watching him as he prepared a cocktail of champagne and brandy for her – it had been her very favourite, and he had known that. Then, he had quickly excused himself and the next moment, he returned in the manifestation of Olsten.

He smiled wickedly, standing over her as she had sat there slightly swaying from side to side in her tipsy state.

'There you are my darling girl. I am so happy that you accepted my invitation, and we certainly will not be telling Lewis about our little clandestine meeting of the mind, body and soul, will we?' he had said, as he held out one hand to help her to her feet.

She had stumbled slightly as she stood up and literally fell against him. He had wrapped his arms around her and led her straight through to the bedroom.

'I certainly will not be telling Lewis any such thing, I am having too much of a fabulous time,' she had said, looking up into his face.

She had been in a daze as he had carried out his seduction in a brutal and indifferent manner having no regard for her somewhat inebriated state. All the while, he kept whispering in her ear that she was to break off her engagement to Lewis and she was to save all her love and passion for him and only him.

Later, in the early hours of the next morning, when he had driven her back to her house, he had been satisfied that the ball had been set into motion and his mission could be swiftly concluded very soon. She had been his perfect victim and would be the ultimate ruin of his adversary.

Chapter Thirty-One

Sister Claudia raised herself up from her kneeling position after saying her prayers, kissing the cross around her neck and crossing herself as she stood up from the hard stone flooring in the huge, whitewashed chapel of the nunnery.

Not even the harsh, tightly wrapped coif around her head, fitting closely against her cheeks, could hide her beautiful classic Nefertiti-like features. Over the years, she had become accustomed to the stiff headdress although in the beginning she had found it very uncomfortable.

She would now find it very strange to remove these garments and leave the convent. It had been a sudden decision, but one that she found she desperately wanted. The convent had been like a peaceful, reclusive sanctuary to her but now she felt it was time to return to her former life. She had awoken that morning startled to see the ghostly form of a strange man standing at the foot of her bed smiling down at her. She had known at that moment that her life was about to change again.

She was still a young woman and would go out into the world again and make a new life for herself. It seemed an age ago when she had first become a nun, and it had been a life she had needed at that time. Now at the age of thirty-seven, she could easily blend back into the outside world; she could maybe marry and have another child, but this time she would not have to give it away.

She could hardly remember that tiny face from all those years ago, but she had known at the time that although she had given birth to the baby, it had never really been her own child. She had known that she had been chosen to be the vessel for the rebirth of a very special child.

Although at the time it had caused her life to come crumbling down around her, she had come to understand she had been chosen very carefully, a special mother for a very special child. But now she felt the time had come to rebuild her own life and to be reborn herself.

She quickly walked through the draughty passageway and as she stepped through to her private room, she closed the door with a sigh of relief. She stood for a long time scanning all her worldly goods, which consisted of a small, shabby suitcase and a picture of a small child that she kept on her small wooden bedside unit. She carefully laid out some garments on the top of her bed, clothes she had kept in a box underneath; clothes from when she had first arrived at the convent. She slowly removed her veil of ordination and then began to pull the full-length apron, scapular and cowl over her head and finally, the main tunic. After removing these heavy garments, she felt a sense of freedom – she felt as light as a feather.

She had begun her day as usual in the very early hours of the morning, clad in her habit, sitting in the pews; hands clasped and face turned towards the altar, deep in reverent thought, followed by half an hour of contemplative quiet and prayer. After breakfast, she had proceeded to the garden for the very last time where she oversaw the flower beds and, most importantly, the vegetable garden. This task had always been her passion that had given her years of mind soothing exercise while in the convent. She would miss this part of her daily life, but it was not something that would be out of her reach in the outside world. She would buy a villa with the biggest garden she could find and have a splendid garden all of her own.

Now as she dressed in her clothes from the past, she felt at peace and although she had no mirror to arrange her short hair, she ran her fingers through her thick, still glossy hair hoping that it was looking presentable, at least until she could visit a hair salon. The thought of being able to walk into a hair salon and have her hair washed and styled seemed wonderful to Claudia now and she smiled at this thought, remembering her former privileged, pampered and luxurious lifestyle.

She picked up a small package that she believed had presumably been left for her by her father and slipped it into a smart, fashionable handbag she had bought with her when she had first arrived. It was a very expensive bag; she suspected it was probably still very fashionable in spite of the number of years that had passed since she had first bought it. She understood that the package contained papers with instructions of where she should go if she would one day want to return to the outside world; there were also official papers with details of a bank account and financial arrangements for her personal welfare.

Although she had been banished from her family connections, she always knew that her father had never truly exiled her from his heart and mind – she had been his little princess.

She glanced around the small room with its stark, whitewashed walls for one final time, pulled on a lightweight jacket and calmly walked out of the door.

There were to be no goodbyes to any of the other nuns. It was a strict regulation in the convent, and it was one that she was not sorry about; she would find it heartbreaking, and she had had enough of heartbreak. She had made many friends amongst the other nuns especially when they were busy outside in the gardens where they could talk and laugh together, enjoying each other's company.

Once outside the convent, she stopped for a few moments to look up at the crumbling old building where she had spent so much of her life. She remembered now that stormy night when she had first arrived as a frightened young girl full of remorse and shame, he knew she had brought upon her family. That was all in the past now and she now held her head high as she turned and walked quickly towards the iron gates which had been left open for her exit.

A man climbed hurriedly out of the waiting car and walked towards her. He held out his hand to take her small suitcase and then opened the car door and she settled herself into the back seat. The smell of the leather inside of the car was heaven to her and she closed her eyes for a second as the car started up and slowly drew away from the iron gates. She felt no regret whatsoever at leaving behind the convent.

She had had some fleeting moments of doubt and dread just before stepping out of her room but now she was absolutely sure that she was doing the right thing.

The driver smiled at her in the rear-view mirror, and she smiled back. He opened the compartment in the dashboard of the car and took out some keys which he passed onto her.

'Those are the keys to your apartment, Madam,' he said. 'We are approximately four hours away, but we can stop along the way in order that you can have some lunch,'

Claudia was amazed when she realized that the keys were the original keys to her old apartment where she had lived from time to time in Florence with her beloved Gregory, in between staying at her parent's various opulent homes on special occasions all those years ago.

Her thoughts suddenly went to Gregory, she had not allowed herself to think about him in such a long time, years in fact; she had denied herself the luxury of those wonderful memories. She now wondered how life had been for him during the past years. She imagined that he had obviously married and now had children; she felt her eyes brimming with tears thinking of the image of his face.

He had been a waiter at one of the celebrated restaurants that she frequented in those days as a young sixteen-year-old girl with her parents and from the very first moment that he and she had laid eyes on each other; they fell in love. He would by now have acquired himself his very own restaurant as he had promised himself all those years ago. He had always told her they would live their life together independently without the wealth of her parents. They had conducted their clandestine relationship seeing each other in Florence when they could, without the knowledge of her parents who they had known would not approve of her seeing a man who was not in the very affluent circle of their family and friends.

For a time, they were immensely happy planning their future together, but when Claudia discovered that she was pregnant everything changed, and she was forced to be separated from Gregory and banished to America for the duration of her pregnancy. It had been a shock to both her and Gregory at the time as they had always been careful knowing that a pregnancy outside of a marriage would bring disrepute to her family at that time.

Thinking back, she had known the precise moment when she had become pregnant. After they had made love one night, she had suddenly awoken a short time after to a bright light in her room and had felt a tingling sensation in her stomach. She had immediately leaned over and attempted to awaken Gregory lying next to her. A feeling of euphoria had washed over her, and she had refused to think about the consequences at that time – she just felt overjoyed at the thought of being pregnant.

It had been a lonely time for her when she had been banished from Italy by her parents and sent to a clinic in America during her pregnancy. After giving birth and on hearing that her baby was to be given up for adoption the very next day, she quickly left the clinic in the early hours of the morning with her baby. She had had no idea of how she was going to be able to travel without her passport and money; she had simply known that she had to get away as quickly as possible.

As she had sat in a cold bus station wondering what to do, a tall dark-haired man walked over to her and sat down next to her. Although the bus station had been completely empty of any other awaiting passengers, she had not felt afraid of the man. He told her that his name was Orbido, and that he had come to help her. He assured her that she was not to feel afraid. At the time she had thought it madness to trust a complete stranger, but she had no feelings of fear.

That had been exactly twenty-one years ago and although she had been astonished by what the stranger had explained to her; she had realized that something unbelievably extraordinary had happened, something that she had been ordained to accept.

She had initially been so angry that her life had been completely shattered at the time by what she felt had been a violation of her body, she had felt used for something that had absolutely nothing to do with her. *Why her?* She had asked herself so many times. It was incredulous that not only had she been somehow chosen to be a vessel for the regeneration of another being, but the particular life form was actually from another realm.

True to his word the stranger in the bus station had taken care of everything and she was grateful to him in the circumstances. The situation was certainly beyond belief, but she knew that he was a very special person who had come into her life when she most needed help.

The journey was long and as they sped along, she glanced at her watch and noted that it was exactly four in the afternoon. She closed her eyes and relaxed right back in the seating of the car feeling a sense of peace and tranquillity. Suddenly, a blinding flash of light erupted before her eyes. She heard a loud whooshing sound, and her eyes snapped wide open. She felt as if she had awoken from a long, deep sleep.

She smiled, then, tears rolled down her face as she turned to see Gregory sleeping peacefully by her side in her beloved shabby chic bed. Leaning over, she kissed him all over his face; she felt as if they had been parted for a long time, and she never wanted to lose sight of him ever again. As she gazed at his young face, she was overwhelmed with a sense of elation.

He stirred at that moment and opened his eyes, puzzled by the tears streaming down her face and dripping onto his own.

'Ciao Bella, why are you crying? Has something happened while I have been sleeping,' he asked, smiling up at her.

Chapter Thirty-Two

James found himself floating around in a vast, open space filled with a sweet, swirling mist - the sensation was hypnotic. His eyes became heavy, and his eyelids began to flicker until he could not help but close his eyes and allow himself to slowly drift off to a faraway place. He did not struggle throughout the journey; he had no fear, rather he felt at peace and welcomed a tingling sensation slowly flowing through his veins.

When his journey came to a sudden halt, he opened his eyes and was startled to find himself in a huge, brightly lit celestial scientific laboratory. There were rows and rows of tall glass dome containers, enclosing men and women standing rigidly erect inside, undergoing a procedural overhaul process. They were all dressed in the same attire - tapered tight fitting silver apparel, silver boots and each had an identity card strapped to a belt around their hips.

As James looked from face to face, he was astonished by the fact that they were all incredibly youthful. There were no signs of any wrinkles or disfiguring marks on any one of the faces or bodies. These people were all tall and straight in stature and perfect to look at – almost like a batch of beautifully created and perfected living mannequins.

He was then led into a separate area by a high-ranking uniformed officer and instructed to wait. While he waited, he wandered over to a large, double glass door and stood looking out into a huge area of cultivated land with a variety of vibrant plant life. When he heard footsteps marching towards the room, he turned as a tall, regal looking man, who appeared to be the leader of the establishment, entered the room.

'Welcome to our kingdom,' the man said, smiling.

James gasped as he immediately realized that there was no mistaking the extraordinary resemblance; same towering height, same dashing broad smile and there was absolutely no mistaking that voice, and the way he expressed himself.

But, how could they have all possibly known or believed; it was too unbelievable for words and not in their wildest dreams could they have imagined or guessed the reality behind all the bizarre events that had occurred during the past years.

'That's right and I can totally understand how you find all this unbelievable,' the man said, extending his hand out and gesturing him to be seated.

James found himself face to face with Olsten and by his side stood Amitola. Olsten wore a white loose tunic belted at the waist and white pants, while Amitola wore a long, flowing white dress - both wore a crown on their heads. James sat there staring at them with an expression of total shock, his mouth wide open.

'Welcome to our astronomical community and allow me to introduce my wife to you,' Olsten said softly as he smiled at James. 'Queen Amitola,' he continued as he stood aside, and Amitola stepped forward and extended her hand out to James.

James immediately stood up and took her hand in his, drew her towards him and kissed the proffered hand. She smiled at him and there were tears of joy in her eyes. She looked so regal, but there were still signs of the young Amitola that James had come to know so well through the years as an earthling.

James stood gazing from one face to the other in amazement; Amitola appeared exactly the same in appearance but Orbido, or Olsten as he had known him, seemed taller and much younger than when he had last seen him.

'It's a long story —in my last temporary version of myself, as Amitola's fiancé, I was, of course, a lot younger than the version you knew so well during the years we worked together' Olsten said, reading James's thoughts. 'I am sure it must all appear to be so confusing to you, but I will explain everything.'

'What you see before you now,' Olsten began, as they walked back into the scientific laboratory, is the most sophisticated

machinery that you will ever see in your lifetime. This is our control centre where a thorough cleansing and cell renewal program is conducted. In a matter of minutes under the intense surge of electronically charged currents from this piece of apparatus, the cells and organs of a body are entirely regenerated to a state of utter perfection and flawlessness. Or it can be set to completely alter your whole appearance according to what settings you choose. Our people never age like the human body or deteriorate with disease after undergoing a regular renewal procedure. We can live for hundreds of years unless we choose to discontinue treatment, or our body suddenly begins to reject any further regenerative procedures.'

'Now, if there is anything you have always wanted to change about yourself, James, – here is your chance,' he said.

'But, before I explain everything to you,' he continued, 'first, let me offer you some American Bourbon., I happen to have a taste for it now and brought my own personal supply with me,' he said, laughing, as he pressed a button on a bracelet around his wrist.

Immediately, an opening appeared in the marble flooring and a glass dome spacecraft elevator arose to transport them underground.

'Don't worry,' Olsten turned to James as he guided him into the glass dome, together with Amitola. 'This dome will not change you; it's our version of your elevator and this button on my wristband is the key to our personal quarters. We are about to go underground now in a flash.'

'Now I know you are just showing off,' James laughed nervously, as he stood rigidly, almost afraid to move a muscle, once inside the glass dome elevator.

Before James knew it, they had descended into the royal quarters below ground level. As he looked around the huge palatial drawing room within their quarters, he could see various personal effects which Olsten had obviously been loath to leave

317

behind in his various properties on earth. Amitola laughed as she looked at James's obvious look of utter dismay and disbelief as he looked around him.

As James sat down on the white leather seating with his glass of Bourbon in one hand and cigar in the other, he could see a giant screen on the other side of the room slowly emerging from the flooring, the bright lighting in the room began to dim and when the screen was switched on he found himself watching what looked like a home movie featuring a small girl playing with a beautiful ceramic doll and then the film went on to feature a lovely teenage girl attending her graduation ball and then, finally showing a stunning young woman on the day of her twenty-first birthday and engagement.

Amitola had looked so beautiful on the day of her engagement. It had been a wonderful day. James could see all the familiar faces -Mr. and Mrs. Defoe, Millicent, Leon and Aaron and his own darling Danielle, pregnant with their baby daughter, who they had already named Mai at that time. Millicent's mother and father were also there, as was Nancy with her new husband Peter.

When Orbido, as he had been introduced to them, and Amitola had joined hands, a sudden flash had emanated around the room, and they had both vanished before their very eyes.

As James stared at the screen, he could clearly see that they had both been wearing a gold wedding band that had sent waves of energy as soon as their hands had touched. When the blinding eruption occurred, everything and everybody had been caught up in a huge torrent and powerful force that had sent them all back in time.

'We are now in another time zone, far into the galactic futuristic space epoch,' Olsten now explained to James. 'I was transported back in time to your world when we first met, known to you at that time as Olsten Ryder, but my given name here is Orbido – King Orbido. I know that what I am going to tell you may sound unbelievable, but let me explain from the beginning,' he paused now as his put his arm around Amitola's shoulders and bent down to kiss her forehead.

'It all began twenty-one years ago,' he continued. 'In our time zone and on our orb, we were conducting a simple standard rejuvenating program for Amitola – these are conducted on a regular basis. Unbeknown to us and for quite some time, as it turned out, one of our subjects had been in the process of a devious plot to overthrow me from my supremacy here. He had, unbeknown to the operators here, tampered with the program during Amitola's session and sabotaged the procedure by reprogramming the whole process.' He paused for a few seconds to allow James to absorb all the information, realising how bizarre it all sounded.

'During that process, Amitola's body regressed back in time, so much so that she was reborn again on earth. I followed to watch over her and to wait for her to mature to the exact age on earth that she had been when her program had dangerously been tampered with. Olsten, or Orbido, paused again at this point and smiled at James' expression of utter scepticism.

'As you have probably guessed, she was reborn on earth in the natural way and was plummeted down by a powerful gravitational wave and impregnated into a young Italian girl of noble birthright. We thereafter met at a bus station in New York one evening when she was fleeing from a clinic after giving birth and I assisted her and made travel arrangements for her to travel back to Italy with her newborn where she entered a convent and became a nun. At first, she was astonished and terrified when I explained to her that she had been a vessel for the rebirth of my wife and as you can imagine she thought me a mad man. I was finally able to convince her that no matter how

319

extraordinary it sounded, it was the absolute truth, and she put her complete trust in me. The choice of becoming a nun was entirely her own decision and I respected that and although I tried to influence her to go back to her previous life with her parents, she made it clear that it was her wish to become a nun at that time.'

'It's not only extraordinary but near impossible to believe,' James said, rubbing his beard.

'I completely understand how bizarre it all sounds to you,' Olsten said. 'It was agreed that her newborn be left outside a convent of her choice and thereafter placed in a well-established home with foster parents. I delivered the newborn to the convent together with a package of documents with strict instructions as to the baby's welfare. I personally selected Mr. and Mrs. Defoe as the ideal foster parents based on their exceptional characters – I knew and trusted that they were the perfect choice. I monitored the child's welfare throughout her time on earth until she reached the age of twenty-one, at which time I reclaimed her as my wife and together we returned to our natural realm here.'

He again paused; he couldn't help smiling at the expression on James's face.

'The whole situation would have been straightforward if it had not been for my driver Kyle, alias Doctor Jud Durand, no less,' Olsten explained. 'It was my very own brother Jud, who was the mutinous individual that caused all the turmoil and frustrations throughout the final years of my time on earth. When his operation had been successful in sabotaging Amitola's rejuvenating process and banishing her from our realm, he then went through a total physical change himself and followed me to earth to generate as much destruction as he could to attempt to endanger the life of Amitola throughout her lifetime on earth. He first introduced himself into my life when I selected him as a suitable replacement for my chauffeur

Demetrius at the time. It ultimately became clear to me that poor Demetrius had been conveniently removed out of the way in the worse possible way. All these attempts during the waiting period were intended to thwart our return to our imperial ruling here.'

He paused for a moment before continuing. 'Unfortunately, I could not read him, as being my very own brother, he had blocked my ability to scan his mind. Of course, the real victim during the unfortunate period was Celeste,' he said, regretfully. 'Kyle, or should I say Jud, had been able to completely brainwash Celeste and control not only her mind but also her whole life at that time, which he destroyed in the end by terminating her life. She had been the major damaging tool in his attempt to destroy my whole reputation. No matter how baffling it must have appeared to you and the authorities, when I was able to disappear after being detained for further investigation following her murder, I had to go out of sight and examine the matter myself. I could not possibly risk being held indefinitely and quite possibly losing my power to evaporate my presence at will. I never imagined that he would enclose Celeste's body in that life-sized doll to incriminate me in such way that there could not be any shadow of a doubt that I was guilty in the circumstances.'

As he listened to this incredulous story, James gulped back his Bourbon and puffed away at his cigar in total amazement at what he was hearing. He had been puzzled so many times during the years that he had known Olsten, but he could never have imagined all this – it was all so incredibly astonishing and unbelievable.

He had to admit to himself now, though, when he really thought about it, that he had at times felt Olsten seemed to be from another planet. He had dismissed the thought at the time, but now, it all made sense!

'In the meantime,' Orbido continued, 'corrective action has been taken and Kyle, or should I say, Doctor Jud Durand, has

been bought before our Supreme Court of Justice here and is, as I speak, being detained indefinitely in another part of our sphere with no chance of a reprieve. It was initially voted that he that he should be immediately executed for his crimes - sentenced to death under a pendulum or burning under the lava of a volcano, but I decided to be lenient and send him to our toughest detention centre - one that harbours creatures that feed on fear.'

James sat there nodding his head; he was speechless.

'We take mutiny very seriously here and take every precaution to protect ourselves against this type of danger. It will never happen again in our lifetime here. It also came to our attention that Doctor Jud Durand, in his infinite wisdom, was also in the process of stock piling soldiers in freezing tubes and was planning to conquer the universe, beginning with Earth. He planned to unleash his wrath across the entire universe and test his strength and courage to prove superiority. His ultimate hope was to be selected as supreme leader of all alien civilizations. Let's just say he was completely insane. It all began a long time ago when he became deranged and obsessive as a young boy and when we became adults and fell in love with the same woman, he began to hate me when Amitola rejected him and chose me over him; in fact, he grew to hate all women.'

James by now looked ashen and could not speak. He was astonished at what he was hearing.

'You may remember,' Orbido said, turning again to James, 'how we racked our brains about all those times I was under surveillance, and I could never figure out who the person actually was. I mean, you cannot imagine how puzzled I felt when I could not even begin to read that man's mind! I should have recognized that it had to be somebody from my own globe who had blocked the pattern of his brain from my natural mind probing aptitude. All the time I thought that he was *working for Celeste, but he was right under my nose! My own brother. The poor woman never stood a chance under his manipulative power. This type of mind control completely freezes and numbs the victim's brain and the whole functioning of the victim's body is pre-programmed and activated by the controller, who, in this case was Jud, masquerading not only as my chauffeur, Kyle, but as her personal bodyguard, and not to mention masquerading as myself at times. To change appearance so frequently eventually weakened the structure of his mind, Jud was considerably handicapped towards the end while he was actively conducting his reign of treachery on earth. It was for this reason that I was eventually able to scan his mind when his barrier began to weaken and eventually break down.'*

Orbido paused again, before continuing. He was only too aware that it was a lot for James to take in.

'When I was finally reunited with Amitola, my queen, my wife, all the anguish and terrible things that happened to you all during my long wait on earth - twenty-one years to be precise, were erased and all was reverted back to how it was before I met you all.

Chapter Thirty-Three

James awoke with a start at the sound of his alarm clock beeping loudly by the side of his bed. When he lifted himself up from his pillow, his head ached; he swung his legs over the side of the bed and stood up feeling unsteady on his feet. He felt groggy from the deep sleep and bizarre dream that he had just come out of. As he walked into his bathroom to take a shower, parts of the dream came back to him.

He had no idea where such a strange dream could have come from, and he could only think that at some time he had seen a movie incorporating a similar story line that had manifested into his subconscious mind.

After taking a hot shower, he dressed carefully, as today he was due to have a meeting with Danielle Fontaine who owned a huge, successful collectable doll company, and he was hoping that he was going to be joining her empire as her private lawyer.

He had recently just come back from the States where he had been working as a freelance lawyer to several top legal offices in New York. One of his private clients had been a Mr. and Mrs. Defoe, two successful architects who were also returning to the United Kingdom at the same time as he had decided to make a new start. His clients were also looking forward to making a new start. They had recently been able to adopt a baby girl and were due to travel to a nunnery in Italy where a fifteen-year-old girl from the poorest region of Naples had given birth to a baby that had immediately been put up for adoption.

On arrival in the United Kingdom, both James and Mr. and Mrs. Defoe had promised to keep in touch. It was Mrs. Defoe who had given James the contact details for Danielle Fontaine, who she had informed him, was looking for a reputable lawyer to hire as her own personal legal representative.

James had purchased a one-bedroom apartment in the impressive Harbour Central in Canary Wharf. As a professional, the style, convenience and comfort in a new luxury development was perfect for James. All residents had the luxurious access to a private balcony, overlooking Mill Wall Dock and on a good day, he liked to sit out on this balcony drinking his first cups of coffee of the day.

As he was drinking his second coffee that particular morning, his intercom rang and when he answered he was informed that Ms. Fontaine's personal driver was waiting outside to drive him to her office in Berkley Square. He quickly gulped down the remainder of his coffee, grabbed his jacket and made his way down the stairs and out of the large main door where the driver was waiting for him.

'Good morning, Sir. My name is Demetrius, and I am Ms. Danielle Fontaine's personal driver,' he said, as he opened the passenger door for James.

'Thank you, Demetrius,' James replied as he climbed into the front passenger seat.

As they pulled out of the driveway, James again began thinking about his strange dream and how vivid the dream had been – it had all seemed so incredibly real at the time.

When Demetrius pulled up outside the office building and James walked through the front door, the man in the reception area looked up from his desk with a broad welcoming smile.

'Good morning, Sir,' he said when James stood directly in front of the reception desk.

'Good morning, I have a ten o'clock appointment with Ms. Fontaine,' James replied. He noted the man's name on his ID badge was Roy and he had an uncanny feeling that he had seen his face before, but he could not recall where.

After asking James to take a seat, Roy picked up the phone and rang through to Ms. Fontaine's secretary's office to announce the arrival of Mr. Lambert.

Almost immediately a young woman with a mane of red curls tumbling over her shoulders and a sunny face full of freckles came into the reception room to meet James and he was then taken up the stairway towards Ms. Fontaine's office.

When James was shown into Danielle's office, she stood up from her seat and held out her hand to shake his.

'I'm so pleased to meet you, Mr. Lambert, please take a seat,' she said, smiling.

'It's my pleasure to meet with you, Ms. Fontaine,' James said, smiling back. He couldn't help feeling that there was an instant attraction between them. There was a spark when their hands made contact.

'Please, call me Danielle,' she said as they both sat down. She picked up her phone and rang through to her secretary for fresh hot coffee.

As they both began to go over all details of the offer of employment, the secretary came through the door with fresh hot coffee and a plate of Danish pastries.

'Oh, thank you, Millicent,' Danielle said, as her secretary placed the tray onto a large coffee table at the other side of her office.

Danielle stood up from her desk and motioned James to join her to sit on a leather sofa facing the coffee table.

'Could you please remind Lily and the rest of the team that we will have a meeting at two to discuss the latest miniature clothing and jewellery designs,' she then said to Millicent as she walked over to join James on the sofa.

'This is much more comfortable – don't you think,' she said, as she held out the plate of Danish pastries when they were both seated.

'I just love a Danish pastry first thing in the morning with my endless cups of hot coffee. Do have one, please.'

'I don't mind if I do,' James replied, smiling into her eyes. *They were incredibly lovely eyes,* he couldn't help thinking as she poured the steaming, aromatic coffee into two cups.

As they chatted away, the telephone rang on her desk and Danielle stood up, excusing herself to answer the incoming call but before she had even lifted up the handset, there was a loud knocking on her door and then a young woman came bursting into the room with Roy right behind her.

'Sorry about this, Ms. Fontaine, she insisted on coming right up without an appointment *as usual,*' Roy announced, frowning.

'Good morning, Danielle,' the young woman gushed. 'I know I have a bad habit of barging into your office without a prior appointment, but I just had to see you.'

'Good morning, Celeste, and congratulations on your engagement to Lewis,' Danielle said, walking over to Celeste to hug her and kiss her on each cheek.

'Do excuse us, James; this is one of my dear friends and she has a bad habit of charging into my office whenever she feels like it,' she added, laughing.

'I want to invite you all to my celebratory engagement party at the Ritz,' Celeste announced.

'I have invited Millicent, Lily *and* her boyfriend Demetrius - I have just been told they have also got engaged and they are delighted to attend at my engagement gathering – it could be a combined celebration,' Celeste continued.

'Yes, I would love to join you at your engagement party at the Ritz – how exciting. Let's have lunch tomorrow if you have no other prior engagement and we can have a good old chat.'

'I would love to, Danielle; it has been a few weeks since we have had a chance to catch up on everything,' Celeste replied.

'I know you have had a few little niggling differences with Roy on reception at times, but I do think you should perhaps invite him and his wife – we are after all a big, combined family here.' Danielle said, raising her eyebrows playfully as Roy turned and left the office slightly embarrassed, but smiling all the same.

It had been a huge amusement to them over the past year how Roy and Celeste had rubbed each other the wrong way when they had first met in reception. Although initially Celeste had found his manner quite arrogant and overbearing, she had quickly recognised his very unique eccentric, but enormously kind character and they were often found laughing together in the reception area whenever she came to meet Danielle for a luncheon date.

'Yes, of course, you are quite right, Danielle. It wouldn't be the same without him. I'll see you tomorrow then, and we can decide where we want to have lunch. Maybe we could go to Millicent's parents' restaurant – absolutely amazing food.'

'Oh, by the way, Celeste, what would you say to a having a life-sized doll created and modelled in your exact likeness with gorgeous fashionable clothes and jewellery? What an amazing engagement present that would be for Lewis.'

Celeste gasped; she shuddered feeling as though somebody or something had walked over her grave and then started to laugh.

'I can't tell you how much that would positively scare the living daylights out of me – it would give me the creeps. I wouldn't mind a lookalike miniature doll, though, to place on the top of my wedding cake.'

'As you wish. That's something to think about. As you can see, I'm in the middle of a meeting at the moment so I will say au revoir, ma Cheri. Until tomorrow then – I look forward to it,' Danielle said, blowing a kiss in Celeste's direction.

'Wait, just a moment,' she called out as Celeste was about to walk out of the door.

'Before you go, let me introduce you to James Lambert, who is about to be appointed as my personal lawyer,' she announced, as James immediately stood up to shake hands with Celeste.

Celeste took his hand and suddenly in her usual gushing and flirtatious habit she leaned into him and kissed him on each cheek. She paused when she noticed a small tattoo of a crown on the side of his neck. 'I just love a man with a tattoo', she said. *Now where have I seen that before,* she thought as she stepped back from him.

'It's a pleasure to meet you,' James said, slightly amused. He could see that for such an innocent looking young woman, she certainly seemed quite an entertaining and interesting character.

'While I think about it, would you mind if I bring my darling brother Leon to your engagement gathering seeing as he will be in London at the time. I am thinking to do a little bit of matchmaking - I think he and Millicent are perfect for each other,' Danielle said, as she blew another kiss to Celeste as she turned once again to leave the office.

'Why don't you bring that handsome Mr. Lambert with you,' Celeste said, winking at Danielle and flashing her best and most dazzling smile at James before stepping outside the door.

'You will have to excuse my friend, Mr. Lambert, she is utterly incorrigible – completely and hopelessly without shame or self-respect,' Danielle said, with a smile.

That's just the way I like them, James thought as he sat back down, returning Danielle's smile, and his eyes suddenly glazing over.

About the Author

Passing Through is Jacqueline Dixon's debut novel for Provoco Publishing. Signed in 2024, Jacqueline grew up in Gravesend, Kent. After leaving school she ventured into London to work at IPC Magazines as a letter writer for Woman's Own Magazine, and she later moved to another department where she began training for a short period as a proofreader. For a number of years thereafter she worked as a legal secretary both in London and Gravesend before she relocated overseas to work in Saudi Arabia until she retired back to the UK.

Jacqueline had a lifelong dream of becoming a writer and always had a great interest in writing and feeling excited about creating characters and deciding their fate. She developed a deep love of books at a very young age and one of her first very favourite books that she could not put down was the 'The Herries Chronicles' by Hugh Walpole. Jacqueline also has a great admiration for the many stories written by Daphne du Maurier and Agatha Christie. She relishes reading novels and feels that getting tucked into a good book is like enjoying a delicious meal. She has written numerous manuscripts that currently lay dormant, filed away, never having been published, although this may now be about to change.

Currently living in Sandwich, a charming small town in Kent, Jacqueline is looking forward to the seeing Passing Through on the bookshelves and is looking to delve into that pile of 'never been published' manuscripts for her next novel.

More from Provoco Publishing –

FRANK by Zack Robertson

Chapter 0
Loop

The distinct possibility he wasn't going to make it loomed large as Josh rounded the corner at Chappell and Donald Lee Hollowell. Chest burning, muscles churning, and sneakers pounding against cracked pavement, he raced out from the waning shadow of the Baptist church that signaled the start of the home stretch and down the weary residential street. He'd reached his limit: The Grove Park run never finished at this pace, and his body was screaming for a reprieve that his sorry legs were more than willing to grant.

Not on your life, the voice said.

The ambush had occurred at the thirty-seven-minute mark, where the narrow path that skirted Bellwood Quarry rejoined Proctor Creek Trail. Three men in jogging suits and dark bandanas concealing darker intentions had sprung from the brush and rushed him from both sides, and he'd barely managed to shoot the gap before they cut him off. Survival instinct now propelled him past a blur of chain-link fences, overturned trash cans, and boarded-up front doors to the rhythm of Prince's "Let's Go Crazy" blaring in his ears. He dared not look back to see who might be there. Not for a second. His breath caught in his lungs, and the quads threatened to give as the Southern Lakes Condominiums came into view. Caught at a precarious junction between fear and God, a hundred yards became fifty amid prayers of profanity. Then twenty. Ten.

Almost a believer.

Momentum carried him into the parking lot, and he collapsed in a lathered heap onto the asphalt behind the Focus. Sucking in the thick Georgia morning, he pulled out his earbuds and listened. There was no sign of the men, who had in all likelihood given up the chase back at the transit station. Only he and the birds chirping away on the power lines.

He stopped his Timex and stared at the blinking *41:38*. With a final leg like that he'd been expecting sub-forty.

Tuesdays were always your slow days.

The voice had a point: something about the 'eighties always held him back. He peeped over the hood of his car, then rose to his feet in hopes no one had witnessed his cowardly finish. Custom stipulated he proceed to the next segment of his morning, but this was his first brush with crisis since the loop, along with the voice, initialized a year ago. He needed time to process. The loop paused, and he, the dripping monk with pebbles in his shoes, awaited command.

"Stretches."

Yes, that was what came next in the Grove Park loop. Eyes alert for sudden movement, he initiated the subroutine, methodically working from the lower extremities to his neck.

He hadn't written a line of code in two years, but it hung around like an unsolicited companion, worming its way into every unassigned partition of his day. It'd never let him go, he knew. He saw loops everywhere, in everything and everyone. The run around Westside Park was a loop. Grove Park was a loop. Life was *the* loop. They ushered him like a sedated patient from one moment to the next, allowing him no say in the matter. They counted up, they counted down, and no matter how fast he ran there was no getting away.

Stretches had concluded, and he was already seeing the event with more clarity. The men, probably out of work from the lockdowns like everyone else in the neighborhood, had meant no real harm. If they'd had guns, they hadn't used them. No need to involve the police. He was perfectly fine. In fact, it was possible he'd completely misread the situation. They could've been punking him for their YouTube channel, or maybe it was some type of edgy performance art. Those were definitely possibilities.

They'd have beat the white out of your ass.

The voice was not a morning person. Shaking it away, he trudged past the beat-up vehicles with their duct-taped windows and plates up to the second floor of the rotting brown building he called home. He unlocked the door to his apartment and, with a glance over his shoulder, entered the chilled dominion. The deadbolts closed with comforting clicks.

All code required constants: those immutable, known values that remained unchanged regardless of application state. Constants made code predictable and manageable, so he embedded the loop with as many as possible. Everything in the apartment had a place, from the bike propped against the wall by the front door to his outfits arranged by day on the closet floor. Morning, noon, and evening medication times structured his day into a tidy procession of tasks that, as per Dr. Neumann's design, prevented debilitating thought patterns from emerging. Everything, including him, was to remain the same. He took care to avoid eye contact with his reflection during grooming by directing attention to only the pertinent areas. The electric razor—no blades—left enough stubble to demonstrate he was above caring about appearances, and he granted no mercy to the gray strays he plucked from the mass of brown set into a hard part on the left, all the while cognizant a full head of hair wasn't to be taken for granted.

With luck, he wouldn't end up like his father.

The Timex went off at nine, nudging him to the next stage of his morning with its gentle, monotone authority. He rechecked the strap on the watch. It had to be positioned just so.

Guided meditation sputtered at the start, even though he was using the paid version of the app. In tighty-whities damp with shower dew, he awaited serenity on a bare mattress laid out on the floor of his bedroom, contemplating off-color patches the size of fists in the drywall. As the narration took hold, he became discorporate, borders dissolving. He was a bodyless head now, but not for long as he soon separated from that, too. Headless, and still the app was not done. Relaxing waves spirited him higher, and he separated from separation. Less-less. Nirvana. Well worth the three-dollar monthly subscription.

The Timex ended the session at ten, and he biked to the Good Buy Grocer to purchase a week's worth of the discounted frozen dinners they cleared out on Tuesdays and a couple of bottles of the cheapest vape juice they stocked. He exchanged medical-masked nods with the older Black fellow behind the counter at checkout, fully aware they met every week and had yet to say a word to each other. A shame, no doubt, but people needed their social distances.

Outside, he smoked his V2 and watched the masked parade of working poor and younger, fashionably dressed Atlanteans trickle through a glass door at the store's entrance that announced each arrival and departure with an emphatic Dee-Dah! The poorest among them knew they, like the Good Buy store, were losing the battle against time. A block away, a high-end apartment building was nearing completion, and by next year the place would be an organic supermarket where environmentally conscious foodies spent their parents' money on humanely slaughtered animals and gritty soaps that rubbed the skin raw. He released a stream of vapor and marveled at how the unregulated plumes of silver writhed in the sun.

The moment came crashing to a halt when the men from the park got out of a sedan parked across the street and started his way. His body stiffened, rooting him to the pavement with his cig dangling from his mouth like a battery-powered pacifier.

No, only some teenagers.

He scolded himself for the overreaction: he wasn't that type of guy. The boys walked by without giving him a second glance, cutting up and laughing at something on one of their phones. He took a steadying drag from the V2 as the Good Buy scooped them into its welcoming arms.

Dee-dah!

And so, the loop went on.

That afternoon, he rode to the local library and chained his bike to a handicap parking sign outside the entrance of the nondescript brick building. Many weren't aware that request services and select indoor facilities had reopened, which was fine by him. He paused before going inside to mop his brow with the inside of his mask.

Variables complicated life the way they complicated code, and people presented the most challenging variables in the Grove Park loop. The first variable to be navigated when visiting the library was of a finite range variety. Cliff, Deborah, Shandice, or Karen? The culturally diverse staff randomly rotated shifts, so he had no way of knowing whom he'd be interfacing with at the Resource Counter. After giving the Timex one last check, he passed through the automatic doors and turned the corner.

Deborah Jenkins.

An unpleasant sensation arose in his stomach. It wasn't that he disliked Deborah so much as he couldn't pinpoint how she felt about him. Deborah was an obese fifty-something straight out of Grove Park with tightly permed hair and colossal breasts that dominated the conversation regardless of what she happened to be wearing. Today it was a low-cut purple cardigan, so he needed to be vigilant about keeping his eyes on her pink-rimmed glasses. As usual, her mask was pulled below her mouth like a chin strap.

"I'd like to check on a title I requested last week," he said, handing her his library card. He never checked anything out, but you needed an account to request books from other branches.

"Let me see if it came, hon."

Today might be Good Deborah. She swiveled on her stool and, upon accumulating the necessary inertia, launched her body toward a mountain of books tagged with yellow Post-it notes on the back counter.

"Name?"

"Stein. Josh Stein."

"No, I know you," she said, without turning around. "You're in here all the time. I mean your book."

"Being and Time," he answered, careful to maintain a polite smile. The rough manner in which Deborah was handling the books, however, made it clear she wasn't pleased. This could mean Bad Deborah.

True or false: Either his request had arrived, or he would be forced to make do with the Nietzsche he'd finished yesterday. Everything hinged on a single Boolean. He cracked his knuckles as she poked through the stack. Seconds later, her finger stopped at the thickest spine.

"Yeah, it came this morning," she said. She pressed the tome to her bosom as if nursing a newborn while she labored back to her seat, breasts swaying like twin planets in orbit when she turned to face him. "It's heavy! What do you need to be reading this heavy stuff for?"

He was starting to suspect Deborah was a covert Mensa card holder. Her powerful inquiry confounded him initially.

"I'm still looking for the question to that," he said upon deliberation. She didn't appreciate the thoughtfulness, however, and shot him a look like he'd passed gas in front of her before signing his receipt.

"You do know you can check these out? Always coming up in here every day and all."

There was no telling where she was headed with this, so with a meek laugh he took the book and retreated to the reading corner, clear of her line of sight. All things considered; things hadn't gone so badly. He and Deborah were making progress.

You disgust her.

The voice usually stayed out of the library. Was it possible the morning's events had provoked it more than he'd realized?

After wiping down a chair and one of the properly spaced tables, he took out a notebook and pencil from his backpack and surveyed his surroundings. Regulations permitted up to four people in the reading corner at a time. Across the room, an elderly Black woman in a wheelchair was reading the newspaper or sleeping, while an Asian guy sat at a corner table listening to headphones in front of a mess of notes and textbooks. The three highly contrasted amigos it was.

He'd put off Heidegger until today, having worked his way from the novice-friendly works of Plato and Descartes to more demanding thinkers such as Kant and Mill. But his limited grasp of existentialism made for laborious study, and he found himself rereading passages several times before he was on stable enough footing to continue. At six o'clock, he closed the book and stared at the collection of inarticulate notes he'd cobbled together:

to understand being, must understand Being
must access Being through a being that has being

the primary question: not a what? but a Who? for the Dasein

Dasein exists in everydayness

Dasein finds meaning in temporality

He hadn't made a note the entire last half of the introduction. The book would require two solid weeks of reading, if not more. Brain synapses withered, he gathered his things and deposited the book at the Resource Counter, which by the grace of Dasein was unoccupied at the moment.

Lingering May heat drove him into the shade of the building's east side for an unscheduled smoke. He knew he shouldn't, but Heidegger had been a more than formidable foe. Warmth from the beige brick radiating into his skin, he leaned back and savored the deviation from structure one delicious lungful at a time. A quick fix was all he had time for. The sun was closing in on the tops of the surrounding oaks, and Grove Park after dark was one variable he never left to chance.

Halfway into that evening's beef stroganoff and broccoli frozen dinner, his phone rang. With a rubbery strip of meat that would be easier to manage if he kept any knives in his apartment dangling from his mouth, he weighed whether to get up from the foldout table in his kitchen and answer. Only one person would call him at this hour. Or at all, really.

The ringer stopped after a minute of blaring. Satisfied at having won that round, he opened his Foundations log to the next blank entry. His mostly peaceful morning had drifted into long-term memory, and with no video evidence dictating how to interpret it, he elected to put a constructive spin on that morning's events. There was his Milestone check tomorrow, after all, and unnecessary negativity had to be avoided. Signing the form didn't mean anything anymore, but the timestamp still brought a sense of accomplishment.

BLOCK #486
I got at least six hours of sleep the night before. Y
I ate a nourishing breakfast, lunch, and dinner. Y
I took all my medications on time. Y
I was physically active for at least thirty minutes. Y
I properly cleaned and groomed myself. Y
I completed my daily chores. Y
I spent time on something I care about. Y
I avoided unproductive habits and activities.
POINTS: 7 / 8
ACCOMPLISHMENTS: started a new book, avoided potential trouble on my morning run
CHALLENGES: still haven't figured out Deborah
SIGNATURE: Josh Stein
DATE: 5/19/2020

Code and time shared a unique relationship in that although the logic of code was timeless, timing regulated all digital processes and transactions. Most weren't aware that to a computer all time looked the same, derived from the number of seconds elapsed between a given moment and midnight of January 1, 1970, the UNIX epoch. It was people who needed to turn it into meaningful symbols and events. They bookended relationships with notarized slips of paper called marriage and divorce and measured out a life in birthdays and a funeral. Unlike computers or the other organisms roaming the planet, people cared about what time it was and wasn't, and in the Grove Park loop, time was the only companion he had.

And time was counting, always counting, as sure as the tick-tocks of the silent ticker on his wrist. All the days, hours, minutes, and seconds since he arrived at Grove Park had been counting toward tomorrow.

Everything will begin tomorrow.

Maybe it was the leveling effect of the Bupropion, but the comedians who bundled the news into clever soundbites calibrated to offend the right people at exactly the correct doses didn't elicit laughter the way they once did. He'd heard one's sense of humor changed as they approached forty; that, or there was nothing to laugh about lately. The effort-reward calculus of self-gratification was not working in his favor that night, and after checking the day's death tallies, he wound up swirling down the rabbit hole of Hall & Oates reaction videos, comforted in the knowledge so many others were also out of touch.

You people are not interesting.

The voice was a discerning critic, and anything less than the cleverest self-deprecation or wordplay got a thumbs down. Tonight, that meant everybody.

The Timex called out for the final time at nine-thirty, and he took twelve and a half milligrams of Sleep-Tight before preparing for bed. His balance faltered, and tooth pasty saliva dribbled down his chin as the medication took hold. Consciousness flickering, he tumbled onto the mattress and in the safety of darkness set the Timex on a shoebox. Today's iteration had come to an end, slipping away into the past to make way for the next beginning in the Grove Park loop.

As his lids shut, two eyes opened in the nothingness and stared at him in a piercing flash of yellow. But they were quickly swallowed by the expanding annihilation, gone as quickly as they'd appeared. He allowed himself to be consumed as well, to be devoured and saved. To relinquish being.

Hush.
Sink.
Now breathe.
Pain is gone,
as you too must be.
But something stirs, the code breaks down,
and soon you'll see this loop you're running was all a dream.

FRANK, by Zack Robertson will be available in late 2025 from Amazon and all good bookstores.